To Catch a Killer

by

Loretta C. Rogers

A Doc Holliday Mystery, Book 6

To Catch a Killer

Cover Art by *Diana Carlile*

The Wild Rose Press, Inc.
PO Box 708
Adams Basin, NY 14410-0708
Visit us at www.thewildrosepress.com

Publishing History
First Edition, 2025
Trade Paperback ISBN 978-1-5092-5864-2
Digital ISBN 978-1-5092-5865-9

A Doc Holliday Mystery, Book 6
Published in the United States of America

Also by Loretta C. Rogers at The Wild Rose Press
Contemporary Romance
Forbidden Son
Christmas at Hope Ranch

Historical Romance
Bannon's Brides
The Witching Moon
Lady Adel's Captain
Cloud Woman's Spirit
*Taming the Lyon
When Comes Forever
A Little Kringle Magic (novella)
*Isabelle and the Outlaw (novella)
*McKenna's Woman (novella)
Fate Comes Softly (Anthology)

Mystery and Suspense
*Murder in the Mist
*Shadowed Reunion
Doc Holliday Mystery Series:
Book #1-Fatal Passion
Book #2-The Boneyard
Book #3-Lights…Camera…Murder
Book #4-Monster in the Dark
Book #5-8 Seconds to Die
Book #6-To Catch a Killer

*Audio Books

Acknowledgments

The only two things I ever wanted in life was to ride horses and write books. I've managed to do both.

As a single-title author, it was with trepidation that I challenged myself to write a mystery series. The question that plagued me with each book was "Is it good enough?"

Dr. Tullah Holliday, her father John Henry Holliday, grandmother Tanti Crow, and the gang have "lived" for six books. I listened when readers were concerned that Tullah didn't have a special someone in her life. Thus, Detective Clay Wolfchild Bannister was created. Thanks to the dedicated readers who have adopted all of them as friends and family. I cannot thank you enough for your support and positive reviews.

Many thanks to my editor Nan Swanson. Words are inadequate. She has worked diligently to make my books as good as they can be. Special thanks to graphic artist Diana Carlisle for creating the alluring covers for each book in this series. Thanks also to my dear friend Flossie Benton Rogers for beta reading on a moment's notice. And to my publisher, The Wild Rose Press, for allowing me to create characters that don't fit the norm.

I must also acknowledge the Cherokee people and their beliefs and customs that helped develop Tullah's maturity as an empathic woman resistant to her gift. And I mustn't forget about the animals—River, Rascal, and the horses. The love of all animals is the most noble attribute of a human.

A writer only begins a book. A reader finishes it.
~Samuel Johnson
Thank You and Happy Reading!

Prologue

Death is the ebb and flow of life and eventually comes to all of us. Murder is the deliberate and willful act of taking a life.

Fourteen years ago, my mother died. She was murdered. Someday, I will find the resources to give up my career as a veterinarian and become a full-time seeker of the person or persons who took her life.

Her name was Josie Waya Crow Holliday. She was an artist of Native American history and visiting New York to display her work at a major museum. She was later found in an alley. I cannot bear to describe the condition of her body when my father, my grandmother, and I had to identify her.

Over the years my father has made numerous trips to New York, only to be treated with flippant irreverence by the NYPD who give him no respect as a law enforcement officer or as the bereaved husband who desires to bring the killer of his wife to justice.

The day I find my mother's murderer is the day that person will beg to be put out of their misery.

Part I: Tullah Dreams

Dreams are not what you see in sleep;
it is the thing that doesn't let you sleep.
~Abdul Kalam

Chapter One

My yearly pilgrimage to my mother's gravesite is
always a painful event, but born of necessity. I knelt to
brush away the damp leaves and debris that had gathered
around the tombstone, and then I laid a bouquet of purple
cornflowers on my mother's grave. I missed, with an
aching intensity, both her and how she had listened to my
hopes and dreams, and even my despairs. I will never
forget the night we received the call from the New York
Museum director informing us of my mother's murder.

I sat on the damp earth and traced my finger along
the letters of her name: Josie Waya Crow Holliday,
Beloved wife, daughter, and *Etsi*.

In the Cherokee language, Etsi is the word for
Mother. Once her remains arrived at the mortuary,
Grandmother and I honored *Etsi* in the Cherokee way.
We first washed her body and scented it with lavender
oil. We wrapped her in white linen before placing her
inside the coffin. Grandmother tucked an eagle feather in
her daughter's hands because the Cherokee venerate the
eagle as a sacred bird. And because she was born of the

Waya clan, the image of a wolf was etched into the tombstone to watch over her.

It gives me comfort to talk to her. "The years have passed, Mama. In a few months I will celebrate thirty years of life. I was barely sixteen when you went away. Grandmother says the Great Spirit Father needed you more than Dad, and me, and even her. I don't understand. We…I…needed you…here on earth.

"You didn't get to see my prom gown, or watch me compete as you did in barrel-racing events. And even though I knew you were not there, I looked in the audience for you when I graduated from medical school."

I continued talking, telling her about Gandalf, her black-and-white pinto. "He's nearly twenty now but still has the spirit of a wild mustang, and there are times when he is as wily as his name." I allowed myself a small chuckle.

The squish of wet grass drew my attention to a pair of shiny black boots. I looked up to see my dad approaching. After all these years, and even with his recent marriage to Dr. Sunny Sanders, lines of sadness still etch his face. He removed his Stetson. Threads of silver lined his brown hair. At the age of fifty-six, he was still ruggedly handsome, still my hero, and still sheriff of Enigma.

I stood. Dad placed an arm around my waist and drew me close. He coughed to clear the huskiness in his voice. "She will always be in my heart, Punkin."

I brushed a tear from my cheek. "It seems like yesterday that we got the call. Fourteen years, Dad, and the NYPD has let the case go cold." Anger laced my heart. "If Mama hadn't been a woman…a Native

American woman…the police department would have been all over the case like a squirrel gathering acorns."

Dad looked down at me. He brushed another tear from my cheek, then murmured, "She would have been proud of you."

I shrugged with a weary gesture. "But I haven't honored her by finding her killer."

"Josie was a gentle soul. She loved nature, and all things beautiful. She adored you." He tilted my chin upward so I could look at him. "Finding her killer would be a dangerous journey, even if he or they are still alive. Your mother would never expect you to put yourself in danger because of her."

"But Dad…"

"No buts, Tullah Josie Crow Holliday! Losing your mother was painful enough. I could not bear losing you, too. Promise me you will forget this notion of avenging your mother. Promise!"

As I did when I was a child about to tell a lie, I placed my hands behind my back and crossed my fingers. I stood on tiptoes and kissed his cheek. "We should go. A storm is coming, Dad."

Across the cemetery, a curtain of rain moved toward us as we raced to our individual vehicles. Dad yelled above the sheeting drops, "Meet me at Tanti's. She and Sunny are preparing lunch."

I waved, climbed into my truck, and watched Dad pull away in his 4Runner. I'm not sure why I decided not to immediately follow. There is something calming about the rain and the music it makes. I rolled down the window, and as I listened to the rhythmic thrumming, I was startled to see a female cardinal, with her orange-gray wings and red beak, perch on the hood. It shook itself as if to expel raindrops from its tufted crest and feathers. I was even more surprised when it hopped toward the windshield, then pecked on the glass.

Over the years, I have learned to embrace my empathic gift and to heed the messages of the animals and other spirits that visit me. A flash of lightning frightened the little red bird away and left me wondering why such a delicate creature would seek me out during a thunderstorm.

I engaged the ignition and drove to meet my father for lunch. I had barely reached the wrought iron gates when a warrior on a rearing pinto horse caused me to slam on the brakes. In a blink the apparition disappeared.

What did these visits mean? My grandmother and Uncle Charlie would know. As I drove to Grandmother's apartment complex, my mind was filled with the possibilities of why these appearances occurred. By the time I pulled into a parking space near her door, my dad was walking toward me holding an umbrella.

"What took you so long, Punkin? I worried you'd had an accident."

"I'll tell you when we get inside. I have questions for Grandmother and Uncle Charlie."

The downpour had increased, and I was glad to get off the road and out of the driving rain. I greeted each person with a brief hug. Grandmother invited us to gather around the small dining table. While we enjoyed our southwestern quinoa salad and then peach cobbler, I related the incident at the gravesite.

Grandmother didn't hesitate when she said, "The female cardinal is easy. I believe my Josie is reaching beyond the grave." She stretched to clasp my hand. I was struck by how blue the veins in her hands were and how paper thin and wrinkled the skin had become. Those hands had so often soothed away my fears after my mother's tragic death; those hands were now icy cold and chilled me.

A slight scoff caused all eyes to rivet toward Dr. Sunny Sanders. I have always admired Sunny. Her brother, Deputy Tiny Goodbody, has been like an uncle to me—he's one of my dad's oldest and trusted friends— and now, after an exceptionally long courtship, she has become my stepmother.

Grandmother withdrew her hand from mine. Uh-oh, I thought. As Cherokee, we are firm believers in the spirit world, and for Sunny to even remotely deride that belief is like spitting on my mother's grave. Grandmother's dark eyes seemed to resemble molten onyx. Her voice was calm, firm, without malice, but with chastisement.

Grandmother lifted Sunny's hand into hers and said, "You have known us long enough to respect the ways of Tullah, Charlie, and me. But you still have much to learn. As Cherokee we believe that all souls after death continue to live; some manifest through the body of animals while others are unseen. So, when the female cardinal alit on the hood of Tullah's truck and then pecked on the windshield, I am convinced that my Josie is trying to communicate with Tullah."

I asked, "Grandmother, do you know why?"

Still holding my stepmother's hand, she shook her head. "All will be revealed in time, granddaughter. That is all I know."

Grandmother shifted her glance to my dad as if asking him to honor her words. It pleased me that he nodded his assent. She seemed to study Sunny's hand for a moment before releasing it. Grandmother's voice remained soft. "We will continue to follow our path."

Sunny blushed. "I meant no disrespect. Please accept my apology."

I knew from the sorrow in her eyes and the expression on her face that her heart and her words were true. For this I was glad. I offered a smile and a nod to her and to my dad.

Uncle Charlie cleared his throat as if returning us to the conversation. Charlie really isn't my uncle. He and my father have been blood brothers since they were in the sixth grade. Charlie is mostly Apache; his mother was Inuit. The bond between him and my dad is strong and has seen them through their college years, a terrible war in the Middle East, and the soul-wrenching sorrow of my mother's death. He is a confirmed bachelor and the best godfather a girl could have. "Little Sister, you spoke of a warrior on a spotted pony. Were there symbols on either of them?"

I plopped another spoonful of cobbler in my mouth as I nodded.

"Tell me about them so that I might discern their meanings."

I closed my eyes for a moment and called forth the image of the warrior holding a spear as he sat astride a pinto horse that reared and pawed the air.

With my eyes tight, I said, "There was a red handprint on the horse's shoulder, and drops of rain…or maybe they were ice-lets." I shrugged, then continued. "There was a snake, coiled and ready to strike, and…" I drifted away for a moment, fearing the darkness.

Uncle Charlie's voice brought me back. I continued. "I thought the warrior was holding a spear, but now I see it is a very long arrow." I opened my eyes. "There was another hand—on the pinto's chest. It seemed to shift in color."

Dad said, "Punkin, you're pale as a sheet and sweating. Are you okay?"

Sunny pushed from her chair. "I'll get—"

Dad indicated for her to remain seated. "I know this is all new to you, Sunny. Tullah isn't sick, not in the way of man's medicine. Trust me. Someday you'll understand."

I managed a smile. "I'm perfectly okay, Sunny." And then I focused my attention on Uncle Charlie. "I understand Grandmother's words about the cardinal. What do your Apache spirits tell you about the warrior?"

The cadence of his baritone voice was almost mesmerizing. "In the ways of the warrior people, the handprint on the horse's shoulder represents an oath of vengeance. I believe the water marks are hail or possibly snow. These marks symbolize a prayer for the horse and rider to fall upon the enemy like shards of ice. The snake symbol represents stealth when approaching the enemy, and the straight arrow signifies victory."

"What about the second hand—the one of different colors?" I wanted to know.

"Ah, the handprint of any color except red means the warrior has accomplished his mission."

I didn't miss the unspoken communication between Grandmother and my godfather. It would be inappropriate for me to speak. I waited.

Uncle Charlie said, "Tanti, grandmother of Tullah, and John Henry, father of Tullah, the spirits have sought out Little Sister to undertake a dangerous journey. The time to seek out those who killed her mother is rapidly approaching."

He inhaled deeply; his eyes closed for what seemed forever until he exhaled, and said, "In the way of our ancestors, we must prepare Little Sister with a cleansing."

A cleansing, I knew, was to purify my body and soul to make me strong enough to survive whatever enemy I was about to encounter and to emerge the victor. What I didn't know was when.

Grandmother rose and on silent feet padded to the kitchen. She returned with the coffeepot and filled our cups. "Granddaughter, in a few weeks you will celebrate your thirtieth year. In my soul, I believe when the new moon is ready to rise in the tenth month, our Josie's spirit will contact you. But not until then." She looked at Uncle Charlie.

He nodded. "It is as you have said, Tanti Waya Crow."

The morning had played itself out. Dad needed to return to the office. Sunny had received a page that she was needed at the hospital, and it was getting close to the time for Uncle Charlie to open the saloon.

One by one, we said our goodbyes. Grandmother had tugged at my shirt sleeve. I sensed she wanted me to stay behind. When she and I were alone, I said, "What is it you wish to tell me, Grandmother?"

Her eyes clouded with tears. "I believe the Great Spirit Father is preparing you for a long and heartbreaking journey—yes, even a dangerous journey." She clutched my hands to her heart. "And it frightens me."

I too was frightened. What could I say to allay my eighty-year-old grandmother's fears? Her gaze clung to mine as if searching for some reassurance from me.

Finally, I said, "Grandmother, you worry too much." And then I kissed her cheek.

Chapter Two

Thunderclouds were amassing outside the window as I drove home. On either side of my truck, green grass was changing to shades of red and brown, getting ready for autumn, and the muted colors seemed to stretch from horizon to horizon. Slowing my truck, I watched the clouds. Within them were visible the shapes of lightning bolts, and with the distant rumble of thunder I could see the strikes aiming toward me.

The storm perfectly matched my mood. I thought about the predictions from Grandmother and Uncle Charlie. Counting the seconds between the splinters of lightning and the thunder that followed, I calculated the distance of the approaching storm. It would be nice to be safe inside my house, where I would watch the wind twist the treetops into a dance of strength and beauty.

I notched the speed up to seventy, relishing the handling of my truck as I raced the storm home. When I turned into my drive, the strong winds were whipping the treetops and cascades of dried leaves fell, flying through the air and scattering to the ground in flurries. The sense of coming home, the place where my mother was born, and I after her, was a gratifying emotion. I could only pity those people who'd never loved a place, had never felt the satisfaction of roots holding firm in land that nurtures the past and the present.

Even more heartening was seeing my black Lab and

gray teacup donkey sitting on the front porch waiting for my return. The moment I pulled into the yard, the animals darted down the steps and around to the carport to welcome me home.

Once inside, I gave my pets some love, then gathered my laptop and retired to my favorite chair. Although I am a veterinarian, I was gifted with empathic abilities. Not only am I able to sense what certain people are thinking or feeling, I am able to communicate with animal spirits that often contact me either as a warning that a crime is about to be committed or has already happened.

It has become a habit to create a case file when assisting my dad with a crime. Keeping track of potential suspects and clues has more than once helped solve a crime. Perhaps this was why I now created a file and labeled it: Who Killed Josie Crow Holliday?

It took a moment to still the tremors in my fingers enough to type. This was my mother. If I closed my eyes, I could still hear her windchime laughter. The pathways to my brain led me to memories that I did not wish to revisit. I forced my fingers to continue typing. This was not the proper time for fear or reflection.

Victim: Josie Waya Crow Holliday

Age: forty

Ethnicity: Cherokee; Wolf Clan

Parents: Mother: Tanti Waya Crow; Father: Samson Six Feathers Goga (which means Crow in Cherokee language)

Date of death: Fourteen years ago, November twenty-seventh

Cause of death: Gang murder—tortured

Place of death: New York City—dark alley

Status of case: Unsolved!
Evidence: Per NYPD no concrete evidence
Arrests: None
Suspects: Possibly an Aryan gang

My emotions were getting a workout. For a moment I stared at the words—black sticks that meant nothing and yet preordained everything. I closed the lid on my laptop and shut my eyes. Once I was playing in the woods behind my house and had ventured too deeply into the swamp and stepped into what I was certain was quicksand. The sensation of sinking, of being slowly sucked deeper and deeper into the mire that stunk like rotten eggs frightened me beyond belief. I remembered screaming *"Etsi…Etsi"* at the top of my nine-year-old lungs. Mother had raced to my rescue, and oblivious of my slimy and stench-coated body, she wrapped me in her arms, cooing that I was safe.

Behind the darkness of my eyelids, I envisioned my mother lying in a cold, dark alley, afraid—and just as she had held me, I wanted to wrap her in my arms. I heard her call my name—*Tullah*!

Startled, I sat up and opened my laptop. My eyes focused on the word "torture." I think my soul hardened a bit more, because a little voice inside my head snarled, *Karma is a bitch!*

My first inclination was to visit the basement and open the trunk that stores my mother's possessions that we treasured. Also inside that trunk was a manila envelope that held the scrap of evidence about my mother's murder. It had been fourteen years since any of us opened the packet. Even now, the thought of reading the contents and looking at the forensic photos caused my heart to rev into overdrive.

Rolling thunder seemed to match the beating of my heart. I closed my laptop and set it aside, determined to visit the basement, unlock the trunk, and force myself to read the contents of the envelope marked: CFM (Case: Felony Murder).

The moment my hand touched the basement's doorknob, a flash of lightning lit up the kitchen and the lights went out. An instant later, my cellphone rang. Ella's picture showed on the caller ID. I answered.

Ella said, "Are you in the dark?"

"Yes. Maybe the power won't be out long."

"Do you think we should check on the horses?"

Thankful we had no animals in the surgical recovery area, I leaned against the kitchen sink to peer out the window and toward the clinic. Just as I thought—no lights.

I said, "There's no need for you to come out in this weather. I'm certain our old pros are snug in their stalls. I'm concerned about Bella, though. We haven't had this type of storm here since I've had her." I continued, "I'll keep you posted."

I'd no sooner disconnected than my dad called to check on me. He said lightning had struck a transformer and that most of Enigma was sitting in the dark until the electric company could restore power. I assured him I was safe.

"Humor your ol' man, Punkin, and lock all of your doors. And don't go out in this storm."

I knew Dad was remembering another storm. Three years ago, it was on a night like this that Junior Lampson, a monster from hell, broke into my house and tried to strangle the life out of me, just as he'd done to eleven other women that he'd buried in the swamp behind my house.

"Dad, I need to check on the horses, especially Bella. I'll take River with me."

"Don't fault me for worrying about you, Punkin. All this talk about a warrior spirit and you going on a dangerous journey has me a little spooked."

I tried to keep my voice calm because I was also a little spooked. Well, maybe a lot more than I wanted to admit. "I promise as soon as I check on the horses, return to the house, and lock the kitchen door, I'll send you a text."

"Nope, call. Anyone can send a text. I want to hear your voice."

After assuring him that I'd call rather than text, I used the flashlight mode on my phone to guide me to the coat rack, where I donned my rain slicker. River, Rascal, and I sprinted into the night, across the rain-soddened yard, and into the barn, to be greeted by friendly nickers.

Chapter Three

By morning the storm had calmed and all that remained was a light pitter-pat of rain. Ella and I splashed across the yard to feed the horses and open the stall doors and the barn door to let the animals go in and out at will. We were thankful that no clients had called with an emergency.

We discussed our sorrow that we'd say goodbye to Jeff Dempsey, our office assistant, and congratulated him on his acceptance to Eastern Kentucky University to finish his bachelor's degree in middle grades education.

Ella said, "You're awfully quiet, Tullah. Do you think we made a mistake in hiring Jeff's younger sister, Alice?"

Alice Dempsey was a pretty girl, shy like her brother, and like Jeff, interested in continuing as a positive role model for her six younger siblings. "She caught on fast when he was training her, and she's a good-natured girl. No, I was just thinking about the annual 4-H fair and rodeo and all the work that goes into making the events a success, and fun for the kids."

"Ah, come on, Tullah, I know you too well. Something's bothering you and it's not the fair. C'mon, give over."

I wanted to be like Scarlett O'Hara and say I'd think about it tomorrow, except tomorrow was a work day and, rain or shine, the phone would ring off the hook.

Ella urged, "Tullah?"

I shot her my best glowering look. In truth, I didn't want to think about an upcoming event, and it didn't include judging rabbits or chickens.

I looked around the old office, taking in the battered wooden desk, the worn hardwood floor, the general air of neglect that occurred in an old barn that had been renovated into a reception area, animal surgery, pharmacy, recovery area, holding room for small animals, and a place for large animals.

"Ella, I think we should remodel the office. New employee, new furniture."

She cocked an eyebrow. "And I think you should stop avoiding my question—but I do agree about the new furniture. Now, give!"

I took a couple of deep breaths. She was right. I blurted, "I don't want a thirtieth birthday party."

She expelled a loud guffaw. Then straightened. "Who said you were getting a birthday party?"

"Don't act all innocent. I overheard Sunny and Grandmother talking about a surprise birthday party. In fact, I distinctly heard grandmother say Patty was making a German chocolate cake, and that's one of my favorites."

"Maybe you misunderstood. Maybe the party is for one of their mutual friends—like Uncle Charlie."

"His birthday was in March, and he hates German chocolate. This is the last of August, and my birthday is next Saturday. Grandmother knows I despise surprises. Tell me…it's true, isn't it?"

Ella merely shot me a smug look, shrugged her shoulders, and said, "I know nothing, and if I did, my lips are sealed."

I was about to give her the third degree when her phone rang. Dang phone! She answered, "Hi, Andy. You're home? Sure, Tullah and I are finished. I'll meet you in a sec."

Crap! I thought.

I locked the office door and followed Ella into the yard. We were almost to my house when she said, "Tullah…I truly don't know the details because Mother and Tanti know how close you and I are. I guess they were afraid I couldn't keep a secret. All I know is please don't disappoint them. Whatever it is, they've worked hard to do something special for you."

Part of me was pleased and the other part was back to the same old protest of not liking surprises. "Do you know when?"

Rain crystals had begun to glisten on the curls of Ella's short blonde hair. "Honestly, I don't have a clue. When I walked into the room, it was as if they had suddenly morphed into dear little old ladies gabbling about a quilting bee or a new recipe for making strawberry jelly."

With that, she waved and trotted around the house to the gate that separates her property from mine. I scooted inside the kitchen and sat in a chair to remove my muddied boots. My coffee mug and the empty pot were where I had left them, waiting to be refilled. The hands on the kitchen clock glided with electrical smoothness on their course.

I filled the percolator, then started down the hallway to the stairs that led to the bedrooms and bathroom. I looked quickly at each doorway as I passed. What I saw was a remnant of my life—lifeless rooms, beautifully decorated by my mother, where my parents and grandparents had entertained, and suddenly recalling my father lovingly telling guests how Josie had remodeled this old house from the inside out. The only room she hadn't changed was Grandmother's bedroom. And I hadn't touched it since Grandmother had moved to town. I bypassed the room and went straight to the master bathroom, to its cool tiled floor, and shed everything I had on. I stepped into the shower, but not before self-consciously locking the door.

The shower was bliss. With cool water shooting over me, washing off layers of sweat, I was able to forget the passing of time and my mother's death for a few minutes.

I toweled off, dressed in my favorite baggy T-shirt, and slowly combed out my wet hair. Padding barefoot downstairs, I poured myself a cup of coffee, opened the refrigerator, and grabbed the box that contained one last glazed donut, then returned to the living room to settle in my recliner. I didn't feel like working on my mother's murder file, and it was too early for bed. *I'll just sit and enjoy my coffee. Maybe I'll think of something to do to use up the remains of this blasted day.*

My eyes spotted a half-finished book. I considered reading but decided I wasn't in the mood. The book was a murder mystery. I didn't want to think about murder or dead people.

After a moment, I wriggled deeper into the cushy chair, stretching my legs on the foot rest. I sipped some more coffee. I was profoundly bored, yet very tense; not a good combination.

"Okay, toes, relax," I said out loud, suddenly recalling the yoga class I'd once attended. "Feet, relax."

I had worked up to my pelvis when an

overwhelming sensual arousal gripped me with an intensity that left me breathless. Heat rippled over me. I envisioned myself in Clay Wolfchild Bannister's arms, his lips teasing mine, his hands exploring my body. I shivered with longing.

A jolted shock rippled through me when a wet nose touched my hand. My laugh was high and shrill as my black Lab whined and wriggled for attention.

I swear the dog grinned at me when I said, "Thanks, River. You've just interrupted the best awake-dream I've ever had."

It had been almost two years since I'd become acquainted with Detective Clay Wolfchild Bannister, and I hadn't heard from him in nearly that long also. It had to be my imagination that he and I had experienced a mystical connection. When we met, he was still in mourning over the untimely murder of his new bride. He'd made it clear he wasn't interested in an attachment, romantic or non-romantic. In fact, he'd as much as said he was indefinitely unavailable.

River nudged my hand again, and whined. He stood, turned to look over his shoulder, then walked to the kitchen. I followed. Smart dog. He stood staring down at his empty food dish. Rascal, not to be left out, trotted into the kitchen. He emitted one of his cute snuffling brays. I filled his dish with a handful of sweet feed and was rewarded with a series of donkey farts.

Since I was at loose ends until morning, I refilled my mug, returned to the living room, and opened the novel. My mind lingered on the handsome detective. Why, after all this time, had he entered my thoughts?

A nagging from somewhere deep inside informed me that this was no mere daydream but an omen, and that whatever was coming somehow involved Clay Wolfchild Bannister.

Chapter Four

A small town is a hard place to be different. Enigma has always been a good place because you know everyone who is anyone, and their business. I had grown from the sheriff's little half-breed girl to a respected veterinarian. I'm not so egotistical that I thought a surprise party was being planned specifically for me. Thankfully, my work week had been filled with several emergencies, plus a couple of appointment scheduling mistakes by our new office assistant. These incidents kept my mind occupied on tending to sick and injured animals rather than the fact that I was leaving one era and entering another.

I hated the thought of turning "middle aged." This morning, I'd actually spotted a gray hair. My first thought was to snatch it out and toss it in the trash can. Then I remembered my grandmother's saying that for every one gray hair pulled out, two more return in its place—and worse, I had examined my face for wrinkles.

Today had arrived and there were no phone calls from Dad or Grandmother wishing me a happy birthday. Part of me was relieved, but I must admit I was also disappointed. As much as I'd protested to everyone about not wanting a surprise birthday party, I thought perhaps I'd objected too much and my wishes were being honored.

I was about to whip up a peanut-butter-and-jelly

sandwich when my cellphone rang. "Hi, Ella, what's up?"

"Tullah, can you come get me? My truck won't start. I think the battery is dead. Andy is on patrol, and Mother is on call at the hospital. I'm stranded."

"Sure. Where are you?"

"At the fairgrounds—barn number three."

I remembered that she had volunteered to help set-up the small animal cubicles for next week's 4-H fair. "I'll be there in twenty minutes."

I was about to suggest that we drop by the Whitehorse Saloon for one of Uncle Charlie's famous BBQ rib plates. Then I remembered that he'd decided to close the saloon for a few minor renovations. I allowed myself a "woe is me" sigh and berated myself for griping too much. It seems I had truly protested my way out of a birthday celebration.

By the time I'd pulled up in front of barn number three and parked next to Ella's pickup, the moon was a ball of white. In spite of yesterday's storm, as soon as I stepped out of my truck a wave of heat engulfed me. A trickle of sweat inched its way down the nape of my neck. A horsefly landed on my arm. Automatically, I slapped at it. It buzzed away only to be replaced by one of its pesky companions.

"Damn flies," I muttered as I tramped toward the barn's closed double doors. Part of me was annoyed that Ella hadn't met me outside. Of course, I rationalized that it was much cooler inside, and that perhaps she was finishing up with a few last-minute details.

I exerted my muscles and rolled one of the heavy doors aside. Like a fool, I stood riveted and staring at the ghostly images as my eyes tried to adjust to the dim interior.

A cacophony of voices burst into song with, "Happy birthday to you," following a cloud of floating balloons, all in various colors, and all with great big red three-o's on them. "Oh, panther piss!" I muttered. My hair was pulled back in a ponytail, my face was void of any makeup, and I certainly wasn't dressed for a party. The surprise really was on me.

To my horror, that note of kindness tipped me into an emotional abyss. A gullywasher of uncontrollable tears sprang from my eyes. I twisted away to hide my face, covered my mouth to muffle the ugly sound. I hated for anyone to see me crumple. Me, the epitome of stoicism, boohooing all over myself.

Dad opened his arms. Without hesitation I walked into his hug. I whispered, "I don't want anyone seeing me cry."

"Are they happy tears?" he asked.

I nodded my answer.

"Then let your family and friends see that you appreciate their love for you. Happy or sad, tears do not make you a weak person. They show that you are human."

From nowhere a handkerchief appeared, and there stood my grandmother, dabbing the dribbles from my cheek as she had done so many times when I was a child. Then someone, I'm not sure who, shoved a glass of wine into my hand, and the crowd began to chant, "Speech...speech...speech!"

I am not afraid of crazed bulls, wild stallions, rabid dogs, or maniacal lunatics, but standing in front of a crowd of grinning people wearing colorful pointy hats and waiting expectantly was an animal of a different color.

I drew in a deep breath and said, "Words escape me…there are so many ways to say thank you, so what I'll say is…from the bottom of my heart…" I held the glass of wine in a high salute and shouted, "THANK YOU! Let's cut the cake."

If anyone was disappointed in my lack of eloquent oration, no one said so. Uncle Charlie and Dad led me to a table where a massive sheet cake covered with white frosting, each corner decorated with fondant icing characters that represented me: a stethoscope, a medical bag, a horse, and a stack of mini chocolate-covered donuts.

I tilted the cake so that everyone could see the masterpiece. Patty said, "It's not German chocolate. I hope you're not disappointed."

I would never hurt the woman that had been like a second grandmother to me. Besides, her food was magical. I said, "My second favorite cake." And then I cut a wedge with the fondant donuts, plopped it into my mouth, and invited friends to the table that was laden with BBQ ribs, fried chicken, and too many delectable goodies to name.

Dad had hired a local band. At his signal they played a slow song. Dad whirled me around the room with Uncle Charlie cutting in. A fast hip-hop was next. Tune after tune followed until I finally made my way over to catch my breath on a stack of hay bales.

It's amazing how lonely one can feel in the midst of a crowded barn. I watched the contentment on my dad's face as he and his new wife swayed to a slow bluesy number. I was still getting used to the fact that Dr. Sunny Sanders, Chief of Staff at Enigma General, was now my stepmother. But I like Sunny. As long as she makes my dad happy, that's all that matters.

My gaze shifted to my best friend and business partner, Dr. Ella Sanders Kemble. She and Deputy Andy Kemble had wed on Valentine's Day, just a month before her mother and my dad married. I've always wanted a sister, and she's perfect.

Standing at the dessert table, slicing cake, stood my grandmother, Tanti Waya Crow, retired former mayor of Enigma, and Patty Sweet, retired vice mayor and former owner of Sweets 'n' Eats Café. These two dear women smiled and chatted with two of their closest friends— Flora and Vera. They call themselves the fearsome foursome globetrotters. A fitting name, I thought. A part of me envied their camaraderie.

From where I was perched, it seemed like everyone in the room had someone, yet here I sat surrounded by friends and family and was probably the loneliest person in the barn. I consider myself a clever woman, and over the years chasing the blues away is a talent I've come to master. Pulling out of my doldrums, I watched my dad, Uncle Charlie, and Andy regroup in a corner with plates of food in their hands, and no doubt discussing crime.

Uh-oh, I thought, when Grandmother and Sunny approached me. The expression on Grandmother's face should have cued me that she was up to something, and I was about to find out what that *something* was.

I was suspicious of their rambling conversation that seemed to meander down a bunch of rabbit trails, and that maybe my eighty-year-old grandmother was beginning to lose control of her faculties.

And then like tiny electrical jolts inside my brain, Grandmother said, "Tullah, how long has it been since you've had a complete physical?"

I was aghast at such a question. "I'm healthy as a horse, Grandmother. Why are you concerned?"

She huffed a sigh. "You've reached a milestone age—thirty. You're single, beautiful, intelligent, well-proportioned, and I'm worried that if you wait too long, your ovaries and womb will shrivel up, and I'll never be a great-grandmother." Grandmother sputtered and pointed toward my new stepmother. "Tullah, I want you to make an appointment with Sunny to make sure your womanly parts are in good working order."

She wasn't quite finished with me. She added, "Far be it from me to criticize, but you need to wear good foundation garments. You keep flouncing around like a butterfly on steroids and your breasts will eventually hang down to your navel. Now, tell me what man would be attracted to saggy boobs?"

It was impossible to tell who was the most astonished by Grandmother's ridiculous declaration. Immediately my eyes flicked down toward my chest. In my defense, I hadn't expected to be the subject of a surprise birthday party. Had I known, I would have dressed more appropriately. Gads, I hoped no one else had noticed the outlines of my bare breasts under the shirt I wore. I steeled my nerves and gritted my teeth to keep from spewing molten lava.

And I tried to keep the growl out of my voice. "First of all, I'd need a sperm donor to fulfill your request. Unfortunately, there isn't anyone in Enigma that I'd have. Secondly, have you been dipping into the spiked bowl of punch? Because it's not like you to talk about my breeding habits."

I blinked back tears that stung my eyes. I'd be

damned if I'd insult my emotions by crying over a dear old woman's whimsies. Poor Sunny's expression was as mortified as I felt. I set my paper plate and cup aside.

When I bent to kiss her on the cheek, my suspicions about the punchbowl were on target. Her breath smelled like a winery. "Grandmother, I love you. When I fall in love with a special man who will love me for all the warts and oddities that make me who I am, and that includes saggy breasts, you will be the first to know."

Before she could retort, the band struck up a note that beckoned everyone's attention. Dad stood at the microphone and said, "Tullah, we know you're not one for a bunch of frilly presents, so we all chipped in to get you a special gift." He added, "Charlie, if you will."

Uncle Charlie walked forward with a huge gift-wrapped box in his hands. With a wink and a sly smile, he set it on the stage.

Suddenly self-conscious about my braless breasts hidden beneath a denim button-down shirt, I reluctantly walked forward and meticulously removed the huge red bow and satiny blue paper from the box. Dad offered his pen knife to help me slice through the sealing tape. I pulled back the cardboard flaps, and this time, I squealed like an excited child opening a special but unexpected gift.

It took a bit of strength to remove the custom-made pleasure saddle that had been hand stamped and tooled with the emblems of the Cherokee Wolf Clan and feathers inlaid with turquoise, complete with a matching bridle. I set everything on top of the box for all to see.

I cleared my throat. It took several seconds before I could speak without rasping. "Thank you. I'm overwhelmed by your generosity, your friendship, and…and for the most wonderful gift ever. I don't think anything will ever top this in the gift department. If I could give every one of you a hug, I would." Instead, I used both hands to blow a double kiss to the crowd of grinning faces.

Grandmother wiped tears from her eyes. I walked down from the stage and wrapped her in a hug. I whispered in her ear, "Don't worry, Grandmother, I promise not to let my ovaries dry up or my womb wither away. As soon as I hear the wolf's cry, I'll know my special warrior is waiting."

Little did I know that I'd just spoken my own premonition.

Chapter Five

I returned home from the party both elated over the saddle and still a little sad. Grandmother's concern about the uncertain state of my reproductive system threatened to take me to a deep dark place known as self-doubt. Here I am, unmarried, just turned thirty, and no prospects. A little voice in my subconscious whispered, *Old Maid!*

A pulse throbbed in my temple as I unlocked the kitchen door and slammed it shut behind me. River and Rascal followed me to the living room. It was late Saturday night. I flopped into my recliner and kicked off my boots. My big toe hurt. I massaged it. Tonight wasn't the first time Grandmother had berated me about giving her a great-grandchild. Her words haunted me. *Make a doctor's appointment. Maybe there's a kink in your tubes. How long has it been since you slid out of your panties?* She'd harrumphed. *Probably not since before Bryce died. You've lost your tender parts, Tullah.*

The moment his name had flown out of her mouth, I'd warned, "Grandmother, you've gone too far." I wasn't sure if I was madder that I couldn't get laid or that she was correct that when my fiancé had died in a freak accident the day before our wedding his death had done more damage to my heart than I wanted to admit.

I trudged upstairs to the bedroom. An array of emotions caused me to kick my clothes across the room the moment I'd disrobed. Forgoing a shower, I climbed into bed, turned out the light, and squinched my eyes tight. I tried to call forth Bryce's laughter, only to have it replaced with the deep, sensual sound of Clay Wolfchild's.

I sat up and stared into the darkened room. I could almost see him standing at the edge of the moonlit window: a striking silhouette, tall, slender, in tight jeans that emphasized his long legs and lean hips. His gaze was sharp and filled with a hint of amusement as he came toward me. My womanly places throbbed.

I grabbed a pillow and flung it at the window. "Get out of my thoughts, Wolfchild! You don't belong inside my head."

The mattress shifted when River leapt onto the bed and nuzzled my arm. He whined and tried to lick my face. I placed my arms around his thick black neck and assured him that nothing was wrong, and then commanded him to get off the bed.

At last, I felt the pull of sleep.

****

In the distance a neighbor's rooster crowed. I groaned and turned on my side to peer at the clock. To my dismay, I had slept through the night. I wanted to burrow back under my pillows, but the fragments of my dream were like pinpricks. I didn't have full recollection of the dream, just that the overall atmosphere had left me with a peculiar emotion.

My next thought was that I was a prisoner in my own bed. River lay snuggled at my feet, and Rascal, who is never allowed on the bed, occupied the extra pillow. Puttering snores from my pets were both endearing and annoying.

I managed to free myself from the tangled sheet. "Okay, you two, off the bed. Go! Scoot!"

My demands were met with stink-eyes and yawns until I physically shoved both animals to the floor. After racing down the stairs to open the doggie door, I ordered them to go outside. Then I decided a morning ride to try out my new saddle took precedence over a shower. I returned to the bedroom and changed out of my nightshirt. However, coffee first. I thought about inviting Ella to join me for a morning ride. A peek out the bedroom window and across the field to Ella's house revealed that Andy's patrol car sat parked next to her truck. Nix that idea, I thought. Newlyweds, and especially law enforcement wives, enjoyed personal time.

After I'd satisfied my caffeine fix, I unlocked my truck and removed the saddle from the box and toted it to the barn. Inside, I opened all the stall doors except Bella's. The other horses ambled outside, did their roll-in-the-dirt routine, then trotted toward the open pasture.

I didn't have a lot of saddle time with the young dappled mare. With this in mind, I eased the new saddle in place and tacked her up. She didn't resist, and I was pleased she showed no signs that the saddle and bridle weren't a comfortable fit.

This was a perfect day for riding, and I led Bella from the barn and to the gate that separated my property from Dolphy's Preserve, the state park property for which I had lifetime-use privileges. In the early days of September, the trees still maintained their vivid green southern attire but had begun teasing nature here and there with fall colors of reds and yellow tempered with hints of orange.

I closed and latched the gate, then toed my boot in the stirrup to apply weight while I watched Bella's ears for signs of agitation. She stood like a perfect lady while I settled into the saddle. With a cluck and a gentle nudge, she obeyed and moved out at a smooth walk.

I never failed to notice the beauty of the preserve's swamp land when I rode there. The smell of the loamy earth was distinctive. Fertile.

I urged Bella into a canter, and then a gallop. Trees reached their limbs like ghostly bones toward a pale blue sky. As we skirted around the swamp laden with its duckweed, snakes, and other dangers, a lot of things crossed my mind—dying ovaries, spinsterhood, and the mysterious spirit warrior. The worst images jumped into my head. The ones I didn't want to see. The ones inside a large brown envelope tucked away inside an old trunk in my basement. The ones of my murdered mother's body. That thought took the wind out of my sails.

River woofed and set out on the trail of a rabbit. In hot pursuit, Rascal joined his pal. I laughed and wondered what a tiny donkey would do if he actually caught up with the little gray bunny.

Perhaps it was the dog and donkey's actions that caused Bella to snort and tug at the bit. I was also in the mood for more than a leisurely gallop. I loosened the reins, leaned in to her neck, and let her sweep me across the marsh in a rhythm of pounding hoofs that matched my heartbeat.

I let her run until her neck was flecked with foam where the reins touched her neck. I allowed her to slow at her own accord. River and Rascal trotted back to join us. River's tongue was hanging out, and Rascal's sides were heaving from a race they had obviously lost. We ambled over to a small rivulet of coffee-colored water. River unceremoniously leapt into the middle of it, then came out to spray us with droplets.

While Bella slaked her thirst, I listened to the trill of tiny songbirds. They flashed through the branches of trees, knocking a few yellowing leaves to the ground. All too soon, summer would yield to winter. I turned Bella toward home.

"River...Rascal," I called. The wind blowing across the open expanse had a chill to it. But the sunshine on my back was almost too warm, and sweat moistened my shirt. Bella rocked my hips in her long-legged Quarter Horse stride. I closed my eyes and simply enjoyed the sensation of sun and movement. My cellphone rang and Ella's picture showed on the screen.

"What's up, Ella?"

"I don't mean to be nosy, but are you expecting company?"

I am no different from any other professional who often puts in sixty or more hours per week. Like them, I value my days off. It was Sunday. I'd left word with my service not to disturb me unless it was a true emergency.

Bella stood patiently while I talked on the phone. I said, "Why do you ask?"

"There's a Jeep parked in your yard and two women sitting on your front porch steps. Do you want me to check it out?"

I nudged Bella into an easy trot. It was difficult to hold both the reins and the phone, and talk, but I managed. "I'm about five minutes away from the house. You might walk over to see if it's a client with an emergency, though I can't figure out why the service didn't call to let us know, or why they would be on my porch instead of outside the clinic."

"Maybe I'll ask Andy to walk over with me. These days it pays to be cautious."

I agreed.

I disconnected the call at the gate, which I then unlocked and led Bella through. River, ever on the alert, raced toward the house with Rascal at his heels. At the barn, I unsaddled Bella and turned her into the pasture, where she galloped off to join her buddies.

I, on the other hand, hurried to the house to meet Ella and the unexpected visitors. My single desire was a shower and then grabbing a cup of coffee.

I stopped dead in my tracks. Andy had River by the collar and was straining to hold the barking dog, while Ella was doing the same with Rascal. I almost laughed at the comical sight of two women backed up against the door of a green military-type Jeep.

"River…Rascal…in the house!" I nodded for Andy and Ella to release the animals. River's hackles still stood like needles on his black neck. As soon as Rascal turned his little butt toward the one woman, I yelled, "Rascal…no!"

Andy covered his mouth and looked as if he were about to choke on laughter. He'd been the victim of one of the tiny donkey's rear hooves. Nonetheless, I put on my best frowny face and pointed at both animals to let them know that I meant business. However, this type of aggressive behavior was out of the ordinary, and I decided to be wary of these two women.

I said, "I apologize for my pets. They can be a little overly protective."

Andy gestured toward a tall, hard-faced woman with short hair. "This is Captain Margie Hinkley, and with her is Lieutenant Dee Shubert."

After the introduction, he excused himself saying he needed to get back to watching his Western movie. Ella asked if I would like for her to stay. I nodded.

Before inviting the two women to join me on the porch, I asked, "Do you have a sick animal?"

The hard-faced woman said, "I apologize for upsetting your pets. We're here to seek your help with selecting animals—horses, specifically."

"For what purpose?"

The lieutenant said, "Do you mind if we sit down?"

I exchanged glances with Ella. I said, "Of course. Forgive my rudeness. May I offer you a cup of coffee?" I figured if Andy wasn't concerned, then perhaps these women were harmless. But they looked as commanding as their military ranks.

Ella said, "I'll make it, Tullah."

Lieutenant Shubert settled in a rocking chair while the captain leaned against the porch rail. I noted the lieutenant's prosthetic leg and said, "Dr. Kemble and I are veterinarians. We treat animals. You need to explain about the 'selecting horses' part of your visit."

Captain Hinkley looked as if her face might crack if she smiled. I also added, "Are you active military?"

Almost simultaneously the women answered, "Army Retired."

Hinkley took the lead when answering my question. "You see, Dr. Holliday, the lieutenant and I are purchasing the old Second Chance Ranch. We plan to renovate the site into a place of rehabilitation and healing. It's a little-known fact that there are plenty of facilities for wounded men veterans. However, very few exist for women, especially those of us who have served in hostile territories and have suffered in both body and mind, as well as spirit."

Lt. Shubert spoke up. "We plan to name our facility Bravera Acres, a Place of Hope and Healing. We've done extensive research on the subject of places for wounded warriors, and what we've learned is that the caring for animals, living things, seems to aid in healing, thus the reason for horses, and chickens, goats, cows, and gardening."

It wasn't my intent to dampen the enthusiasm of these women. Yet my inner spirit was whispering not to get involved. In fact, I shouldn't have been taken by surprise when my owl, the one with eyes of two different colors, landed on the porch railing. I swear the bird winked at me, stretched upward, and ruffled its feathers.

As soon as River woofed a warning, the owl squawked, then flew off to perch on a tree limb where it continued to stare at me.

"What the hell?" exclaimed Hinkley. "I don't think I've ever seen a real live owl."

Ella returned with a tray of steaming coffee mugs. She hastened to reply, "Oh, don't mind him. He visits when…ah…when…ah…unexpectedly. We're used to him, aren't we, Tullah?"

I merely nodded. I was more interested in the ability of two retired Army veterans to operate a rehabilitation center. "Yours is an admirable cause, Captain, and as much as Dr. Kemble and I would like to assist you, we run an extremely busy clinic, as well as being involved in other community services. We simply don't have time to go horse shopping."

I could see the argument forming in her expression, and decided to waylay her. "Do either of you know the proper way to tack up a horse?"

Hinkley and Shubert exchanged glances. Hinkley said, "Not sure what that means."

"It means saddling and bridling a horse."

The women simply shrugged their answer.

I asked, "Do either of you know how to ride a horse or milk a goat or a cow?"

Hinkley seemed to mull my question. "No, but I'm sure there are books on the subject. We can learn."

"That's right," Shubert added. "How hard can it be? I mean, you plop the saddle on, climb on the horse's back, and say 'giddy-up.' I mean, they're just big dumb beasts, right? Look, Dr. Holliday, the captain and I are combat trained; we've seen action and had to be quick thinkers. There isn't much we can't handle. We're told you are the expert on horses. We're willing to pay for your time."

I didn't need to look at Ella to know she was trying not to roll her eyes. And me, my fingernails were biting into the palms of my clenched fist. I sucked in a deep inhale and let it out slowly. Big dumb beasts, indeed!

To quell my anger, I concentrated on sipping my coffee, and I watched the owl watching me. Finally, I said, "It's not about money, it's about commitment to my clients and my patients. There simply aren't enough hours left over in the day to take on extra projects such as yours."

"Okay." Hinkley shifted toward Ella. "What about you, Dr. Kemble?"

"Thanks, but no thanks. I can barely eke out enough time for myself and my husband, let alone taking on the responsibility of finding horses with temperaments suitable for the type of operation you're proposing."

I lifted the mug to my mouth for another sip while on the inside I was smiling, and silently saying, *Go Ella!*

I withdrew the cellphone from my back pocket and searched through the list of contacts while addressing the captain and lieutenant. "Natalie Fletcher, a decorated United States Marine combat medic, mother to a special needs child, and also Founder of Happy Hooves Equestrian Center, is a close friend. Natalie's center focuses on building the confidence and self-esteem of disabled children and adults. A few years ago, she expanded her facility to accommodate men and women veterans who needed healing in the spirit, mind, and body. She is a trained psychologist, an expert horsewoman, and one of the most generous and kind people you'd ever want to know."

I held my phone forward. "Here's her number. Give her a call. I'm certain you'll find her a valuable source of information, and she would probably welcome another facility to help alleviate her load."

Hinkley and Shubert set their coffee mugs aside and stood. Hinkley did a screen shot of Natalie's number. She held out her hand. "Dee and I are disappointed that you can't help us, but we thank you for sharing this information with us."

I returned the handshake and stood next to Ella as we watched them walk down the steps and toward the Jeep. What happened next was a validation that I was correct in my judgment of the captain and lieutenant.

As Hinkley opened the door to the Jeep, the owl swooped down and grabbed a hank of her hair in its talons. I don't know who screeched the loudest, the owl or Hinkley, as she and Shubert swatted at the bird until it released its grip and soared away. Needless to say, as soon as the Jeep sped up the driveway toward the main road, Ella and I could no longer contain our laughter.

Chapter Six

Billowing clouds were massing as I drove toward the fairgrounds. Today was the first day of the 4-H fair and rodeo. On either side of the truck, pastures were turning the colors of autumn. As a child, cloud watching had been one of my favorite pastimes. Those were the times I felt free of judgment from classroom bullies. Slowing the truck, I watched the clouds. They took on the shape of a bird, then an alligator, and then they scudded apart to re-form into the shape of a wolf.

Thunder rumbled in the far distance. An ominous sensation prickled the hairs on my arms. I gripped the steering wheel tighter. I had a terrible feeling that, if possible, I needed to throw up a psychic wall of protection. Tears stung my eyes, but I blinked them back.

This was a warning—of what? No matter how many times I experience these empathic visits, I'm always a little unnerved. I leaned over the steering wheel to look closer at the wolf cloud. It had disappeared, leaving me unsettled.

For the entire week of the fair, Ella and I had arranged to alternate our days at the clinic. I would work on the days she was at the fair judging the smaller animals, and she would take over on the days I needed to judge.

My phone rang, and I spoke to answer the call. "What's up, Alice?"

Alice is our new receptionist. Like her brother Jeff had before he left for college, she is working part-time at the clinic until she graduates from high school. She said, "I know you're on your way to the fairgrounds, Dr. Holliday, but there's an emergency at the horse barn. The horse is lying down and the little girl says she can't get her up. I told her you'd be there soon."

"Thank you, Alice. Did you get a name?"

"Yes, ma'am. Dana Phillips. Her daughter's horse is an eight-year-old Welsh pony mare. Mrs. Phillips said it was okay last night."

"Call her back to let her know I'll arrive in about ten minutes."

We disconnected the call and I pushed the accelerator. At the gate reserved for fair personnel and emergency vehicles, I was waved through. I eased through the parking area and parked as close to the horse barn as possible. Grabbing my medical bag, I dashed through the back door and trotted down the wide aisle until reaching stall number seven.

A sobbing child held the sorrel pony's head in her lap, and stroked its glistening neck. A woman said, "I'm Marci's mother, Dana Phillips. Are you the doctor?"

I offered a smile as I squatted next to the pony. "Yes, Dr. Holliday." I directed my attention to the girl. "Hi, what's your pony's name?"

A tear-streaked face filled with worry looked at me. Her lower lip trembled when she spoke. "Dilys. It means true and loyal. She's my best friend. Please don't let her die."

"That's a great name. What about you—what's your name?"

"Marci."

"How old are you, Marci?"

"I'm nine."

I offered what I hoped was a comforting smile to the child. "Well, Marci, it depends on what's wrong with Dilys. I wouldn't want to make promises that I can't keep, but I'll do my very best to find out what's wrong with her. Then we'll go from there. Okay?"

Marci answered with a nod.

I smoothed my hand over the little mare's swollen belly. She grunted and squealed in pain. Marci did her best to hold the pony's head still. In fact, she leaned forward and kissed the mare. "That's good, Marci. Talk to her. It'll keep her calm."

I placed my stethoscope to the mare's chest and listened. The heart beat was strong, though a little rapid, which I attributed to stress. As my hand rested on the extended stomach, I felt a distinctive bump, and then another. I listened with my stethoscope, then looked up at Marci's mother. "When was she bred?"

Dana Phillips eyes widened in shock. "Never. At least, we haven't…I mean…really?" She placed her hands against her cheeks.

"Mommy, she isn't dying, is she? Please, Doctor, you can't let her die."

Before I could answer, Dilys let out another squeal and thrashed about as if to stand. "Mrs. Phillips, help Marci hold the mare's head." Then I offered an encouraging smile to the little girl. "Marci, your pony is about to have a baby."

"A baby? Oh, can I watch?"

I cast a glance at the mother who nodded and said, "You betcha."

I lifted the little sorrel's tail and did a physical

examination. The foal was in the correct position for an easy birthing. Still, as a veterinarian, I knew to never take anything for granted. I asked, "About when did her pains begin?"

Mrs. Phillips said, "She seemed okay until about two hours ago. Marci was trying to braid Dilys's tail to get ready for the show and the pony couldn't seem to stand still, which is out of character because she's such a calm little dear."

"Are you Dilys's first owner?"

"No, we purchased her about seven months ago from a Mr. Norstrand in Pennsylvania. We brought her papers with us to present to the judges for registration verification. You don't think there's a problem, do you?"

"Not at all." Again, I offered a smile. "Is this the first time you've owned a horse?"

"Yes, and we searched for months before settling on a Welsh pony, and Dilys. Why do you ask?"

"Apparently, Mr. Norstrand either didn't know the mare was pregnant and sold her without knowledge, or he knew she was pregnant, and possibly not bred back with another Welsh, and didn't want to have to contend with an unregistered foal, so perhaps deciding to sell the mare was his best option. Either way, in about ten minutes you and Marci will add to your animal family."

"Oh, dear, what can I do to help?" Mrs. Phillips wanted to know.

"Just stay calm and try not to hover. Dilys is fully dilated. She'll do all the work in about—" I began a countdown with my fingers. "Here we go. You are about to witness the miracle of birth. Marci, once we know if it's a colt or a filly, you'll have to think of a special name."

I was rewarded with a dimpled grin, and then a scrunched frown. "What's a filly or a colt?"

I briefly explained the difference and was rewarded with a nod of understanding.

Once Dilys got started, she pushed the foal out in less than five minutes. A spindly-legged, copper-colored foal made its entrance into the world.

Marci clapped her hands in glee. "Is it a boy or a girl?"

Because the mare was still lying down, I gently moved the foal to her head so she could lick and bond with the new baby. I said, "Dilys's licking will stimulate the foal to extend its front legs, and then in an hour or two it should be able to stand. Don't worry if it's wobbly and falls down. Just like all new babies, it takes a while to get the hang of standing and walking."

"Yes, but is it a boy or a girl? I need to know so I can give it a name."

Oh, the impatience of the young. How well I remembered myself at Marci's age. "Let's give Dilys time to clean the foal, and then in an hour or so, when it stands and begins to nurse, I'll come back and check to see how they're doing. Maybe then I'll be able to answer your question. Until then, mother and baby need time to get to know each other."

Dana Phillips said, "Showing her today is out. How long before Marci can ride Dilys?"

In my mind, I went through a laundry list of dos and don'ts before saying, "At least six to eight weeks. Mares are no different than human mothers. They need to rest and to heal before any rigorous activity."

I disposed of the rubber gloves on my hands and closed my medical bag. "Mrs. Phillips, I'll speak to the head show judge and explain about Dilys so she won't be disqualified for being a no-show. I'll also ask if your entry fee can be returned."

"That's gracious of you, Dr. Holliday."

As I said my goodbyes, with the assurance that I would return to check on Dilys and the foal before I left the fairgrounds, Marci enthusiastically said, "I don't care if it's a colt or a filly, I'm gonna name it Copper Holliday because it's the color of a brand-new penny, and after you, Doctor."

I bent to give the little girl a hug. "I'm honored and flattered, Marci. Thank you."

Before exiting the stall, I handed my business card to Mrs. Phillips.

I left the barn and headed straight to the judging stand where I spoke to a longtime friend, the head judge, and explained about the mare. She made a note in her judging book next to Marci and Dilys' names with a promise to issue a refund.

Today was one of those feel-good days of accomplishment as I examined livestock, checked their health records, and answered a bevy of silly to serious questions from 4-Hers of all ages. I had also satisfied my affinity for carnival food with cotton candy, funnel cake, a sausage dog laden with peppers and onions and slathered in mustard, and enough pink lemonade to float a boat.

The sun was setting and my day was officially over, unless an emergency arose. I was ambling toward the parking lot when an elfin voice called out, "Tullah Crow!"

It wasn't a question but more like a command. I stopped, turning. Beside and slightly behind me stood a diminutive woman of undeterminable age. She was clad in a blue silk robe imprinted with golden stars and crescent moons. I was almost disappointed that she wasn't wearing a pointed hat to match her robe. Although her hair was covered with a blue swami turban, I was drawn to her eyes—obsidian but benevolent, and familiar.

"Do I know you?"

Her voice was matter-of-fact. "Perhaps…perhaps not."

"How do you know my name?"

She held a deck of cards forward. "The cards told me."

"Who are you?"

I saw loneliness in her face. She didn't appear old, but circumstances seemed to have aged her. "I am called by many names. For now, you may call me Madam Zahrani."

My memory banks were drawing a huge zero. I didn't trust myself not to sound snarky. "Madam Zahrani, I have no need to have my fortune told."

"It is not your fortune I wish to tell, but rather a warning I wish to give you."

Mere seconds ago, I had strolled past where she now stood. Unless I'd been lost in a daydream and missed seeing her, she had magically appeared, it seemed. After having experienced numerous unusual phenomena in recent years, you'd think I'd no longer be surprised by these unexpected visits. It was enough to drive a sane person to drink, and I'm not talking about apple cider.

I turned to walk away.

This time her voice was stern when she called me back. "Tullah Crow, long ago you received a fortune cookie. All these years you have kept that small slip of paper with this message: 'A golden egg of opportunity will fall into your lap. Wait for it.' "

Those words stopped me in my tracks. I turned my head so fast I almost gave myself whiplash. The hairs on my arms and on the back of my neck prickled. It had been years since I'd thought about that slip of paper. This female wizard had my full attention.

There was no malice in her slight smile. She said, "Come…follow me."

It was as if I'd been tele-transported from the parking lot and across the midway. I found myself inside a conical tent where I expected to see a crystal ball in the center of a table. My mind filled with questions.

Madam Zahrani invited me to join her at a table, minus a crystal ball. She snapped her fingers and a teapot and cups appeared. Okay, I commanded myself to awaken from this dream. She poured and my nose inhaled the tea's aromatic scent.

"Do not be afraid to drink, Tullah Crow. I am not a malevolent wiccan, and I do no evil nor bring harm to those whom I have been sent to warn."

"I'm not afraid. I'm merely surprised to be contacted by a wizard when my usual forewarnings come to me through animals or…" I thought about the warrior spirit that had presented himself to me the day I visited my mother's grave, and the time Shadow Woman had visited me in a dream.

"Forgive my impatience. Unless you've broken into my house and searched through my belongings, there is no way you could know about the fortune cookie message. So let's cut to the chase. Who are you—really—and why are you warning me?"

This wizened woman lifted the teacup to her pale lips and sipped. She seemed to study me as she drank. Maybe she was trying to decide to kick me out of her tent or cast a spell over me.

Finally, she said, "Be careful who you trust. Salt and sugar look the same."

Oh, panther piss, I thought. "Stop talking in riddles. Just spit it out…or I'm gone from here."

"Sip the tea, Tullah Crow. It will calm you."

I had to admit I admired Madam's brevity. To placate her, I dared a small sip. "Why do you call me Tullah Crow and not my full name?"

"Because it is your mother's spirit that beckoned me."

"A sorceress and not a Cherokee Spirit woman? I don't understand."

Her voice was succinct and her eyes stern. "You have wasted too much time with your doubting. I can do no more. Your ears are closed."

She stood and walked around the table, and with a swoop of her arm flung back the tent flaps. "Goodbye, Dr. Tullah Crow Holliday. Yes, I know who you are. I know about your mother's murder, for her spirit has sought me out."

Madam Zahrani morphed into a slender woman with a flawless coffee complexion, hair the color of a raven, and almond-shaped eyes. She no longer wore the silken robe but was clad in a buckskin dress. Around her neck was a turquoise necklace with a crescent moon and star pendant.

"Shadow Woman," I whispered. "Why have you appeared as a woman wizard?"

She cocked an eyebrow. "A woman wizard does not

draw attention at a fair as does a Cherokee woman."

"But you're not real…you are a spirit."

Her laughter sounded like tingling bells. "Believe what you believe, Tullah Crow. Now, heed my words. Your journey begins. It is a dangerous journey. Beware the skinheads."

Her image began to fade. I beckoned her. "Please…I'm confused. What journey…where am I going…and what the hell are skinheads?"

"It's not what, Tullah, but who."

"How will I know them…these skinheads?"

Her voice wavered like faint echoes. "Your mother knows. She will guide you."

In a wisp she was gone, and I stood alone in the parking lot. A surge of panic rippled through me as I struggled to rein in my thoughts.

"Hey, Dr. Holliday, did you forget where you parked?" Russ Albright, the fair's security officer, approached me.

Stunned and befuddled, I said, "Yes, I guess I did. It's been a long day."

He pulled out a handkerchief and wiped his brow. "Yeah, tell me about it. By the way, you parked next to the horse barn." He turned and pointed in the opposite direction from where I was facing.

Chapter Seven

It wasn't until I had parked under the carport and reached to turn off the ignition that I realized I was home. Although I'd become accustomed to theatrical appearances and vanishings, I still jumped when Ella rapped on the truck's window.

As soon as I opened the door and stepped out, Ella wrinkled her nose and pointed toward my rubber boots. This was her first year as a 4-H judge, and tomorrow was her initiation day. I grinned up at her as I sat on the back step and removed my boots.

It didn't matter how clean the students kept their animals and the inside of the stalls, there was always lots of fresh, oozy poop. I wriggled my freed toes. "I can't wait to see your face when you get home tomorrow evening covered in animal poo." I cocked an eyebrow and shot her my best know-it-all smirk.

While I rinsed off my boots, I regaled her about the surprise foal and how I'd overly indulged in fair food. I also warned her about the addiction of cotton candy. She simply nodded. "I'm a little nervous about tomorrow. It's my first time judging, and I don't want to hurt a child's feelings."

I assured her she'd do great. We chatted about her day at the clinic, and that Alice was doing a great job of running the office. I asked, "Do you have time for a cup of coffee?" In actuality, I wanted a hot shower and some alone time to think about the visit from Madam Zahrani aka Shadow Woman.

"I'd love to, except I'm meeting Andy at the Whitehorse Saloon for supper." She snapped her fingers. "Why don't you join us?"

I declined, feigning exhaustion and needing to catch up on paperwork, which wasn't a lie. We said our goodbyes, and I wished her luck on her first day as an official 4-H judge.

I was tired but not sleepy, so I decided to trudge upstairs for a long, refreshing shower. Passing through the kitchen, I had a sudden memory of my mother sitting at the table with her sketch pad and a cup of hot tea growing cold next to a neat row of colored pencils, a faraway look in her eyes as if she were living what I could not see. This made me smile. I closed my eyes and let the memories slide over me. A pang of loss hit me hard in the heart. I missed my mother. She had shaped my childhood, and my view of right from wrong, and she taught me to value my dad because he was a man who stood up for principle.

There was no doubt that as sheriff of Enigma my dad had dealt with the bottom-feeders of mankind. He had shielded me the best he could from the worst kind of people, especially the schoolyard bullies. He'd often advised me never to fear the bigots and to stand up for what was right. A little voice inside my head cautioned that standing up for right was often dangerous.

This brought me to the question that my family and I had asked so many times—why had my mother been murdered?

As I stepped over a sleeping dog and donkey, the animals barely lifted their heads to give me a woeful look. River then stood, arched his back, turned in a circle, and settled in the same curled position but faced the opposite way. Before going upstairs, I shed my stinky clothes and tossed them in the washing machine.

Once in the shower, I closed my eyes and managed to shut out the world as I relished the cascading water. Afterwards, dressed in my favorite oversized T-shirt, I found my stomach demanded something absorbent, so I took myself down to the kitchen where I heated water for a mug of hibiscus tea with ginger syrup and fixed a bowl of oatmeal with brown sugar and sliced banana. Then I made my way to the living room and into my recliner.

After scraping my bowl clean, I set it aside and opened my laptop to the murder file I had created about my mother. I read through all the previously written information and created a new tab and labeled it "Ponderings."

I'm not a very trusting person, so I understood what Madam Zahrani aka Shadow Woman meant when she warned, "Be careful who you trust." However, I was stumped by her statement, "Salt and sugar look the same."

My fingers flew over the keys with the thoughts and questions humming inside my brain like angry bees.

Who are the skinheads and how will I know them?
When will my mother contact me?
How will my mother contact me?
How am I supposed to solve her murder when she was killed in New York and I live in Kentucky?

I set the cup aside to massage my aching temples. Where were my spirit animals? In every case I'd helped my dad solve, either an owl, a murder of crows, a raven, or a wolf's howl had contacted me with a forewarning.

With the silence that slid over me while I sipped my tea, I wondered if they had abandoned me.

None of this mattered. What mattered was finding out the truth. By this time I'd finished typing my thoughts, so I shut down my laptop and strode to the kitchen to rinse my soiled dishes and set them in the dishwasher. I was exhausted. What I needed was a night of undisturbed sleep. I climbed the stairs like a woman twice my age.

****

Between alternating our days for the clinic with the 4-H fair, the remainder of the week sped by, leaving Ella and me exhausted and ready for a quiet weekend. I looked forward to doing nothing. I didn't have enough energy to take Bella for a workout.

It was still early on Saturday morning when the chiming cellphone yanked me out of a groggy dream about a garbage-strewn alley, blood splattered everywhere, and the looming shadow of a wolf. I fumbled the phone to my ear and heard Grandmother talking a mile a minute…something about a dream, and being on her way with…I thought she said jelly-filled donuts.

Click.

She hung up.

I could have slept longer but decided it was time to rise and shine, so I dressed, and hurried downstairs to turn on the coffeemaker. I opted to wait for Grandmother on the front porch, and to bide my time, I settled in the porch swing, opened my laptop, and searched for "skinheads." The definition "violent, right-wing youth gang—a hate group" was like a pitcher of ice water down my spine. I knew from my studies that groups like this were extremists of the worst kind. According to the research, most of the skinheads were hate-motivated against minorities.

My head snapped up at the warning woofs and brays, and the sound of an approaching vehicle. In a matter of minutes, Grandmother's blue sports coupe parked under the sprawling oak tree. Oaks are messy trees, especially when shedding their leaves in the autumn, but I love them in all seasons, even in the winter when their limbs reach toward the sky like ghostly arms.

My mind was still on the bit of information about youths often affiliated with neo-Nazi groups. I decided to keep this piece of information to myself. There was no need to upset my grandmother.

She opened the car door and waved. "I hope the coffee's on. Patty brought an assortment of our favorite donuts."

Morning light slanted through the branches as she and her best friend exited the blue coupe and walked up the steps.

Grandmother wrapped her arms around me in a bear hug, but her tremble was evident. I finally extricated myself, then looked her dead in the eye. "What's got you upset, Grandmother?"

I looked over her head toward the woman holding a large pink pastry box. Patty pursed her lips which was her way of saying she knew but her lips were sealed.

Grandmother said, "Let's go inside. I feel a bit chilled."

I opened the screen door and followed my two favorite ladies to the kitchen. Patty made a production of collecting saucers while I poured the coffee. It'd been a week since I pigged out on the 4-H fair's junk food. My stomach was finally back to normal. If asked, I would have admitted I'd rather have had a plate of biscuits and gravy in front of me instead of raspberry-filled donuts and chocolate éclairs. But I wasn't about to turn up my nose at them.

I waited until Grandmother had licked the éclair's chocolate icing off her fingers before I said, "Grandmother, you didn't drag me out of bed at the crack of dawn to share donuts with you and Patty. What gives?"

She finished off the coffee in her mug and held it forward. My patience was waning. She was stalling, and I needed to know why.

She babbled away in Keetoowah. Tears streamed down her bronze cheeks. Although I can hold my own in the Cherokee dialect, I was having difficulty following Grandmother's gush of words. I shot Patty a questioning look. She merely arched her eyebrows and shrugged.

I handed Grandmother a paper towel to wipe her eyes and blow her nose. I also refilled her mug.

She stammered, "Tu…Tu…Tullah, I had the most horrible dream." She spouted, "You died. The killer was young, and he had a bald head."

Grandmother's shoulders shook with sobs. I pulled my chair next to hers and wrapped my arms around her trembling body. Madam Zahrani's image flashed before me; her warning echoing inside my mind.

"It was only a dream, Grandmother. It's not like you to let a nightmare upset you."

Her gaze snapped to mine. "The secret sense is the wisest part of us. It knows when something's not right and steers us clear of what is bad for us. It also guides us toward what *is* right, and sometimes it's hard to tell which is which. Sometimes, Tullah, dreams are omens. You should know."

I released Grandmother and walked to the kitchen window. Morning sun slanted through the window. I half expected a spirit animal to appear to validate Grandmother's dream. Across the yard, Gandalf stood with his neck draped across Bella's. An eeriness crept over me. Gandalf had belonged to my mother, and while she was alive, he would let no one but her ride him. It was almost as if the gelding was protecting the young mare. Perhaps this was the substantiation I needed to support Grandmother's dream. Yet it didn't make sense. I had no significant other to protect me.

It was Patty who interrupted my musing. I grabbed the coffeepot and returned to the table. She and Grandmother waved away my offer to refill their cups again. Patty Sweet is a no-nonsense, intelligent woman. Like my grandmother, she was a widow who never remarried, but she'd never had any children. She and my grandmother gravitated toward each other and became best friends, and then Patty served as vice mayor during my grandmother's mayoral term. Last year, she sold Sweets 'n' Eats, her pastry shop and café, and officially announced her retirement. Still, at eighty years young, these two vibrant ladies are my idols.

Patty said, "Far be it from me to poke my opinion where it may not be wanted, but I think you should discuss this with Charlie. Dreams, strange sightings at the cemetery—maybe it's nonsense, or maybe it's a paranormal warning. Who better than he, a Native American, from outside the Cherokee people, to know about such ideologies."

She nailed me with a serious gaze. "Tullah, with

Tanti's background as a crime reporter, and with this mystical gift you possess, I know and you know that she doesn't scare easily. Whatever she saw in her dream has frightened the bejeebers out of her. For her sake, and yours, don't sluff it off."

After a long pause, and to set their minds at ease, I said, "There's no need for either of you to worry. However, I promise to call Uncle Charlie."

Chapter Eight

I stood on the porch and watched the blue sports coupe travel away from the house and toward the highway. I tried to push aside the darkness of Grandmother's words. I told myself I wouldn't let Madam Zahrani's warning or Grandmother's dream get inside my head, but of course that was impossible.

After fourteen years of whatever evidence existed lying cold in a dust-covered cardboard file box inside a New York police precinct's storage room, the person or persons who had tortured my mother were evidently long gone, but her case still needed to be solved. She deserved justice.

Having a degree in forensic psychology, and working with my dad to solve several heinous cases, I was aware that once killers tasted blood they thirsted for the next kill. Psychopaths were born and bred, created from both nature and nurture. They would keep coming, and nothing I or any officer of the law attempted could deter them from their destructive path.

There was much that neither I nor my father knew about "Unsolved Homicide Victim Holliday, Josie Waya, NYC, NY." The large brown folder lay dormant inside a trunk in my basement. Fourteen years ago, I was a teenager and barely capable of comprehending the violence inflicted on my mother's body, much less read and absorb all the information listed in the homicide report.

Until now.

I brought the coffee cup to my lips and realized it was empty. The weather was too hot for me to remain on the porch, no matter how much I enjoyed the view, and I needed something absorbent in my stomach anyway. Returning to the kitchen, I opened a can of biscuits, then laid several strips of bacon on a cookie sheet and popped them in the oven. The delectable aroma brought my black Lab skittering to the kitchen. While I waited for my breakfast to cook, I sat at the table and glared at the door that led to the basement. Grandmother's dream and Patty's advice to contact Uncle Charlie played like an incessant tape recording inside my head. Inundated in my musings, it wasn't until I smelled burning bacon that I realized I had completely forgotten to set the oven timer.

While rushing to rescue my breakfast and to keep from setting my house on fire, I tripped over River, and in the process of falling knocked myself silly when my head collided with the corner of the counter.

I must have lost consciousness. The next thing I remembered was Ella, who had a damp cloth pressed to my forehead and was calling my name. When I opened my eyes, River's paws were on my chest and he was whining and licking my face.

"What happened? Are you okay?" Ella asked. She removed the bloodied dishcloth. "I don't think you need stitches, but let's get you to the hospital. I want to make sure you don't have a concussion."

She helped me to a chair once I managed to shove my concerned dog aside enough so I could stand. As a doctor, I'm well aware that animals as well as people experience moments of post-traumatic stress disorder. Perhaps it was the bloody cloth and the blood on my shirt and the blood on Ella's hand that brought my mother's death back to me, full force. I was sixteen, standing in the morgue with my father and grandmother, weeping over my mother's mutilated body.

I blinked to clear my vision. "I'm fine, Ella."

"No, you're not. Don't argue. I'm pulling rank on you." She placed her arm around my waist.

The moment I stood, the room began to swirl, my stomach turned upside down, and I teetered. I don't remember much about the ride except Ella must have broken every speed limit between my house and the hospital.

By the time we arrived, a gurney was waiting at the emergency room entrance with my dad, Grandmother, Uncle Charlie, Andy, and my stepmother, Dr. Sunny Sanders Holliday, waiting like sentinels. Except for a massive headache, and a lump the size of a bantam egg, I almost felt like a celebrity being greeted by doting fans.

While I was being wheeled down the hall to x-ray, Ella said, "Sheriff Holliday…um…Henry…sorry, I keep forgetting you're my stepdad…anyhow, on the way to the hospital, Tullah kept mumbling something about skinheads, and salt and sugar looking the same."

I have no clue how Dad responded because Sunny banished my concerned entourage to the family waiting room. An hour later, I was wearing a hospital gown and lying in a hospital bed with an IV in my arm, and gladly swallowing a pain pill to alleviate the feeling that I'd been hit in the head with a sledge hammer. Sunny declared that as a precaution she was keeping me overnight.

When I protested, Sunny said, "You have a concussion, Tullah. As Chief of Staff, and now your stepmother, I'm pulling rank on you. As a medical professional you know the consequences of a concussion, mild or serious. Besides, think of the perks—you get to wear the latest fashion in patient attire and enjoy the hospital's gourmet cuisine."

When her pager sounded, she patted my hand and promised to check on me later. Thankfully, the pain medication had kicked in. I looked at the concerned faces staring at me. I wanted to set them at ease by making a joke or some comical remark. Nothing came to mind.

Uncle Charlie winked and said that later tonight he'd bring me a BBQ sandwich and onion rings.

Ella told me not to worry, that she and Andy would feed the animals. Since tomorrow was Saturday, I could rest easy. She also assured me she could handle our caseloads until Sunny gave the okay for me to resume work.

I lamented, "I feel positively foolish tripping over River. I hope he enjoyed the burnt bacon and biscuit."

Her blue gaze met mine. She shook her head and smiled. To my further amazement, huge tears welled in her eyes and one slid down her cheek before she turned away and followed Andy out of the room. I was touched by her emotion.

When Uncle Charlie headed toward the door, I said, "Don't go. I need your help."

I didn't miss the questioning glance he shot toward my dad and Grandmother. At the moment I was about to explain why I needed him to stay, an aide walked in with a tray of food—yum—red gelatin, a banana, clear broth, a cup of coffee, and saltine crackers.

The aide offered a wan smile. "Sorry. You were admitted after the lunch hour. It's the best I can do until dinner."

Nonetheless, I thanked her and peeled the banana. "Grandmother, even though it's upsetting, I'd like you to tell Dad and Uncle Charlie about your dream—in detail and as much as you remember."

I feasted on my meager meal while she related about a youngish man, bald, attacking me with a knife. "You were in a dark alley." Her voice trembled as she spoke.

Hmm, I thought, a dark alley; that coincides with my dream. Perhaps this is the omen I'm expecting.

Grandmother continued. "I also remember there were numbers and letters tattooed on the knuckles of each hand, and a symbol on the top of his head and the side of his neck."

Dad said, "Do you recall the numbers and letters or the symbol?"

She didn't so much as crack a smile. "Oh, yes, Henry. They were all quite vivid."

I was so intent on listening to Grandmother that I'd finished my meager meal without realizing it until I drained the last drop of bitter coffee from the cup and shoved the bedside table aside. A light rap on the door interrupted Grandmother. The same aide who had delivered my meal entered to collect the tray.

As soon as she left, dad prompted Grandmother to continue. I noticed she was having difficulty containing her emotions. I wanted to beat someone to a pulp for putting such fear into my grandmother.

She closed her eyes; her voice was low and succinct. "On the right hand—N.A.S.H. and on the left—S.P.3.7." After a deep exhale, she added as she touched the top of her silver-streaked hair, "Two large lightning bolts covered his entire bald head. And…"

At her hesitation, I prompted, "And…what, Grandmother?"

She buried her face in her hands and shook her head. "I don't want to say—it might come true."

Dad scooted his chair closer and wrapped his arm around her shoulders. "It's best that we know everything you remember Tanti."

Uncle Charlie agreed. "Dreams are often omens that guide us to the truth; good or bad."

She stuttered her answer. "He…" Her voice dropped to a nearly inaudible whisper. "He scalped Tullah." The wail that rose up from her throat reminded me of a wounded animal.

It was the same sound she'd made the day we had to identify Mama's body…the most forlorn cry I've ever heard, and it sent ripples through me because it was the sound of my heart breaking, too.

A nurse, with my stepmother on her heels, rushed into the room; concern lacing Sunny's face. "What happened…Tullah?"

I pointed. "It's Grandmother. She's a little overwrought. Please give her something to calm her nerves." Grandmother's desperation tugged at my heartstrings.

Sunny issued an order. The nurse hustled from the room only to return in minutes with a small white pill cup. She poured a glass of water and held the disposable container to my grandmother. The abruptness of her tone startled me when Sunny said, "Henry, it's time for Tullah to rest. Perhaps you or Charlie will take Tanti home for her to also relax."

Although my head throbbed, I objected. "Not yet. We need to figure out…"

Dad cut me off. "Sunny's right, Punkin." He stood over me and planted a kiss on my forehead. "We'll see you tonight."

Uncle Charlie shot me one of his rare smiles. A smile that didn't hide the concern in his ebony eyes. He quirked a look at my stepmother and said, "No offense to the hospital kitchen staff, Sunny, but I promised my goddaughter a BBQ sandwich and onion rings, and I never go back on a promise."

Sunny returned a conspiratorial smile. "My lips are sealed only if you bring me one, too."

"I think that's called blackmail."

A nurse entered carrying a small silver tray that held a syringe. I've given plenty of injections to animals, but I've never been a fan of being on the receiving end. The nurse inserted the needle into my IV. All she said was, "Doctor's orders."

Within minutes I was alone. Just me and the slow-drip-plunking IV. I tried to concentrate on the information Grandmother had related from her dream, only to find the numbers and letters swirling inside my head like leaves on a windy day.

Chapter Nine

The problem with lying in a hospital bed is having too much time on your hands. I've never been one to wallow in a blue funk. Today is an exception. In the deep-dark, down-and-ugly blues, not even the bright pink hospital gown cheered me up. I briefly closed my eyes, hoping all of this was a bad, bad nightmare. Deep in my soul, I knew better.

I puzzled over the letters Grandmother had described on the baldheaded guy's knuckles. Obviously N.A.S.H. and W.P.3.7 were gang codes, but what did they mean?

My head ached. The dripping from the IV seemed to echo inside my ears.

To relax and allow the sedative to work, I tried to envision myself astride Bella, racing across the swamp, the wind whipping my hair and her mane. Instead, I slogged my way through lightning bolts and leering alphabetic letters.

I hadn't realized I'd drifted to sleep until someone tweaked my big toe. A delectable aroma tantalized my starving tastebuds. The idea of onion rings and pulled pork made my mouth water.

Uncle Charlie stood at the foot of my bed. His flint eyes stared at me. "You know how much I hate breaking promises." He opened a bag and withdrew a round container and removed the lid. "Truth is, I decided to fix you shrimp and grits, and hot buttered biscuits."

The dream had disappeared yet left me unsettled. I felt weak, the way an invalid must feel after a long and debilitating illness has passed its crisis. I shifted restlessly.

He raised the bed to a sitting position. I managed to smile. "Food fit for a queen. You're forgiven."

I scooped the grits over the top of the shrimp, and indulged myself. "Thanks, Uncle Charlie. So much better than gelatin and broth."

Dad strolled in toting a cup carrier with three large coffees, and a pink box. He said, "Chocolate fudge courtesy of Patty."

To say I felt extra special is an understatement. After I'd scraped the last morsel of grits out of the bowl, licked the biscuit butter off my fingers, and consumed three pieces of fudge, I was ready to be sociable. Except socializing wasn't on my mind.

My brain was still a bit foggy and I couldn't think of a way to start the conversation. I felt like bursting into tears, which was so unlike me. In a bid for time, I lifted the coffee cup to my lips and sipped.

I shifted my gaze between my dad and Uncle Charlie, and said, "Do you think there's any validity to Grandmother's dream?"

Dad crossed and uncrossed his long legs. Finally, he said, "I've run the letters and numbers through the national crime data base. It'll take about twenty-four hours to hear back." He fiddled with a wrinkle in his jeans. "Honestly, I think with the anniversary of Josie's death approaching, it's sent Tanti into an emotional spiral. Tanti's nearing her eighty-first birthday. That may also contribute to her frame of mind."

A heavy pattering drew my focus toward the window. I half expected to see a crow or a raven tapping at the glass. My first thought was—tears. Instead, raindrops splatted and slid down the pane.

As if reading my thoughts, Uncle Charlie said, "Well, Tanti is Cherokee. Perhaps the Great Spirit beyond has reached out to her because you have made it clear that you no longer wish to be contacted by the spirits, and the only way to reach you is through Tanti."

He leveled his gaze at me. "You asked if there is validity to Tanti's dream. When I was a little boy living on the White Mountain Apache rez, I remember the shaman telling me that dreams and the truth often walk hand in hand. Little Sister, open your internal eye, the one that looks into your soul, to find the answer to your question."

He stood and patted my shoulder. "I must go now. The saloon does not run itself."

I wanted to hug him.

Before he exited the room, Sunny entered. She asked me to follow her finger as she flashed a light in my eyes, and then she offered a smile. "You can go home tomorrow morning."

"Aw, gee, Doc, and I was just beginning to enjoy my vacation." It was a lame statement and my failed attempt at humor.

Dad said, "Speaking of vacations, Punkin, when was the last time you actually took one?"

His handsome face is marked by time. He hasn't fully recovered from last year's knife wound to the heart that nearly took his life. The thought of losing him causes me great concern. For a moment we let the silence gather around us, and then I said, "What about you, Dad? When was the last time you took a vacation?"

Sunny arched her eyebrows. "Yes, Henry, neither of us could carve out enough time for a honeymoon."

He accepted her hug, and before she left she kissed him on the cheek. "The perks of being public servants."

He drew a deep raspy breath as he readied to leave. I searched for words to delay him and Uncle Charlie. Emotion caught in my throat, a lump impossible to swallow, and I asked them to stay.

"What's wrong, Punkin?" Dad said, "Your face just went all white."

Uncle Charlie shot me a worried look.

Both of them pulled their chairs closer to the bed, and I managed to relate the warning and the mysterious visit from Madam Zahrani, and how she had morphed into Shadow Woman.

"Dad, sometimes it seems like yesterday that we looked at those horrible pictures of mother." A deep dread settled over me. "With Grandmother's dream and Shadow Woman's warning, I think it's time to revisit the case file. We were all so distraught after her murder that none of us had the wherewithal to remain objective about evidence or lack of it. The large brown envelope is tucked away inside the chest where it has remained all these years."

Emotions played across his face and his jaw worked in agitation. "As a lawman, I understand your reasoning. As a man devastated by the senseless mutilation of his beloved wife's body, I'm grappling with the idea."

I glanced down at my clenched hands. The look of my twined fingers, combined with the hospital's antiseptic smell and the scrape of Uncle Charlie's boots against the floor, ripped the cover from a well of memories. For a few minutes I was no longer wearing hospital garb, lying in a hospital bed, but standing in a morgue nervously waiting for the mortician to fold back a blindingly white cotton sheet to reveal the corpse of a once-vibrant woman.

With a terrible effort, I wrenched myself back into the proper place and time. As I struggled not to break down, I listened to the timbre of my father's voice as he finally said, "It's time. When?"

He lifted his head as if he'd just won a battle.

A chill went through me as I replied, "Tomorrow. Uncle Charlie, we need you to come also, and Grandmother."

The heaviness of this commitment made me want to cry. I managed to hold back my tears. As soon as Dad and Uncle Charlie said their goodnights, with promises to escort me home tomorrow, I pushed the call button.

A nurse answered, "How may I help you?"

The dull ache behind my eyes threatened to explode into a chronic migraine. "This is Dr. Holliday. I need something for a headache."

Within minutes a gentle voice spoke my name. I looked into a pair of kindly eyes as the nurse handed me the pill cup and a glass of water. She said, "You're going home tomorrow."

It wasn't a question just an attempt to make polite conversation. I swallowed the medication and answered with a painful nod. At this point all I wanted was for the narcotic to kick in, and to lose myself in a mindless void.

I drifted in and out of relieving sleep and painfully vivid images. Visiting hours had ended and the noise level in the hallway was winding down for the close of day. A nurse entered my room and dimmed the light. I asked her to completely darken the room. She did.

My mother's face flashed before me and faded just as fast. I remembered the shape of her eyes—almond, and with a hint of mischief. She had a dimple in her right cheek that deepened when she smiled and was part of her infectious laughter. She'd never see another sunrise…never capture life on a canvas…ever again. And for the rest of my life, I would miss her.

I must have coasted off to sleep, because the next thing I was aware of was waking. I woke just a little, though; just enough to realized I'd been asleep, just enough to rationalize something unusual had roused me. A soft whisper.

"Tullah."

It wasn't a nurse because they all referred to me as Dr. Holliday.

The voice came again. "Tullah."

My eyes opened wide in the darkness. I lay stiff, listening. I could see through the darkness much more clearly now.

I scooted higher on the pillow, and spoke to the shadowy figure standing at the foot of my bed. "Who are you?"

I strained to focus on a figure that faded in and out like an old-fashioned intergalactic movie character. Had a monster somehow slipped past the nurse's station and entered my room? The rational part of my brain scoffed at the idea; the drug-mired side suggested otherwise.

Despite the dreadful hammering of my heart, I again commanded, "Who are you?"

I willed myself to be still. The figure yo-yoed in and out of the cosmic aura, making it difficult to decern whether my intruder was man or woman.

A voice that reminded me of brittle leaves said, "Do you not know me, Horse Girl?"

I was trembling from head to toe. Only one person had ever called me by that name. When I was a little girl, horses were the center of my young world. I loved horses so much that my mother called me Horse Girl. I was almost afraid to speak and responded cautiously, "Etsi?"

"It is I, my daughter."

Talk about warring emotions. I didn't know whether to jump out of bed and wrap my arms around my long-dead mother or seek help from a psychiatrist. I yanked myself out of this anxious silent yammering.

"There is so much I need to know, Etsi...names... names of those that..." I couldn't bring myself to finish saying, "those that killed you."

"Hush, my daughter. Open your ears, for the Great Spirit Father and Shadow Woman have granted me a small space of time to visit you. I have much to tell. Listen without speaking."

I nodded my acquiescence to her command and hung on every word. I didn't want to miss any important details. I watched as she tried to shoved away the darkness that threatened to recapture her essence.

"I wish you could be with me always, Mother."

"I have never left you," she said. "I am the owl, the crow, the raven, and even the horrid pallbearers in the sky."

Part of me wanted to rail in anger because I'd felt cursed rather than blessed to have these warnings that led me to murdered victims and sometimes seemingly unsolvable mysteries.

To curtail my temper, I bit the inside of my cheek. Still, it was difficult to keep the edge out of my voice. "I don't understand. There were moments when I questioned my sanity. Why would you saddle me with such gruesome responsibilities?"

There was a shift like fog or a misty cloud. My mother's image began to fade. She waved a ghostly hand in the air. I had once read that good souls shied away from controversy. I cried out, "Don't go. Forgive me. I must know—why?"

I wanted to hold on to the soft misty touch of her hand. The sadness in her eyes reached deep inside mine. She said, "It was never my intention to disturb your mental being. *Uyaga* is an evil earth spirit which is invariably opposed to the forces of right and light. I only meant to prepare you for a dangerous journey—to find those who took my life and bring them to justice. It is ordained that in the circle of seven only a woman warrior can avenge the death of a sister warrior. Do you understand, my daughter?"

I nodded. "How will I know *Uyaga*?"

"Be careful who you trust. Salt and sugar look the same."

Those were the same words Madam Zahrani had spoken. "I don't know what that means."

"You will, my daughter. You will see with your own eyes."

I decided not to question her further lest she fade away. "I am afraid."

"Fear is a good thing, my daughter. It keeps you vigilant, but the Lakota known as *Shunkaha,* the wolf, will appear when you are in the most danger. He will protect you—forever. Do not be afraid."

Some call what I have a gift. Regardless of my mother's explanation, I still consider seeing spirits, even my mother's, a curse. The problem with me is that ever since the first time the owl—or should I say, my mother—visited, my empathic gift seemed to become more acute whether I wanted it to or not.

Her essence began to flicker. I called her back. "Etsi, what else…what else should I know to help me find your killers?"

Little spits of light seemed to encircle my mother. She was surrounded by fields of looming shadows. I had often seen these same shadows while sitting in my porch swing during the late evening when only the fireflies flittered and winked, and all else was quiet. Innately I knew not to call her back. She was returning to the great beyond.

I sensed rather than heard her voice. She had not answered my question but rather had said, "*adageyudi uwetsiageyv,*" which in Cherokee roughly translates into *I love you, daughter.*

Before mother had shifted into a wisp of vapor and disappeared, I whispered, "I love you, too, Etsi."

A knock sounded at my door. Light from the hallway enveloped the room. A nurse entered. Absurd, but the rap sent alarms rushing through my bloodstream. She stood next to my bed. "Are you okay, Dr. Holliday? I thought I heard voices."

She lifted my arm to check my pulse. "It's a little elevated. Perhaps I should notify Dr. Sanders."

I assured her that I was okay. I said, "Sometimes concussions cause people to experience bad dreams. Perhaps I was having one and talking in my sleep. There's no need to bother my stepmother."

The nurse stared at me oddly. She handed me the call button and, with authority in her voice, said, "Buzz if you need anything."

She opened the door, turned to give me one last look, then pulled it shut behind her. My eyes shifted around the room. I was alone.

I had to admit I was a bit shaken. I knew the visit from my mother wasn't a hallucination. I was fully awake, and ghosts didn't open doors—they walked through them.

Chapter Ten

Yesterday, Ella had brought me a clean change of clothes. Today, I was up early. I needed to wash away the lingering effects of last night's visit. Big time. I slid out of bed and padded to the bathroom, making sure to lock the door. I shed the hospital gown and stepped into the shower to stand under a spray of delightfully warm water.

I was dressed and ready by the time Dad entered the room. Checkout time. I needed coffee…good coffee…something other than weak as water brown liquid. I almost objected to being escorted downstairs in a wheelchair. Then I thought, *Why not?* I knew it was hospital policy and I'd only waste my breath protesting.

By the time Dad drove down my driveway and parked next to a black truck, I spotted Uncle Charlie and Grandmother sitting in the porch swing. River and Rascal rushed to give me an exuberant welcome, and Dad had to steady me to keep them from knocking me off my feet.

"Grandmother," I said, "you have a key. Why are you waiting on the porch?"

Although the temperature was pleasant, I sensed the tremors running through her body like a bird coming back to life after a cat had left it for dead. She said, "I have visited many times since Josie's death, but I have never felt the memories as I am feeling now. They are almost like labor pains coming close together and forcing me to remember what I've spent years trying to forget. I don't want to see the pictures. Not ever again."

Her eyes reflected my own sorrow and fear. The last time I heard that grief in her voice was the day I stored the large brown envelope inside a wooden chest down in the basement and vowed to leave it buried forever. I had handed the key to my dad. The sound of it turning in the lock had grated like anguish in my heart.

Uncle Charlie helped Grandmother from the swing. I said, "Don't worry, Grandmother. There's no need for you to relive the horror."

She nodded. As soon as she entered the house, she walked straight to the kitchen. "I'll make the coffee." She glanced at the sacks Uncle Charlie held. "We'll eat first."

As anxious as I was to share about last night's encounter with my mother's spirit, I respected my grandmother's wishes to delay the revisitation of an ugly past.

We had all stored up the hurt these many years. I thought we needed to do this to be free of the uncertainties that had placed a stranglehold on our lives. We deserve to know the truth and to have the murdering animals brought to justice.

Animals…yes! What they did to my mother no sane person would have the stomach or the balls to commit.

The soothing aroma of coffee filled the kitchen as Grandmother bustled about setting the table and removing bacon and egg biscuits from Uncle Charlie's bags and putting tater tots on plates. She waved away my offer to help. Grandmother is an expert worrier, and I try not to give her anything to concern herself over. I understood that bustling about kept her mind busy and off what was to come.

After we were seated, Dad cleared his throat and said, "We might as well address the elephant in the room. Prolonging the reason we're here won't make reviewing the evidence file and photos any easier."

With that, he chugged down a gulp of hot coffee that sent him into a coughing spasm. He grabbed a napkin to keep from spewing us. Uncle Charlie stood and pounded him on the back with enough force to knock out a prize fighter.

Dad sputtered between coughs. "Charlie...I'm...okay."

While watching my dad choke on coffee and gasp for air wasn't exactly funny, the comic relief was enough to ease the tension that hovered over us. It was now or never.

"Something odd happened last night," I began. "One is that a ghost visited me last night."

Grandmother smiled as if she thought I was joking. When she figured out I wasn't, she repositioned herself in the chair, her posture arrow straight.

"It was Mother. The things she told me relate to your dream, Grandmother."

Dad frowned. "That's number one. What's number two?"

Grandmother clutched my arm as if I were a life preserver. She looked doubtful.

My voice shook to match the chattering of my teeth. "She also gave me the exact same warning as Shadow Woman did when she came to me as Madam Zahrani."

Grandmother grimaced. "What did she say?"

I twisted a strand of wayward hair and pushed it

behind my ear. "She said, 'Be careful who you trust. Salt and sugar look the same.' "

The look on Uncle Charlie's face matched Grandmother's and confirmed that I wasn't exaggerating.

I asked again, "I know that salt and sugar look the same but taste different; I know they are both used to season food, and I know that too much of either one is unhealthy, but what does it mean pertaining to Mother?"

Uncle Charlie said, "It is similar to the phrase 'Don't judge a book by its cover.' It usually refers to there being much more to people than you can see just by looking at them."

Instantly the words Mother had said about trusting Shunkaha slithered over me. A brief quiver returned. When she'd said that he would protect me, did she actually mean the opposite? Salt and sugar… A brief quiver returned. Who was I supposed to trust?

Grandmother scooted closer to the table. She looked flushed. I said, "I'm sorry, Grandmother. I didn't mean to reopen old wounds"

She looked at me with renewed worry. Her attempt to smile failed. "We have stored up all this hurt from years ago. It is good that it is coming out," she said. "Best thing you can do is not be afraid of it. Whatever *it* is."

Dad sat quiet—listening. A breeze had come up and whistled an eerie mourn around the house. At the same time, sounds and pictures from the past came without my bidding. Waves of panic rose and then fell. As I did when I was a child, I counted them. Ten. Eleven. Twelve. I waited for more, but the trembling stopped.

Though I wasn't a teenager anymore, I felt like I was sixteen again, the age of the memories. Grandmother rubbed my back, offering every bit of comfort she could. I'm not sure what I would do without her and my dad.

Through all the talk, we had somehow consumed our breakfast. I can't speak for the others but mine clung like sawdust in my throat. I shoved from the table to reach for the coffee pot to refill our cups.

Grandmother grabbed for my hand and gave it a squeeze. "Grandmother, it's been a while since you visited Moon. Instead of torturing your emotions, why don't you saddle him and go for a ride while Dad and Uncle Charlie and I sift through the contents of the evidence envelope?"

I glanced at Dad. He returned a nod to indicate he agreed with my suggestion, so I moved to the door that led to the basement. "I know exactly where the envelope is. I'll only be gone a few minutes."

Before I retreated, Grandmother expelled an audible breath. "Absolutely not. Moon can wait. As difficult as this is, I'm no coward."

I flipped a switch and grasped and turned the door knob. The light cast eerie shadows against the stair walls. I had never considered entering the basement as ominous. Until now. My palms actually sweated. Years ago, I had remodeled the room from a storage catchall into a darkroom. When cameras became obsolete, I converted the area into an office, which mostly went unused. Months had passed since I'd ventured into the cheery room decorated with bits of my mother's artwork and a few of her paintings. My favorite is a generational portrait—great grandmother—Chenoa; grandmother—Tanti; mother—Josie; and me, a little girl of six. Four generations encircled a rare white wolf denoting our Waya Clan.

I walked over and removed the cushions that adorned my mother's hope chest. *Hope*, I thought. What had my mother hoped for? Certainly not to die at such an early age. I opened the chest. On top lay a series of magazines, their covers still crisp and clean. Inside, Josie Crow Holliday's work was featured along with articles about an up-and-coming Native American artist whose paintings and artwork told the story of the Cherokee.

I lifted one of the magazines and opened to a paperclipped page. Mother's image stared back at me. The photographer had captured a mischievous glint in her eyes that, like the famous Mona Lisa, held a secret. What was the secret? It was a logical question, but logic is never a girl's best friend. I returned the magazine to its resting place.

Dad's anxious voice called, "Punkin?"

"Coming, Dad."

I reached beneath a layer of treasured items and searched until my fingers touched a paper package that sheltered years of sorrow, and hopefully clues to a killer.

The envelope was bulkier and heavier than I remembered. Upstairs, I handed it to Dad, who opened it and emptied the contents onto the kitchen table. My first reaction was to swallow the urge to barf my breakfast when I recognized the crime scene pictures of my mother and the tremendous damage that had been done to her.

"Grandmother, there's no need to upset yourself by looking at these. Remember her as she was…not…not like…this."

She inhaled deeply and held her hands to her breasts. "I am asking Great Spirit Father for courage."

I sifted through the stack, willing my stomach to stay calm and my emotions to remain cool. I knew one thing though—if these photographs were allowed in a courtroom, a jury would surely lose all sympathy for the killer or killers. It wouldn't matter that she was dead. There was no statute of limitations on murder. The prosecution would put these images to good use.

Dad's jaw worked back and forth, his brow knitted into a scowl, as he gathered the pictures and placed them back inside the envelope. Then he removed the criminal case file.

I embraced my grandmother as she emptied herself of tears. Mine joined hers, and new tears came in ripples like on a river. As I blew my nose on Uncle Charlie's bandana, which magically appeared, my headache escalated to a throb.

A part of me wanted to run out of the house and keep running. Another part of me felt bolted to my chair. The two parts battled in silence.

We all exchanged looks as we remained silently seated around the table. Grandmother started to stand and the chair crashed to the floor with her in it. I leaned over her. "Grandmother, are you hurt?"

Uncle Charlie lifted her into his powerful arms. I pointed to her former bedroom located next to the kitchen, and followed as he laid Grandmother on the bed. She protested that only her pride was hurt. She sat up and swung her legs over the bed's edge. And then she said, "Life hurts us all. We must find the strength to find my Josie's murderers. I want them punished." She raised her voice, and though Grandmother never rails, she shouted, "I. Want. Them. Dead!"

She skewered me with a defiant look. "Tullah, help me to the kitchen, and where is that special bottle of Irish Crème?"

Dad immediately went to the cabinet where I kept the container out of sight. The Irish Crème was for special occasions only. He refreshed our coffee and laced it with the chocolate alcoholic beverage.

Grandmother raised her cup. "To the sons of *Uyaga*—sooner or later you will sit down to a table of unmitigated consequences, and then I will sing the song of victory."

I have never seen such malice in Uncle Charlie's dark eyes. He said, "My Apache blood boils. In the days of my fathers, I would have striped my face with warpaint and sought to avenge my sister in spirit." He lifted his cup and drank deeply.

A knot grew in the pit of my stomach. My gut twisted together, a tingling premotion that something was about to happen, grew. I blurted, "Mother and Shadow Woman both said I would go on a dangerous journey. I asked when, and only was told that I would know."

My secret sense started like a vibration in my chest and then extended to my fingertips like a small charge of electricity. I cried out in frustration. "I'm so weary of the innuendos. Why do the spirits tease me with puzzles?" My voice rose. "In the name of the Great Spirit—just tell me!"

I held my head as if the puzzle just got harder.

Dad's cellphone rang. He fumbled to remove it from his pocket. "What is it, Tiny?"

Deputy Tiny Goodbody answered, "The information from National Crime Database came in."

"Can you send it to me in an email?"

"Sure, can, Henry."

Dad thanked him and disconnected the call.

As soon as the phone chimed to indicate the email had arrived, Dad opened the attachment. The scowl returned as he previewed the information he'd requested regarding the initials Grandmother had seen in her dream.

Chapter Eleven

Dad's fingers flew over the keypad. He said, "Punkin, I'm sending this to you so you can print it out."

I nodded and rose to race down the stairs to my office to collect the copies for Dad and myself. He glanced over the info, then said, "Tanti, I'll never understand this psychic connection you and Tullah have with the unknown, but the numbers and letters in your dream exist."

He read off the information: N.A.S.H. according to NCDB stood for New York Area Skin Heads. According to the report, the numbers three-seven indicated it was a subculture of the most secretive gang, known as the one-sevens. The one-sevens managed and enforced the gang codes and the laws, even from prison; they were known as the men of blood, the most dangerous in the Aryan gangs.

He lifted his gaze and looked at Grandmother. "The lightning bolt is their insignia."

While we were trying to digest this information, I flipped to the second page. My eyesight blurred and it took all my mental strength to read the gang's initiation requirements for young recruits.

Because of the fall weather, the windows and doors were open to air out the house. The wind blew through the trees, and for a moment I thought I heard my mother's voice. A squirrel chattered in a nearby tree.

Though the pain had lost its edge, my head still ached.

Dad lifted the medical examiner's report. He sighed with resignation. "In the war, Charlie and I've seen brutal things before."

Uncle Charlie nodded his acquiescence, his voice a whisper. "We've seen men ripped apart by explosions. Sometimes more than we could count."

Dad continued. "Sometimes there were hundreds of unidentifiable bodies. But this…"

I cast an intense glance to my dad and then toward Grandmother. I didn't want to increase her anguish any more than she had already suffered. Apparently, her eagle eye didn't miss my silent cue. She said, "What is it that you don't want me to see?"

It was difficult to accept that the pieces of the body on the gurney, in the morgue, had been a real woman, all in one piece, with no chunks of flesh gone, no bisection, no horrible gashes in her mouth.

When we didn't answer, Grandmother snatched the sheet of paper from my hands. "I'm a former crime scene reporter. There's not much I haven't seen."

Her color shifted from a rosy tan to ashen. She had difficulty getting the words out. "I had forgotten the tortuous cruelty done to Josie." Without another word she passed the paper to Uncle Charlie.

Renewed anger glinted in his eyes. He growled his response. "I would give these sons of hell-dogs the pain they deserve. I would bind them in the hot sun, then stretch them naked over anthills, and then I would slather their bodies with honey. I would turn a deaf ear when they cried out for mercy, and smile as I walked away. It is the way of my ancestors."

The loud slam of Dad's palm against the table

startled all of us. His top lip lifted into a snarl. "Five times I have been to New York seeking information…begged for help to find the monsters who did this. And five times I've been disrespected as an officer of the law and as a grieving husband, only to be told that ours isn't the only case and they're doing the best they can. Bullshit!"

There was little else to say.

Dad's cellphone rang. "Yeah, go ahead, Ramsey."

Three years ago, Deputy Wayne Ramsey took a bullet that left him with a permanent limp. Rather than letting him take a forced medical retirement from his Chicago precinct, Dad had hired him to man the Enigma office. Deputy Ramsey is invaluable, especially with his knowledge of the law.

Ramsey said, "Sheriff, we have a ten-sixty-five in progress with shots fired. Deputy Kemble and Goodbody are proceeding to the scene."

In his no-nonsense voice, Dad responded, "That's a ten-four. On the way!"

Dad and Uncle Charlie raced to the front door. Uncle Charlie is an auxiliary deputy as well as Enigma's fire chief. He often assists Dad when an extra deputy is needed.

I promised to take Grandmother home. She and I clasped hands as we stood on the porch and watched the two trucks speed toward the highway. Ella raced through the gate to stand with us. The worry in her voice was evident. "I heard Andy's name on the police scanner. What is a ten-sixty-five?"

I said, "It means a robbery in progress with shots fired."

Ella's knees buckled. Grandmother and I caught her

before she collapsed. I've been a sheriff's kid since I was fourteen. You'd think that by now I'd be used to these emergency calls.

I'm not.

A long time ago, I vowed to never fall in love with a lawman; yet it wasn't a bullet that killed my fiancé so many years ago. I tried to keep the fear from my voice. "They know their jobs, Ella, and won't take any unnecessary chances."

Her hands were icy cold. "That doesn't make it any easier."

Grandmother pulled Ella around to face her, her voice stern. "Ella, never let Andy see your fear. Never tell him about your fear, and never chastise him for doing his job. When you said yes to his marriage proposal, you also said yes to his career as a lawman. Someday, and I'm no predictor of time, but someday he may become sheriff, and that comes with an even heftier responsibility. You must decide now to stick it out for the long run, or…"

She left the rest to remain unsaid. Ella drew in a deep breath as she hugged Grandmother, and said, "For better or worse, through sickness or sorrow, until death do us part. When I said those vows, I meant it. No matter what the future brings, Andy is a keeper, and I am no sniffling crybaby of a wife."

My heart swelled with pride for my stepsister and business partner. "You can spend the night with me, if it will make you feel better." I flashed Grandmother a questioning look. "You, too, Grandmother. It's been an upsetting morning."

As soon as we entered the house, I gathered the criminal report and slid the pages inside the envelope.

"Excuse me while I put these away." I raced upstairs to my bedroom and shoved the envelope under my pillow.

When I returned, Grandmother stood holding her purse. "Let's go to Sweets 'n' Eats. My nerves are screaming for a pumpkin spice latte and a pumpkin muffin stuffed with extra vanilla nutmeg custard. Afterward, you can drop me home." Before I could protest, she held her hand up. "I know you love me, and you worry about me, but I need to be alone. Understand?"

I did understand. A part of me also wanted to be alone. As much as I never again wanted to look at the crime scene photos of my mother, I knew if I could detach myself from the gory mutilations, I might find clues that had either been overlooked by the NY investigating team or ignored because my mother was a stranger in town and they were biased against a Native American woman. Clues that would help my father when he decided to return to New York once again.

The drive to town was silent, as if we each were lost in our own thoughts. Ella broke the quiet by saying, "I hope it isn't the bank that's being robbed."

"Or maybe the jewelry store," Grandmother added.

At the main crossroads, street signs now show the names of the roads. When I was growing up, they were unmarked. Everyone knew the names already. I braked at a shiny new stop sign. New pavement covered the road leading to town.

Grandmother lamented, "If given a choice, I wouldn't want to stay in Enigma, though I'm not sure where I would go. I feel like Patty and I created a monster when we were pushing so hard to bring industry here." She let out a long sigh.

My eyes widened as I turned to look at her. It was as if she were reading my thoughts.

However, dredging up the good ol' days wouldn't solve the increase in population and crime. I pulled into an empty parking spot in front of Sweets 'n' Eats.

Worry dug a trench along my grandmother's brow. I switched off the truck's ignition and mustered a smile. "Grandmother, Enigma was a forgotten town dying a slow death. You were not only progressive but a wonderful mayor, and as vice mayor, Patty stood staunchly behind you when the city councilmen were satisfied to sit on their lardasses and let the town wither away."

Although I didn't mean it to be funny, "lard asses" elicited a snigger from Grandmother. I continued, "Because of your efforts, Enigma has new shops, more jobs, sustainable housing, and a community college. You breathed life into Enigma."

I paused. She touched my hand and frowned again. "And crime."

To make light of her distress, I said, "At least our sidewalks still roll up by seven o'clock."

I think Grandmother and I had forgotten about Ella until she laughed at the not-so-funny joke.

A thump on the window startled all of us. Ella squealed. "Andy!"

My immediate thoughts concerned my dad's safety. We all piled out of the truck, and Ella practically threw herself into her husband's arms. He looked over her head. "Everything is under control. Once Dr. Sanders-Holliday gets finished picking birdshot out of the perps, we'll make them comfortable in the jail."

In perfect harmony, our voices joined together and

asked, "Who was robbed?"

"The least likely place—would you believe it?—Jackon's gas station. Old man Jackson said the boys walked in with masks on, pointed a pistol at him, and demanded he open the cash drawer. He reached down for his sawed-off shotgun and pulled the trigger. Blew a huge hole right through the counter. Peppered both boys in the legs. All of that for less than fifty dollars. It was Tommy—Jackson's grandson—that called it in."

"Are the boys anyone we know?" I asked.

I shot a sidelong glance at Ella, who seemed to have stopped breathing. Andy made a sound of disgust. "Remember Mrs. Pierson? It was the same boys that shot her mare with an arrow last year. Apparently, the short visit to juvie didn't teach them a lesson."

We had followed Andy as he talked. Before we entered the pastry shop, I didn't bother to hide the disgust from my voice. "Those boys are no longer juveniles. I hope they're ready to really face the music."

Andy replied, "Yep, felony with a firearm will give them more than a slap on the wrist."

Inside the Sweets shop, a waitress showed us to a table. After we'd placed our orders, I asked, "Was Mr. Jackson or Tommy hurt?"

The waitress returned with cups and filled them with coffee. Andy said, "Mr. Jackson sustained a wound to the head, but he wasn't shot."

The waitress hovered with the coffee pot, listening.

We all leaned forward, our mouths agape. Grandmother scolded, "Well, don't keep us in suspense. How was he wounded if he wasn't shot?"

It was obvious by the Cheshire-cat grin on Andy's face that he was deliberately prolonging the suspense.

"The Haines boy managed to fire off a shot, which hit a bowling trophy on a shelf behind Mr. Jackson. The trophy flipped off the shelf and landed on top of his head—you might say he was *bowled* over. Anyhow, he suffered a minor gash, no stitches required."

We laughed at the unintended pun, which seemed to relieve a bit of my earlier tension.

****

Ella and I checked on our post-op patients, then called the horses in. Once all the animals were tended and fed, we strolled across the yard with River and Rascal trailing behind.

Ella said, "Tullah, you look tired. I'm concerned about the dark circles under your eyes. Tomorrow's appointment load is light. You've barely had time to rest since being released from the hospital this morning. As long as there are no major emergencies, I can handle the clinic."

I didn't hesitate to accept her offer. Instead of entering the house through the kitchen, we walked to the front porch. I said, "Andy's still on duty. Want to stay awhile and chat?"

She followed me to the porch where we settled in the swing. For a few minutes we were quiet until I blurted out, "Ella, do you think there's anything wrong with my ovaries?"

At first, I thought she was going to laugh out loud at my absurd question. In fact, I was surprised at what had just flown out of my mouth. Instead of laughing, she said, "This is totally out of character for you. Why would you ask such a question?"

My head wasn't the only thing that ached. "You heard what Grandmother said at my birthday party about my ovaries shriveling up." I tried to wave away my doldrums. It didn't work. "Don't take this the wrong way, Ella, but I think I'm a little envious of all of you."

She responded, "Really? How so?"

"Grandmother has her fearsome foursome group, you have Andy, and Dad has Sunny. There are times when I feel like the outsider looking in." Again, I waved my hand as if swatting away the miseries. "Pay me no never mind. You're right. Falling and knocking myself silly has made me…well…silly. Forget everything I just said."

Ella shifted so that she faced me. "Tullah, before you became my business partner, then my sister, you were and will always be my best friend. Please take what I'm about to say with a grain of salt because I'm saying it with love. Okay?"

I nodded. "Sure, hit me with all you have."

She worried her bottom lip. I surmised that she was trying to find a way to be tactful. I waited. She said, blushing, "A long time ago you gave me a piece of advice about my appearance. I'm returning that advice to you."

There was a long sigh. Finally, she said, "Stand in front of the mirror and take a good look at yourself. There's nothing wrong with your ovaries. The truth is, you could be a knockout with blue eyes against your bronzed complexion, and your bone structure, and your figure. But, girl, you're a mess. Your hair slicked back in a ponytail, no makeup, always dressed in jeans and boots… It's almost as if you are deliberately making yourself ugly. You act like you've given up on yourself. Forgive me for saying this, but a mummy would be more enticing." Ella fanned her face with her hand, though a cool autumn breeze riffled through the trees. "Oh, sorry."

"Ella," I said earnestly, "You've given me lots to think about."

I'm sure she had more to say. Fortunately, I was saved by a deputy's car rolling toward her house. She stood and graced me with a woeful look. "You're not mad, are you?"

A flash of the old days, before my fiancé, Bryce Meyers, was killed by a fractious stallion, nearly knocked me off my feet. I had always been the tomboyish type, but still took pride in how I applied my makeup and coifed my hair. Bryce was a ruggedly handsome man, like an old western movie star. We complemented each other in almost every way. When he died the day before our wedding, most of me died with him.

I gave Ella a sisterly peck on the cheek. "Never be sorry for being honest."

Chapter Twelve

Long after Ella left, I sat on the porch swing and watched the last rays of sunlight stream through the trees. It would be dark soon. Lightning bugs would blink across the field like tiny stars come to earth.

My thoughts kept me company. Grief, I decided, comes at a great expense. I shrugged to myself and pondered how the sadness of losing Bryce and my mother never went away. It just faded over the years like the colors in my favorite flannel shirt. I told myself not to cry, that I was being ridiculous, and the voice inside my head sounded a lot like my mother's.

It was late September in Enigma, and the oak tree leaves seemed to race each other to the ground. A gust of wind sprinted over the front pasture, bringing a twister of leaves to dance at the front steps.

When the whispers started, I told myself it was just the wind blowing through the trees. But it sounded more like women sobbing than the wind. Goose bumps rose on my arms and the hairs prickled at the back of my neck. I left the swing and opened the screen door. The whispers called me to come back. They weren't ready for me to leave.

I obeyed. Late afternoon sunlight danced off the green and gold oak leaves. My mother smiled at me. I read the sadness in her eyes, and I remembered the anniversary of her death was rapidly approaching. She stood there, her eyes dark and narrow as though looking through a portal into the past.

My heartbeat accelerated and memories chased after me. First, my mother, then Bryce, and now the ghosts of five women I've never known all stood in my front yard.

"Tell me what you want," I practically shouted.

Mother looked straight at me and says, "Limbo is a lonely place, my daughter." She spread her arms wide, and amongst the swirling leaves are the women, weeping. "They, like me, cannot cross over the bridge of eternal life until those who took our lives are no more."

I wanted to cry out, "Why me?" but I knew the answer. I'll never truly understand why I was cursed with this gift of communicating with the dead.

I pondered a strategy. "How can I find your killers when I don't know any of you?"

My mother's ghost was silent for several seconds, as if paying respect to the spirits of the dead everywhere. Her eyes didn't leave mine, as though she challenged me to a game of truth or dare. "The answer is in the papers you keep hidden. Our killers are all the same. You are clever, my daughter. Secrets get buried all the time. Look to the papers. Our secret lies among the words."

If I was to be free of this curse, to have a life without spirit animals leading me to the dead, to relax in the evening hours without hearing whispers in the wind, to find love again, then I had to speak to make it so. I gathered courage. "Mother, I will do my best to do your bidding, on one condition."

She looked at me with intense eyes. Eyes that, even when I was a child, never let me get away with anything; like she already knew what I was about to say, and she said, "Tell me."

"I love you, Mother. My heart tells me these women were also cherished by their families. I cannot control the law. I cannot control the law's decisions. I cannot control what punishments the law will give the murderous hellions. What I will promise is that I will find them, and then let the law do its duty. But you, and they"—I spread my hands toward the swirling clusters—"must promise to leave my life, forever! I am weary to the bone of this curse foisted upon me. I yearn to move forward with my life."

A gust of wind brought down a flurry of leaves that gathered in a dusty whirlwind before dancing away. Voices echoed and faded. I was almost certain the voices said, "You are our only hope…we…promise."

But something told me the trouble was far from over. My breathing went shallow. I entered the house and went upstairs to retrieve the envelope I had hidden under my pillow. Mother had said the answers were in the papers.

Downstairs again, I brewed myself a cup of hot tea laced with ginger syrup. I opened the envelope and removed the criminal case file to spread the pages side by side as I opened my laptop to the murder file I had created for my mother.

My anger kicked up dust that no broom could touch. It was not Mother and the spirits that I was angry with. It was the world. A world where women, especially ethnic women and women of color aren't always given a choice, or respected for their talents and intelligence. Women who are murdered for being who they are.

The first lines on the case file blurred. The pain in my head intensified. My mental energy was exhausted. Ella had been correct. I needed a day to rest. I sent her a text taking her up on the offer to manage the clinic, with the promise that if an emergency arose she should call me.

She responded immediately with a thumbs-up emoji.

River and Rascal followed me upstairs and settled in their beds. I closed the door to my bedroom, effectively shutting out the pages strewn across the dining table, and the voices in the wind.

The house was silent.

****

To my surprise, eight hours later, I awoke wide-eyed. I'd slept the entire night without seeing ghosts in my dreams, hearing voices, or even a trip to the bathroom.

A hot shower put a new complexion on the morning. I opened my bedroom window and inhaled the sweet aroma of jasmine. The sun was warming a brisk September day. This was perfect weather for a horseback ride, or sitting on the porch with a mug of hot chocolate and reading a good book, just about any other thing than searching through the criminal file, looking for clues that would give birth to multiple murders, and that would, hopefully, lead me to the killer or killers.

I dressed in black jeans and a black pullover sweater. The moment I grabbed the brush and pulled my hair back into a ponytail, Ella's words roared in my ear: *It's almost as if you are deliberately making yourself ugly.*

I looked in the mirror, and gulped down a lungful of oxygen. The image that stared back at me echoed Ella's words. *Girl, you are a hot mess.*

I touched the image and admonished myself.

"Tullah Josie Crow Holiday, I promise to do better. After I solve the case and can get on with my life."

The image winked then smiled at me, and Mother's face emerged. In a split second it faded back to my reflection. Swearing under my breath, I gathered myself together.

I skipped down the stairs to the kitchen, turned on the coffee maker, grabbed eggs, bacon, and a can of biscuits from the refrigerator, then busied myself preparing breakfast. Anything to avoid delaying the task of sifting through the papers on the table.

I decided that dining on the front porch was far more attractive to my digestive system than mixing death with scrambled eggs and bacon. With that thought in mind, I laced two hot biscuits with generous amounts of butter and healthy dollops of orange marmalade.

River's and Rascal's tails whipped back and forth with the expectation of receiving handouts. I opened canisters labeled for each pet. For River, I grabbed a large doggie biscuit and for Rascal a couple of nicker doodles, which are carrots and apples compressed into nuggets.

Once I had settled in the swing, and the dog and donkey were enjoying their treats, I relished a healthy bite of biscuit as I looked across the pasture. In the Cherokee culture, sky and land rule. A ray of sunlight broke through the clouds to cast a speckle of shadows across the yard.

Odd how an angle of light can evoke an avalanche of memories. I thought of my parents sauntering down the driveway after they'd walked to the mailbox on such a morning, walking hand and hand with me skipping along beside them. I can still hear my mother's laughter when my father playfully nuzzled the side of her neck.

Or the September day that I sat in the porch swing with Mama and Bryce came galloping down the drive on Cisco, an incredibly handsome blood bay gelding he'd bought with the money he earned mowing yards. The light had caught Bryce's strawberry blond mullet haircut and made him look like a Viking warrior.

He had dismounted, a box of chocolates in one hand, and like a gallant knight had dropped to one knee, thrust the chocolates forward, and asked me to the annual 4-H festival's dance. I was thirteen and mortified at such blatant attention. But it didn't stop me from accepting the candy, or accepting his invitation to the dance.

And then there was the day he'd mimicked that, now many years ago, to appear on bended knee again. Only this time, it wasn't a box of chocolates he'd offered, but a blue velvet box containing an engagement ring—a single diamond with a turquoise band to honor my Cherokee heritage.

The problem was that I had once known lust and love. And I missed both. I used to daydream about being married and having children. I had it all planned out, how it would be, how I would feel. The trouble was that every man I met left me feeling…empty.

My life was captured in moments, some of them occurring down this long driveway with its rich pastured land on each side. Somehow, I knew the past was more appealing because the present was so hollow.

I am a doctor, and as such, I had diagnosed my disease of loneliness; it was the cure that eluded me.

Perhaps Grandmother was right. Perhaps my ovaries had shriveled up and left me without hormones, the ones that desire to attract a man. When I was a child and would beg for some nonsensible items, Mother would say, "Your wants won't kill you," or "You can't miss what you've never had."

Thank goodness, though, I had no more time for reflection. I had wiped my plate clean, my coffee cup screamed for a refill, and the papers on my kitchen table held secrets waiting to be discovered.

Chapter Thirteen

Before delving into the content of the criminal file, I decided to phone my dad with an idea the leaf women had stirred in my brain.

"Morning, Punkin. How's your head?"

"It doesn't hurt as much as yesterday, and I slept like a log last night."

"Good to hear. What's up?"

Without going into exaggerated detail, I explained about Mother's and the leaf women's visit. All he said was, "Hmm, interesting."

"Yeah, exactly. That brings me to my reason for calling. Would you search the crime data base to see how many women of ethnic origin were murdered since Mother's death, and if these women's cases are closed or cold?"

He said, "You're specifically interested in women murdered in the same vicinity or borough as your mother?"

"Yessir; same time frame up to present day."

"You're thinking there is a connection or a pattern pertaining to what?"

"I'm not sure, Dad. Maybe they were killed by the same gang, or perhaps investigated by the same precinct." I shrugged my shoulders. "The leaf women that visited this morning all said the same thing—they couldn't cross over until their murderers were found. I'm also interested to know the motivation behind the killings…" I stumbled over my next words, "or if the women were also tortured."

Dad's heavy sigh echoed in my ear. He said, "Money can buy a verdict or kill an investigation. Remember that, Punkin. I've never had the courage to thoroughly read through your mother's criminal file. The bereaved husband part of me overruled the lawman in me. Whatever answers you find in the report, be satisfied. I'll pass the information on to the proper authorities. It's time to move on with your life."

"But, Dad…"

"No buts, Tullah. You are all I have left. Your mother and I created you. I can't lose you, too. Promise!"

Dad had called me Tullah rather than Punkin. He never used my real name unless he was concerned, angry, or serious. His worry touched me deeply.

River and Rascal barreled out the doggie door. A loud rap followed, and a voice called, "Dr. Holliday, it's me, Alice."

"Gotta go, Dad. Alice is at the door. I hope nothing's happened at the clinic."

"Tullah, heed what I just said."

"Love you, Dad. Talk to you later."

Saved by the bell, so to speak. Alice's knock on the door had saved me from making a promise I had no intention of keeping.

I swung the door wide. Our young receptionist stepped in with a smile. The flutter in my heart calmed down. I said, "Everything okay at the clinic?"

"Oh, sure." She thrust a square white envelope forward. "This came with the office mail. It looks like an invitation of some sort."

A dimple in her cheek deepened as she smiled again. "I mean, the envelope looks like the kind we got with our high school invitations. I showed it to Dr. Kemble. She said it was okay to bring it to you."

I gathered the pages into a pile and slid them under my laptop. Alice Dempsey was shy and naïve like her brother. "How is Jeff?" I asked.

"Oh, he's really liking the university." And like her brother, she blushed easily. "I wish I was smart like him."

"Give yourself more credit, Alice. In a few months you'll be graduating, and like Jeff, setting a great example for your younger siblings."

She accepted the cup of coffee I had offered. I suppressed a grimace when she loaded it with four teaspoons of sugar. "Here's the thing, Dr. Holliday. I don't want to go to college. I'd rather keep working for you and Dr. Kemble. Besides, more schooling takes money, and I only work parttime."

She sipped the coffee. "You got any milk?"

I opened the refrigerator and offered her the carton of cream. Then I said, "Alice, you are smart, and a fast learner. However…"

Tears formed in her eyes. She set the cup on the table. "Oh, no, you're gonna fire me 'cause I don't want to go to college?"

I grabbed both of her hands. "Let me finish, Alice."

She nodded, and blinked back the tears.

In my best reassuring voice, I said, "College isn't for everyone. However, as the clinic continues to grow, so will the business end of it, such as having monetary accounts that require business mathematical skills, and updated computer knowledge. If you are willing to attend vocational school and earn a certificate in office management and bookkeeping, then I'm certain Dr. Kemble will agree with me that you will be a valuable asset to the clinic."

Her voice was soft when she answered. "You'd do that for me?"

I nodded.

Then she said, "Jeff got a scholarship. Do they give scholarships for vocational school?"

With six younger siblings, an absentee father, and a mother who barely made ends meet with a meager salary, I understood Alice's concern about money. Still her question threw me off balance.

"Ask your school guidance counselor. She'll know. If not, then perhaps, arrange to take evening classes, because I'm certain that, when you graduate in March, Dr. Kemble will agree to hire you full-time—with the provision that you live up to your end of the deal by completing all courses and receiving your Business Certificate in a timely manner."

Her unexpected pounce nearly knocked me off my feet, and the tight hug caused me to gasp for air. "Thank you...thank you!" She squealed. "I can't wait to tell Mama, and then Jeff."

She opened the door. "I'd better get back. The phone's been ringing off the hook all morning."

She skipped down the steps. Watching her dance across the yard to the clinic made me want to dance, too. Instead, I sighed and pulled the paperwork from its hiding place and then sat down to begin digging into a puzzle that needed solving.

Generally, I'm not a procrastinator. I'm not sure why I continued to delay reading the crime report.

Perhaps I was afraid of reliving the horrors my mother had endured, or perhaps we were all so distraught we'd initially skimmed over the truth, leaving us with no mystery to solve.

I rose and rinsed the syrupy coffee from Alice's cup and set it in the dishwasher, then refilled my cup. Sitting down again, I opened the square white envelope. The return address piqued my curiosity. Art Museum of New York. The same museum that had displayed my mother's artwork, and the reason she had gone to New York.

I carefully opened the envelope and removed the card and a folded letter. It was, indeed, an invitation. My excitement grew as I read the letter:

Dear Holliday Family,

My name is Armand Toussaint, the museum's new curator of art. It is with great sadness that Monsieur Jean-Claude Gradasso retired and returned to France. While I was inventorying the art pieces, I came across the exquisite Native American pieces created by Josie Crow Holliday. Please accept my sincere and belated condolences. Monsieur Gradasso apprised me of her tragic passing.

With that being said, in honor of Native American and Indigenous Peoples month, the museum is hosting an exhibition of marvelous works created by such artists as Ms. Holliday. It is with pleasure that I extend an invitation to your family. This gala extends the entire month of November.

I wanted to raise my arms and do a Cherokee ceremonial dance of thanks around the kitchen. "Thank you, Mother!" I whooped.

She and Shadow Woman had said I would know when the time had come for me to go on my journey. A dangerous journey, they had warned. The dangerous part slightly dampened my enthusiasm. My only dilemma— to share this invitation with my grandmother and Dad, or keep it a secret?

I knew Dad and Grandmother would insist on accompanying me; and why shouldn't they? After all, this invitation was to celebrate a momentous occasion. My head began to throb.

No more procrastinating. I decided to be like Scarlett O'Hara—I'd think about it tomorrow. So I picked up the Criminal Case File for Josie Crow Holliday recorded in the Borough of Brooklyn, State of New York, dated fourteen years ago:

Investigating Officer's Brief Summary:

Approximately zero one hundred hours on fifteen November, Officer M. Boswell and I, Officer T. Rice, of Brooklyn Heights Precinct responded to a 9-1-1 call. Location of crime scene: Union Street alley; no specific address.

Arriving at the Scene:

Upon arriving at the scene, Officer Boswell and I discovered a darkened alley littered with trash and the following:

Deceased victim: nude; Gender: female; Hair color: unknown; Race: undetermined; possible: Hispanic or Asian; Name: unknown (no immediate identification); Address: unknown; Witnesses: (possible) C. Dewitt; address: homeless.

About This Case:

The victim was found nude and brutally murdered. It appears the victim was killed at this location. Items collected at the scene revealed no specific evidence. However, carved in the victim's chest was a jagged slash that resembled a lightning bolt and carved on the victim's forehead numbers that appeared to be two-seven. The victim had been scalped. No evidence of the victim's hair found at this location, which is where the crime is believed to have occurred.

The motive was unknown. Emergency medical personnel declared the unidentified woman dead at the scene. While at the scene, Office Boswell and I observed a trail of blood leading to a connecting alley.

Scalped! Oh my God!

I railed. "What kind of fiends would do this?"

Air clutched my lungs. I couldn't breathe. The words on the paper blurred. A strange ringing in my ears escalated the throb building behind my eyes. I tried to clear my lungs, and told myself—breathe. To inhale, then exhale. Don't faint. Don't faint.

I closed my eyes and willed myself to remain calm—focused.

I continued reading:

The witness, C. Dewitt, age forty-eight, states he is homeless. Dewitt is the one that reportedly found the deceased. C. Dewitt states that at the time of the murder, he was dumpster-diving. When he heard male voices laughing and taunting, he was scared and hid beneath the garbage until he heard nothing, at which time he slightly opened the dumpster's lid. He states that he saw four men, he thought they might be juveniles, but couldn't say for sure. They were running out of the alley. He didn't see their faces. It was too dark to identify their clothing. He said, the men or boys seemed to be angry because the woman wouldn't cry out.

The witness states he heard male voices repeatedly shouting, "Cry, damn you!"

When asked how he knew the victim was a woman, C. Dewitt states that he didn't until he climbed out of the dumpster and looked at the body. He states that he ran to find a buddy, another homeless man, and used the man's cellphone to dial 9-1-1. C. Dewitt said he didn't want to get involved because he was afraid of what the boys or men might do to him. In his words, "This is a bad, bad neighborhood. Gangs, you know."

Asked if he could identify the assailants as gang members. Did he see gang colors? To which he answered: "It was too dark. There ain't no street lights in this part of town."

At this time, the investigation is pending until the autopsy report.

I had to stop reading. My blood boiled and my heart ached. The report read as if my mother was a piece of unwanted trash thrown in an alley. Hispanic or Asian? How dare those lamebrained imbeciles! She was a human being.

I walked to the sink and splashed cold water over my face. In no mood for interruptions of any type, I put my cellphone on silent and turned off the house phone.

It wasn't until River bumped my hand and whined that I realized I was staring off into space—lost in a horror story with no ending. I squatted, wrapped my arms around his neck, and hugged him. I refused to cry. Now wasn't the time for tears.

After assuring my loyal dog that I was okay, I opened the refrigerator. What I needed to calm my nerves was sugar. My eyes spotted a box of waffles and a bottle of wine. I reached for the wine, then mentally slapped myself. To digest all the information, I needed a clear head, so I grabbed the box of waffles. While waiting for them to toast, I glanced at the clock. I still had plenty of reading time before Ella closed the clinic. I hoped she wouldn't stop by the house to check on me.

After satisfying my nerves with an overdose of maple syrup and another cup of coffee, I finished reading the report.

Missing Persons Report:

Date: Twelve November

Time: Nineteen hundred hours

Report: Jean-Claude Gradasso, Master Curator of the Museum of Arts, appeared at this precinct to file a missing person's report on one Josie Crow Holliday. Mr. Gradasso reports that Ms. Holliday was a Native American (Cherokee). Her artwork was on display at the museum, and she was to give a presentation. When she did not show, he telephoned the hotel where she was staying. The receptionist stated that Ms. Holliday had not spent the night in her room, nor had she checked out of the hotel. Report taken by Desk Sergeant S. O'Toole.

It was all so impersonal. Except for Mr. Gradasso, it felt as if no one gave a damn about my mother. I wondered if the police had also dismissed each of the leaf women as just another casualty of crime?

My hands trembled when I picked up the autopsy report.

Autopsy Report:

Decedent: Josie Crow Holliday

Autopsy authorized by: Dr. J. Eckleburg, for City of Brooklyn

Identified by: Fingerprints and dental impressions

Race: Native American

Age: approximately forty years old

Stature: Five feet and four inches

I skimmed through the description of articles of clothing and focused on external examination.

External Examination:

Well developed. Well-nourished Native American female with multiple deep lacerations to the upper extremities. There are lacerations of face and calvarium, skull base, and facial bones. There are multiple penetrating injuries of the anterior thorax and left thigh. There is partial evisceration of the large intestine. Markings on the skull evidence of scalping. Amputation of left ring finger.

I wanted to scream, lash out, punch a hole in the wall. What good would it do? None! I skipped past the detailed x-ray information and the pathological diagnosis to the official cause of death.

Summary: This approximate forty-year-old female victim appears to have lived an estimate of five minutes before succumbing to multiple injuries sustained from a brutal beating.

Cause of Death: Crushed cranium and hemorrhage.

Manner of Death: Homicide

Over the years, Dad had made five different trips to the NYPD precinct in charge of investigating mother's death. I lifted the last summary report, dated four years ago, which didn't say much:

Communication:

Police have not identified a possible motive and continue to investigate. Brooklyn Police Chief Wilson T. Stoddard said the killing has left many unanswered questions, and he has asked the family to be patient as investigators examine all available evidence.

I railed, "Asked the family to be patient! Fourteen years? How much longer must we be patient?"

My stomach roiled. I rushed upstairs. River and Rascal raced behind me. Somehow, I managed to get to the bathroom, drop to my knees to hug the commode, and unload everything I'd eaten today. Fully clothed, I crawled into the shower and turned on the faucet. I sat with my knees drawn to my chest and allowed my tears to comingle with streaming beads of cold water.

Chapter Fourteen

Functioning through a wooly fog of mental fatigue, I managed to stand and undress inside the shower. I left my sodden clothes where they lay. I had just managed to pull on my oversized T-shirt and crawl into bed when Ella's voice called my name.

I felt old and tired, and not in the mood for company. "In the bedroom. Come on up."

By the time she entered, I was sitting on the end of the bed. River and Rascal had broken the forbidding rule about getting on the bed; they lay close to me. It was their way of trying to give me comfort.

Ella held the crime report in her hands. I can't begin to describe the horror in her eyes. She said, "I wasn't snooping, honest. I thought maybe this was a medical report on one of our patients. When you didn't answer my text or the phone, I was worried and decided to check on you."

She sat next to me and grabbed my hand in hers, and laid her head against my shoulder. Compassion filled her voice. "I had no idea. Someone was crazy, or unbelievably vicious. Or both!"

Yeah, I thought. I have a neat tidy life in a messy world, and sometimes I suspect I'm trying to fulfill the stereotype of a small-town female veterinarian, pretending to fit into a world that accepts me for who I am, not as the sheriff's daughter, or the fact that my blue eyes don't match my Cherokee heritage.

"Tullah, you're awfully quiet. Are you all right?" Then she huffed. "That was a stupid question. Of course you're not okay. Should I call Tanti or Henry?"

I said cautiously, "I'm pretty much okay." A slight exaggeration but close enough to the truth. "And no, don't call Grandmother or Dad. I don't want to upset them."

I suddenly wanted to say something indelible to my stepsister. The only thing I could think of wouldn't bear utterance. So I said, "The pain in my head has lessened. I'll feel okay enough to come to the clinic tomorrow. Really."

The fact is, I just wanted to be left alone with my emotions. I hoped she hadn't seen the invitation.

"Okay, Tullah, but if you need time off—take it."

I had a sudden spurt of emotional energy after Ella left. I looked around and decided to put it to good use picking up, putting away, and rearranging the bedroom furniture. I placed my wet clothes with a load and headed for the washing machine. Downstairs, the guest bedroom was pristine, as usual. The basement was my next victim. I trotted downstairs and began gathering old magazines, outdated reels of film, and trash in general, enough to fill two large garbage bags. I straightened and restacked books on the bookshelves, and decluttered my desk.

When I looked at the clock, it was well past my normal bedtime. I trudged upstairs, showered off, and climbed into bed. I stared at the ceiling and thought about the autopsy report. I wasn't thinking about my mother being dead, about the reality and finality of her death. I was thinking about the brutality of her death, the way *they* had left her body nude and exposed had been deliberate. And suddenly I knew what had been biting at me through all the horror.

I thought faster than I had ever thought before, and I didn't feel sick anymore.

****

Due to Alice's overly zealous appointment scheduling, Monday whizzed by in a blur. In between patients, Ella and I barely had time to scarf down a pack of crackers. The upside of staying busy allowed me to shut out the crime scene photos, autopsy report, and the unhelpful crime report.

Alice, a high school student participating in the diversified career track program, leaves at noon to attend classes. By the end of the day, as I locked the clinic doors, I groaned when the phone rang.

Ella grumbled, "Let the service pick it up."

My fatigued brain and massive headache agreed with her; my empathic instinct said otherwise. I answered, "Holliday Animal Clinic."

A woman's voice said, "This is Dr. Madilyn Hagar, Dean of Academics and veterinary residency placement at University of Kentucky. May I speak with Dr. Ella Sanders?"

Ella's eyes widened. She switched the phone to speaker, then said, "Dr. Hagar, this is Ella. I've married since leaving the university. I'm now Dr. Ella Sanders Kemble. How may I help you?"

After the congratulations and other yadda-yadda, Dr. Hagar got to the point. I could have jumped for joy, and from the expression on Ella's face, I knew she was just as excited. Ella said, "Hosting a first-year intern is an exciting opportunity, Dr. Hagar, and one I certainly advocate. However, in all fairness, I must discuss this with my partner, Dr. Tullah Holliday. I'm certain she will be onboard also. May I get back with you in the morning?"

I jotted down the phone number as Ella repeated it. As soon as she disconnected the call, we both jumped up and high-fived each other. She and I had often discussed contacting one of the schools of veterinary medicine to participate in an internship program. With our patient load growing, extended vacations were out of the question.

Ella lamented, "Maybe I should have come right out and accepted the offer."

I assured her she had made the correct decision. "This will give us enough time to formulate a few questions. We want to make sure the intern is a good match for our rural community, and we need to make certain there is affordable housing available. And speaking of housing, will the intern expect a salary, and how much?"

My grin widened as I added, "Of course, this is a smoke-screen, because we will certainly accept."

Ella squealed. "I can't wait to tell Andy." Her expression grew serious. "Andy and I have been married eight months and haven't taken time for a honeymoon. And, then, of course, you haven't had a vacation in like—never."

It had been a long day. A day filled with unexpected emergencies and surprises. My next thought was to send up a silent prayer of thanks to the Great Spirit Father. Bringing in an intern would allow me to accept Armand Toussaint's invitation to the museum, the perfect excuse to go to New York. The question I wrestled with was whether to invite Grandmother or not. My mother was her only child. The two of them were extremely close. When mother died, I watched a great deal of life drain from my grandmother. Did I have the right to deny her the opportunity to enjoy the wonderous works of her daughter?

I didn't know the answer—yet.

Friday, I received an email from Dad with detailed information regarding the number of women murdered in the same proximity as my mother. I wasn't surprised when I read the number of cold cases—five. I also wasn't surprised when I read the five women were of ethnic origin: two Hispanic, one Asian, and two Middle Eastern.

I settled in the recliner and invested myself thoroughly in each woman's crime and autopsy report, making notes of similarities as I read. By the time I'd finished, it was well past bedtime. What I had to tell Dad could wait until morning—but it wasn't necessary to wait, because my phone pinged, alerting me to a text.

Dad: *What conclusion have U drawn over info I sent U?*

Me: *Don't fully agree with hate crime motive. When r u available?*

Dad*: Tomorrow. Six P.M. Whitehorse. My treat.*

Me: *Ask Uncle Charlie to join us.*

Dad signed off with a thumbs-up emoji.

Upstairs, I climbed into bed. Although my mind hummed with ideas and conspiracy theories, I somehow effectively managed to shut out the darkness of forensic details, every commonality and difference of each female victim, including my mother.

I continued to mentally flip through my notes, thinking I might have missed a relevant clue. One thing

I was certain of: there was more than one killer. The question was whether they wanted the victims to die within that particular city area for a reason, or was it mere convenience?

My last thought before succumbing to exhaustion was—these victims needed justice.

Chapter Fifteen

Getting up and going to work the next morning wasn't easy, but it was reassuring. I slipped into my regular veterinary attire, black jeans and, for the cooler weather, a dark blue long-sleeved shirt with the HVC logo encircled with a stethoscope, and I finished by braiding my hair.

A look at the clock told me it was time to open the clinic. I caught myself humming as I strolled across the yard. Alice pulled into her usual parking spot and beeped her car horn.

Ella sprinted to catch up with us. We shared our usual good morning greetings. I said, "I had a thought about the new intern—we can offer two options."

Ella followed me inside. While we shrugged into our white medical coats, she said, "I could barely sleep last night. Andy is also excited for us." Then she said, "You go first."

I tossed out the possibility and convenience of the intern living on premises in the airstream, versus renting an apartment in town with the added expense of gas money for traveling back and forth to the office.

Alice grinned as she held up a pink box. "My treat." Donuts!

We thanked her for her thoughtfulness, then offered a gentle chastisement. I said, "Save your money for vocational school, Alice."

She bit into a chocolate-covered donut, nodded, and said, "Yes, ma'am." Then she quickly added, "First appointment is a spay for Dr. Sanders Kemble at nine-thirty, and for you Dr. Holliday, a game warden from Wildlife Fish and Game Services is bringing in a coyote carcass for necropsy. Possible rabies. Nine-thirty."

Alice reached to answer the ringing phone. Ella and I retreated to our individual ORs to prep for surgery. We barely had time to finish our coffee when the first patient arrived, with the game warden following. He toted a large black canvas bag. Alice directed him to my operating room, and I assured him that I'd give the necropsy priority.

I'm thankful we made noon to one-thirty a mandatory closing for a much-needed break. After notifying our answering service to receive calls, Alice left for school, while Ella and I propped our feet up and made key decisions regarding our intern.

She made the telephone call to her former professor and was all grins when she had disconnected. "Dr. Hagar approved all of our terms. The intern was in her office as we spoke. He agreed to a lower salary since we are providing on-premises housing and he'll save gas by not having to commute."

"When does he arrive?" I wanted to know between bites of my tuna sandwich.

"Arrives on the twenty-ninth. Starts first day of November. His name is Jesse Delight."

We both giggled. Ella said, "Dr. Delight. Cute."

The date was music to my ears. I explained to Ella about the art show in New York commemorating my mother's artwork along with that of other Native Peoples. "I know it's premature to go on vacation, and I hate to saddle you with a newbie so early into his internship…"

She cut me off. "I'm taking two weeks off in April, remember?" Her smile upside-downed into a concerned frown. "Just promise me one thing, Tullah. Don't go getting yourself killed. I'm not fooled one little bit. There's more to this trip than visiting a museum."

She reached over and grabbed my hand, and held it tight. "You're more than my best friend. You're my sister."

Before we could get all gushy, a voice yelled, "Help! Doc Holliday, I think this little dog is dying."

Ella and I rushed to the office. A middle-aged man held a bloody towel. I said, "What happened?"

His voice quivered. "I saw this little guy on the side of the road. He must've been hit by a car. Some S-O-B left the poor thing to suffer. I pass by here every day on my way to work. I figured you would help."

I lifted the dog from the man's hands. He said, "I hate to run off like this, Doc, but I gotta go. My shift starts in fifteen minutes. You understand, don't ya?"

"Thank you for bringing him in."

"My name's Ernie Gilford. I work at the soft drink plant. Will there be a charge?"

I assured Mr. Gilford the dog was in good hands and there was no charge. He dashed out the door, then just as quickly hurried back inside and held his hands forward. "Doc, do you mind if I wash my hands?"

Ella pointed him to the bathroom. He was in and out in a flash saying, "On my supper break, I'll call to check on him."

And that's the way our day ended. Before we had time to examine the extent of his injuries, the little terrier drew its last breath in my arms.

*****

After a quick shower and a change of clothes, a glance at the clock told me it was almost time to meet Dad and Uncle Charlie. I slapped on some lip gloss and grabbed my laptop satchel from the door peg, then bounded downstairs to stuff my laptop inside the brown bag and locate my keys, all the while muttering facts about the leaf women and my mother.

It also crossed my mind to feel sorry for myself that Ella had someone to go home to, not just a dog and a donkey.

By the time I arrived at the Whitehorse Saloon, parking was a scarce commodity. Since the growth of the town and Uncle Charlie's reputation for the best BBQ sandwiches in all of Kentucky, and his award-winning chili, the saloon has become more of a restaurant than a honky-tonk, except for the weekends.

Earsplitting music greeted me as I pushed through the doors. I stood for a moment allowing my eyes to adjust to the dim interior. My gaze drifted around the room until I spotted Uncle Charlie wending between the tables toward me.

I yelled, "Is Dad here?"

He pointed to the earplugs in his ears and hooked my hand through his arm. I nodded my understanding and followed him to the backroom reserved for private parties, where we usually met to discuss private matters. Within minutes, Vera, Uncle Charlie's waitress, arrived with a large soft drink for me and coffee for him and Dad. She also set a pitcher of cola and a carafe of coffee on the table.

"Vera," I said, "I honestly don't know how you can

stand the noise."

She grinned and pointed to her ears. "Cotton. Muffles the racket but lets me hear the customers when they order." Then she said, "Charlie's already ordered for you. Double order of onion rings, extra crispy, pulled pork sammie with dill pickles, extra coleslaw, and two chocolate éclairs. Right?"

I returned her smile. "He knows me too well."

She hustled off.

After slaking my thirst, I removed the laptop from my satchel.

Dad said, "Did you find a correlation between any of the women?"

I sighed as I often do when I think of my mother. "Enough to determine that their murders were more than hate crimes."

Dad and Uncle Charlie exchanged glances. "Explain how you came to that conclusion," Dad said.

"All of the women were killed in or near the same vicinity, and all were left in an alley. I've asked myself multiple questions, such as did the killer or killers want the victims to die within the particular city limits for a reason, or was it mere coincidence? As new cases piled high, the leaf women's cases went to the bottom of the stack."

Uncle Charley frowned. "Leaf women?"

"They appeared to me as swirling leaves. Thus, the name."

He smiled and nodded. "Good analogy."

I continued. "Each woman, including Mother, was scalped and the ring finger on the left hand amputated. Additionally, each victim had the number seven carved into their foreheads."

I stopped to sip my drink, and to calm my mind. I continued, "Dad, you confirmed that the numbers two and seven in Grandmother's dream were Aryan gang numbers. Bear with me while I use a bit of history to explain my theory."

I shifted toward Uncle Charlie. "In the olden days, the days of the plains Indians, when it was time for the young boys to prove they were warriors, they were sent to an enemy tribe to count coup. Touching an enemy who was alive, for example, earned a warrior higher honor than touching a wounded or dead enemy. Am I correct, Uncle Charlie?"

"You are, Little Sister. On the Plains, the feat of counting coup on enemies was an achievement that allowed warriors to gain different levels of prestige and status through acts of bravery. Counting coup could be done by touching—or, more likely, striking—an enemy with a coup stick, club, bow, or hand; by touching an enemy's defensive structure; or by stealing an enemy's weapons or his horses tied up in camp. Counting coup often was humiliation enough on those touched— warriors who practiced this often did not proceed to kill the enemy."

Dad looked confused. He sounded a bit impatient. "Nice history lesson, but what does this have to do with our case?"

Uncle Charlie and I merely shook our heads. I was thankful he understood. He said, "Patience, my brother. Continue, Little Sister. My heart is filled with joy to talk about the old days of my ancestors."

Vera arrived with our food. I waited until she left the room, with the door completely shut, before I continued. "Coups were usually recorded by putting notches in a coup stick. In some tribes, a warrior who won coup was permitted to wear an eagle feather in his hair, and if he was wounded in the attempt, he was required to paint the feather red to indicate his failure to best his enemy."

Dad picked up his sandwich and chomped into it. I knew by his expression that he wanted me to get to the point. "Dad, please, bear with me. It's important, and once I finish, you'll completely understand. I promise."

He drained his coffee cup and refilled it. "Okay. Fire away."

I helped myself to an onion ring. "Eventually these young men resorted to different levels of counting coup such as taking a scalp, slitting a throat, or wounding the enemy several times. This was their rite of passage into manhood."

Dad raised then lowered his sandwich. He stared at me. "I'll be damned."

Uncle Charlie said, "Exactly."

I ignored the fact that the ketchup on my onion ring looked like blood. It'd been a long day with little to time to eat, and my hunger was getting the best of me.

I remained silent long enough to let the information really sink in. "Think about the similarities of young Indian boys—proving they were men so they could join the elders in war parties—to our particular villains."

Dad reared back in his chair. He pursed his lips, and squinted at me. "Initiation? That's what you're saying?"

"That's exactly what she's saying, Henry. Our Tullah is a smart girl. She should have been a detective." Uncle Charlie held up his hand as if defending himself. "Not to say that you're not a great veterinarian, because you are and the animals are damned lucky to have you."

Dad lifted his napkin and wiped his hands. "It makes

sense. The women were all ethnic, their victim profiles are the same, and the number seven." He beat his fist against the palm of his hand. "Damn. Damn. How in the hell did the NYPD not figure this out?"

Frustration laced his voice. "All these years, and no one figured out that my wife and the other women were tortured because a bunch of depraved, asshole juveniles wanted to get initiated into…into a gang! Where the hell were their parents, or teachers, or priest?"

His face suffused a reddish-purple. A vein in his neck pulsated. Fearing he might have a heart attack or a stroke, I stood and wrapped my arms around him. We both needed comfort. "Not just any gang, Dad. The skinheads. And you yourself said that the one-sevens were notorious, secretive, and the most dangerous of all the NY gangs. The question is, what do we do now?"

Dad merely shook his head. "I don't know, and that's what pisses me off."

I shrugged a shoulder. There was something niggling my brain. Something was off. If only I could reach out and grab hold of it.

Uncle Charlie's voice protruded into my thoughts, and whatever it was that I was trying to call forth disappeared. He said, "All of this happened fourteen years ago. If those punks were in their teens, they'd be what…in their late twenties, early thirties? How do you even go about identifying these thugs?"

I snapped my fingers. "That's it. That's what's missing."

Dad and Uncle Charlie stared at me like I had grown two heads. I wolfed down a large bite of my sandwich, and spoke between chews. "DNA! That's what's missing. Nowhere in any of the autopsy reports was there mention of DNA."

I savored a large sip of drink to wash down my food. "I can't speak for the leaf women, but I know Mother would have fought her attackers until she drew her last breath."

"That's right, Punkin. Josie was a kind and loving woman, but true to her Cherokee heritage, she was no coward. She would have given those young bastards the fight of their lives."

I wanted to scream my frustration. Instead, I sighed. "Where does this lead us? Without DNA, we have diddley-squat."

Uncle Charlie's voice deepened. "Some prick dropped the ball. Under the fingernails would have been the most obvious place to find DNA. Fourteen years is a long time. How many more crimes have been committed by this gang and gone without punishment? It makes me think there's wormy apples in the police department. Maybe tied to this gang."

I suddenly knew exactly what Madam Zahrani meant when she said, *Be careful who you trust. Salt and sugar look the same.*

It was as if Dad and I had a mind-meld. We both knew he planned to make another trip to New York. No, no! I railed. He wasn't the one destined to go. I needed to think of a way to stop him from interfering with what Shadow Woman and the other spirits had ordained.

But how?

Chapter Sixteen

Friday night, and it was ridiculously late. I should have been sleeping. It was difficult to sleep, though, after tonight's discussion with Dad and Uncle Charlie. It made sense to research the Aryan gangs. I settled at the kitchen table to study the profiles of the different groups. The NY police said they had investigated possible serial killers, and different Hispanic gangs. They also said they believed the killer might be one person possibly obsessed with young ethnic women.

After sifting through the crime reports, again, I found no mention of investigating Aryans or skinheads.

Saturday morning early, my phone rang. It seemed to be coming from far, far away. I awoke with a start and slid off the kitchen chair—landing hard on my rear end. For a moment, I felt lost—in a fog. I had no idea where I was or why I was on the floor. Obviously, I'd fallen asleep at the table.

I grabbed my phone. Dad's photo smiled at me. Clearing the rasp from my voice, I wondered why he'd be calling me at two in the morning. Unless…the hairs on my arm prickled. A premonition.

Over the years I've learned not to ignore my secret sense. Death was on its way. Death was coming. I had a vague recollection of several years ago when Junior Lampson broke through my kitchen door and tried to kill me. Of course, death was coming, and I would be the intended victim. But not today. Who then? I didn't want to know.

All hell broke loose with River's frantic barking and scratching at the doggie door as if demanding I open it so he could get at the intruder. Between the barking and Rascal's braying, I wanted to scream, *Shut up*!

A voice yelled, "Tullah, it's me, Ella! Open the door."

Simultaneously I unlocked the door and answered the phone. My imagination ran wild. "Dad, what's wrong?"

"Tullah, it's Sunny. Get to the hospital ASAP— Henry's had a heart attack!"

Death rides a pale horse rippled through my brain. "I'm on my way, Sunny." I prayed to the Great Spirit Father to not take my dad. Not yet…not yet. I needed him!

Ella said, "That was my mom, right?"

Emotions threatened to strangle me. I couldn't speak when she said, "Andy called Uncle Charlie. He's bringing Tanti to the hospital. Uncle Tiny is already there."

I grabbed my keys from the hook by the door and commanded, "Let's go!"

I barely waited for Ella to strap into her seatbelt before I backed out of the carport and barreled up the driveway to the main road. Time seemed to move in slow motion. I checked my speedometer. I could almost hear Dad's voice ever cautioning me to avoid speeding. What the hell. I pressed the accelerator.

A large red eye—a light rotated in the darkness. Andy's patrol car waited at the end of the driveway. He rolled down his window and motioned me to follow.

Never mind that the speed limit was sixty, he escorted us to the hospital's emergency entrance, siren blaring, speed limit be damned.

Andy exited his patrol car. He said, "Give me the keys, Tullah. I'll take care of parking your truck. Sunny's waiting for you." I sensed he wanted to give me a reassuring hug, except I didn't have time. I'm not even sure I smiled at his offer as I raced toward the double automatic doors.

A mixture of fear and stoicism lay on Grandmother's face. Braids draped over her shoulders, her face devoid of makeup, she wore a red robe over a flannel gown, and red felt beaded slippers. She reminded me of an aged little girl. A contradiction—yes. She opened her arms wide and wrapped me in a hug.

I pulled away. "Where's Sunny?"

A tall, skinny man dressed like a doctor jogged toward us. "I'm Allen Byers, Dr. Sanders' Physician's Assistant. Please follow me. We have a private family waiting room for you."

Like a gaggle of geese, we followed this white-coated leader. "What about my dad?" I wanted to know.

He opened a door and, obediently, we followed. "We're prepping him for surgery."

I'm certain mine wasn't the only puzzled expression in the room. I said, "But who's doing the surgery? There's no cardiac surgeon at this hospital."

"I can answer that." Sunny wore a haggard expression.

Her PA excused himself. Sunny presented herself as a doctor void of emotion. Part of me completely understood. As a doctor myself, I knew the importance of putting on a non-emotional front to help keep the family members calm. The other part of me was irritated. She was my dad's wife. They'd been married less than a year. I wanted to rail at her to show some friggin' emotion for criminy sake.

She continued. "Henry's heart has never fully recovered from the knife wound he sustained. Enigma has no helicopter service, and there's no time to get him to Lexington in an ambulance."

At this point her voice began to quiver. I watched her struggle with her emotions and felt ashamed of my earlier thoughts about her lack of feelings.

She heaved a soulful breath. "Dr. Chen Lei Yue is the chief cardio-surgeon at Lexington Memorial. She and I have been friends for many years. We attended medical school together. Her success rate surpasses many other cardiologists. I trust her completely. She will arrive in about fifteen minutes by helicopter. I will be assisting. I want Henry to know that, no matter what the outcome, I'm with him all the way."

We both allowed ourself tears. At this point, I embraced her. "I'm taking it that this is no simple bypass surgery?" Although I knew the answer, I needed to hear it verbally.

She stepped back and shifted into doctor mode. "Quadruple, and possibly with stents." She folded her arms against her chest, then looked me straight in the eye. "It's the old stab wound that nicked the aorta that worries me the most."

Allen Byers, PA, cleared his voice. "Excuse me for interrupting. Sheriff Holliday is asking for his daughter, Charlie Whitehorse, Tanti Crow, and Undersheriff Goodbody."

I looked at Sunny. She simply nodded her approval

and led us down the hall to the pre-op room.

I cannot explain the pain that wafted over me as I stood looking at my father's pale, almost waxy complexion. Waxy as in pre-death. The emotions welling in my throat threatened to strangle me. This tall, handsome, virile man resembled a shrunken caricature from a movie set. I kept my voice soft when I spoke. "Dad?"

Someone pulled a chair next to the bed. Dad's eyes fluttered open. I clasped his lifted hand. At first his voice was a raspy whisper. I leaned forward to better hear him. He cleared his throat. He said, "Tiny."

Deputy Tiny Goodbody stepped forward. He lowered the bed rail to lean closer. Dad said, "Tiny, you're the undersheriff. The county is in good hands with you at the helm. Look after Sunny and Ella."

Tiny offered a reassuring smile. "You just concentrate on getting well, my old pal. I'll happily vacate the chair when you're ready to get back in the saddle."

Dad coughed. I feared the light was fading from his eyes. Tiny released Dad's hand. He came around the bed and placed his hand on my shoulder. "You need anything, just ask."

I nodded. Dad waved me forward. He said, "Where's Charlie?"

"I'm right here, my brother."

"Charlie, look after Tullah and Tanti. Contact Judge Michael Duvall...he has my will."

"Aah, Henry—" Uncle Charlie clipped off the sentence, knowing now wasn't the time to waste words on platitudes like *You're gonna make it*, or *Hey, ol' buddy, you're too ornery to kick the bucket.* Instead, he said, "Tanti and Little Sister are my only family. Their needs are my needs."

Dad managed a smile. He spoke between rests. "Charlie, if I make it, let's go fishing."

"It's a promise, Henry. Count on it."

When Uncle Charlie turned to leave, Dad said, "Stay. I need you to hear this." And then, he waved Grandmother forward.

He clutched her hand. "Tanti, thank you for giving me Josie. Thank you for loving me like a son. Thank you for helping me raise Tullah to be the wonderful daughter she is."

Dad closed his eyes and was quiet. Panic flittered my heart. I laid my hand on his chest to make sure he was still breathing. I think Uncle Charlie, Grandmother, and I collectively held our own breaths.

Finally, Dad opened his eyes. His voice now barely audible. "Punkin, I don't have enough words to say how much I love you. Every time, I look at you, I see your mother. You have always been the best part of both of us."

He shifted his glance to Uncle Charlie and Grandmother and said, "We all know about Tullah's special gift." He hesitated.

I wondered why he'd mentioned my special talent. He'd never truly embraced this…whatever it is I was either cursed or bless with.

He shifted his look toward me, then said, "I am asking her to use it."

He reached to grab a strand of my hair and rubbed it between his thumb and forefinger. Tears clouded his eyes. "I wanted to be the one to go to New York to find the bastards that killed your mother. As a man of the law,

I would never ask you to commit a crime using whatever these special powers are that you possess. As an angry man, I want to rip out the hearts of those animals and feed them to the vultures. God forgive me for such heinous thoughts."

Dad's chest rose and fell. His breathing seemed to become shallower. "Charlie…Tanti, whatever Tullah decides, support her. Do not hold her back. This is her destiny. I have my God, and you have your Great Spirit Father. I believe they are one and the same. He will protect her, but I need the two of you to call on the spirits of your people to shroud my daughter in an impenetrable armor so no harm will come to her as she makes her decision to undertake this journey."

Grandmother wiped a tear from her cheek. She and Uncle Charlie exchanged a brief glance and a nod. She said, "You have our promise, Henry."

Dad's grip on my hand was lessening. Where the hell was the helicopter? It seemed the machines attached to him had become louder, and were echoing in my ears. "Dad, hang on. Please. I'm not ready for you to go."

"I'm just tired, Punkin. So very tired." His eyes cleared, and for a moment I felt a vibrancy in his clutch. "Peace or vengeance, never regret your decision. And, when it's over, find a good man. A man worthy of you. You deserve happiness."

I heard the womp-womp of rotor blades. The helicopter had arrived. I breathed a prayer of thanks.

Sunny entered the room. An entourage of attendants followed behind her. The area became a hive of activity. We raced down the hall behind the gurney. The long trip toward the operating room seemed miles longer than I had remembered. I wondered if other patients' loved ones had felt the same way.

Sunny held Dad's hand the entire way. At the double doors, she said, "I'll keep you informed. There'll be coffee and refreshments in the waiting room. Make yourselves as comfortable as possible."

"How long?" I asked.

She merely pursed her lips and shook her head. "As long as it takes."

And then she disappeared. My dad disappeared. I felt as if a huge part of my life had also disappeared behind those two doors.

Chapter Seventeen

Uncle Charlie paced about the room. He reminded me of a caged animal. Finally, he said, "How long do you think this will take, Little Sister?"

I glanced at the large walk clock. Twenty minutes seemed like hours. I had never participated in a heart bypass. This was a new area for me. "Honestly, my best guess is somewhere between three to six hours."

I didn't want to sound morbid, but Dad had always taught me to never hedge the truth, so I added, "But it may take longer depending on how many blood vessels are being attached, and if the old stab wound to his aorta doesn't create problems."

Uncle Charlie pulled up a chair and sat in front of me. He gathered my hands in his. The expression on his face was both compassionate and serious. He said, "You know I would never abandon you...ever! My Apache blood trembles cold with fear and burns hot with anger. Tullah, I must go to my cabin by the lake. I must seek the Great Spirit Father and ask him to breathe new life into my brother. I need the quiet to hear the Creator's voice. Do you understand?"

Because he never called me by my given name, the seriousness of his appeal didn't escape me. My heart ached. Instinctively, I wanted to plead with him to stay with me and Grandmother. I would like nothing better than to close my eyes and wish all of this away because

I wasn't sure I could face hearing news that my dad hadn't survived the surgery.

I caught myself. My fingers, no longer held by Charlie's, gripped the edges of my chair so tightly my knuckles hurt. It seemed as if I had to unlock my jaws in order to speak. "Go without worry, Uncle Charlie. Grandmother and I lend our strength to your journey of prayer. Stay as long as it takes. I will send a text or phone you…"

I couldn't bring myself to say *if Dad dies.* Instead, I said, "When we have good news."

Without another word, Uncle Charlie grabbed his battered cowboy hat, situated it on his head, and with a sad smile, opened the door and quietly closed it behind him.

To break the silence, I asked Grandmother if she would like a cup of hot tea or coffee. Her reply was, "Neither. A glass of chardonnay, but since it's not on the table, I'll settle for hot tea."

I helped myself to a large coffee and a glazed donut. For the first time in my life, one of my favorite foods tasted like cardboard.

We sat in silence. To keep my mind off the snail-crawling time, I focused on the crime and autopsy reports, and found my mind had drawn a blank. I inwardly castigated the so-called gift of mine. Where the hell were the spirits when *I* needed them? Where was *my* owl?

Grandmother patted a chair. "Tullah, sit next to me. I have made an important decision."

Grandmother reminded me of a small child sitting in that large brown recliner. The stern softness in her voice commanded my attention. I obeyed.

"What's on your mind, Grandmother?"

She grimaced when she sipped the tea. "Cold!" And handed the cup to me.

When I offered to refresh it, she waved away the request.

"Tullah, you are a strong-minded woman, but never foolhardy. You have the strong will of the Cherokee and the stubbornness of the Irish. I have often watched you battle the two traits to see which one you would let win."

I wondered where she was going with this analogy. The Cherokee often make their point through stories. It's true the Irish side of me tends to get impatient while I wait for the topic to come to fruition. Usually, I'm very tolerant of my grandmother's meandering through stories. Today wasn't one of those days.

"Grandmother…" I heaved an impatient sigh. "Please, just spit it out. Say what you have to say."

Her ebony eyes sparked with irritation. "All right! Henry said to support you in whatever decision you make about going to New York. Well, here's my decision. I'm going with you."

She held up her hand to stop my protest. "I read on the internet that the Museum of Art in New York is hosting a showing to honor Native American Heritage Month. Josie's name was mentioned."

She pierced me with a look that said *Don't challenge me*. "My years on this earth are not long. I have a right to see my daughter's work honored. I am going to New York. Patty is going with me. We can all go together or not. She and I have already made reservations at the hotel on Fifth."

"Grandmother—"

"Tu-llah!" Her voice snapped.

I knew better than to test her, especially when she spoke my name in syllables.

"Grandmother, I'm going for a walk. I feel as if I'm suffocating."

I turned to leave. She clasped my hand and held it tight. Tears clouded her eyes. "I didn't mean to snap."

"I'm not angry, Grandmother. Please understand that Dad and I are of the same mind that mother's killing was racially motivated. It's also my belief that the reason her killers were never brought to justice is also racially motivated."

"What do you mean?"

"I believe someone in authority knows the killers. Someone with enough power to impede the investigation until the case went cold. Grandmother, you and Patty are vibrant, independent women, capable of looking out for yourselves, but—" A voice inside my soul silenced my argument. Who was I to deny my eighty-year-old grandmother the right and privilege to see her only child's artwork on national display? How selfish of me.

I wrapped her in my arms. "Give me the dates of your flight. We will go together. It's been many years since I've seen mother's artwork."

I left with her smiling.

The hospital is surrounded by a densely populated forest. There's an arched bridge that leads over a shallow stream to a peaceful area with wrought iron benches. The garden club ladies placed a plaque to identify the place as *Serenity Gardens*, a place for meditation and solace.

On the path in front of me I retrieved a perfect red maple leaf, its color bold in the early morning sun. I put it in the front pocket of my jacket to later dry and place on my mother's grave. A gust of wind urged some leaves from the trees, and they race each other to the ground where they crunched underneath my feet, releasing the perfume of fall.

Sixteen years ago, on my fourteenth birthday, Mama gave me a necklace she'd had since she was a girl. It was shaped like an eagle feather, emblazoned with turquoise. She said her grandmother, Chenoa Waya, had given it to her, and the necklace had been handed to Chenoa by her grandmother, who had asked the Shadow Mothers to bless it. It was a sacred treasure, and I was to keep it safe to hand down to my daughter.

I touched the necklace where it nestled between my breasts beneath my shirt. Although she had never implied the pendant held mystical powers, in my young girl's mind, I had believed it was so, especially when I heard voices in the wind. Voices I was too young to understand.

And then Mama had died. The voices did not die with her.

At the center of the bridge, the whispers started. I told myself it was just how the wind sounds when it blows through the trees. Except it sounded more like human voices than a gusting breeze.

A gust raced over the bridge and my long hair flew wild around my face. I automatically clutched the feather pendant beneath my shirt. I was unable to discern if what I heard were ancient voices or new ones whispering their secrets.

The bridge creaked when I stopped to gaze into the clear, colorless water bumping over brown stones. For a moment, I listened to the soothing sound of gurgling water, then continued until I settled on a bench at the pool's edge.

I wrestled with my thoughts. Madam Zahrani, the disguised Shadow Woman, had warned me of a dangerous journey. Mother and the leaf women had beseeched me to find their killer. Dad wanted retribution, but had left to me the decision of choosing between vindication or accepting a circumstance beyond our control. The decision felt so ominous, I almost expected the spirits to bombard me with their whispers.

For the longest time I sat and stared at the water. In this early morning hour, a gossamer film of fog hovered over the forest. The snap of a twig drew my attention. Nature's beauty came alive as a doe and fawn ventured silently to the pool for a drink.

Two cottontails and several squirrels joined the early morning show. My thoughts kept me company, but the solitude was interrupted by the anxious squawking of two bluejays. I watched the birds dive frantically, flitter away, scold, and repeat the process. As if a call to rally had been sent out, two more bluejays swooped in to join the fracas.

I scanned from left to right searching for the intruder. It was the whirring that caused my body to tense. Perfectly disguised among the amber and brown leaves was the thick, tubular body of a rattlesnake. Leaves fell away as the viper coiled in defense against its attackers.

Goose bumps rose on my arms and the hair at the back of my neck prickled. To avoid becoming an innocent victim, I carefully lifted both feet and swiveled my lanky frame to fit fully on the short bench.

Icy chills slithered through me when the rattler reared, its triangular head turned in my direction, its hooded eyes seeming to stare directly into mine. I held tight to my necklace.

The snake's tongue flicked in and out. I knew it was sensing me. In many Native American cultures, the People believe the snake is a creature from the Underworld, the realm of darkness, evil, and eternal death. The whispers returned, louder, until I was certain my ears would explode.

My secret sense dropped into my gut. The snake knew I had made my decision.

It lunged. And I screamed, "Shunkaha!"

A warrior astride a rearing black-and-white tobiano stallion appeared. On the shaft of the warrior's war lance, the deadly viper writhed in protest of its own death.

Sunlight seemed to dance off red and gold leaves. Tree branches swayed over my head. I felt caught in a nightmare, but deep inside I knew what was coming would be more dangerous than anything I had ever before experienced.

When I returned to the hospital waiting room, Grandmother caressed the side of my face like she always does. "You are pale, Granddaughter. What has frightened you?"

I wrapped her in my arms and sought comfort in her embrace. "It doesn't matter, Grandmother."

It seemed as if I'd been gone for hours. The wall clock begged to differ.

I didn't have to ask because Grandmother already knew the question and merely shook her head. Sunny hadn't sent word of Dad's condition yet.

Chapter Eighteen

At five o'clock, Patty Sweet appeared with a basket of goodies. She said, "I figured the cafeteria wouldn't be open at this early hour." She reached inside the basket and removed several wrapped sandwiches, saying, "Egg salad, PBJ, blueberry bagels with cream cheese, and lots of crispy fried ham."

Patty also held up a carton of hazelnut coffee pods. She smiled. "Never fear. I brought enough pods to last all day, if necessary."

She touched her finger to the tip of my nose like she has done since I was a toddler, and then embraced Grandmother before choosing a chair in which to sit. "What's the word on Henry?"

"It's been hours." I huffed a frustrated sigh in reply as I helped myself to much needed sustenance.

"Uh-huh. Where's Charlie? Thought sure he'd be here."

I explained about Uncle Charlie's need for alone time to think and to pray. She said, "He's a keeper, that Charlie."

I was glad the chitchat no longer included me. My head throbbed, and I was still shaken by my experience in the serenity gardens. Every now and again, Grandmother smiled to let me know she hadn't forgotten me, but mainly I was left to my own thoughts. Thoughts that even when I was full of good food challenged me about why I was chosen to carry this burden of communing with spirits—and who was the regal warrior on the black-and-white horse?

At five forty-five the door opened. I think we all held our breath, expecting Sunny with news about my dad. A woman entered.

The woman offered a congenial smile and her voice was soft. "Good morning, Holliday family. I'm Sally Woodberry, the hospital's family-patient liaison. You've had a long, anxious wait to hear about Sheriff Holliday." Again, she smiled. "The surgery was a bit more complicated than expected. Dr. Sanders-Holliday explained about the previous wound to his aorta."

At our worried looks, she hastened on. "Not to worry. All is going well. I'm here to let you know that perhaps another hour in surgery, then another hour in recovery, and then he'll be moved to a room. I'll continue to keep you updated, and if you need anything, here's my extension number." She turned to indicate the phone on the wall.

I glanced at Grandmother and Patty huddled in their chairs. "It's really cold in here. Blankets for my Grandmother and her friend would be appreciated."

"Yes, ma'am, you got it."

As promised, she returned with a blanket for each of us. When she left, I softened the room's light to semi-darkness and curled up in my chair in hopes of shutting out visions of warriors and snakes.

I awoke with a start. Sunny had lightly touched my shoulder and whispered, "Tullah?"

The blood-splattered smock shouldn't have startled me, but it did. Seeing my reaction, she hastened to say, "He's okay. Due to the extensive damage to his heart, and for his own safety, we've placed him in isolation. He's in ICU to keep him as germ-free as possible."

Whatever else she had to say came out in the form of tears. "Oh, Tullah, I was so afraid we would lose Henry!"

We sought comfort in each other's arms.

Thank goodness it was Sunday. After depositing Grandmother and Patty at their apartments, I sent Ella a text letting her know I was on my way home. She answered back that the animals were fed, there were no post-op patients in the clinic, and for me to get some rest.

****

The next week seemed like an eternity. Uncle Charlie was still at his cabin in the woods to pray. Dad's recovery was inching along at a snail's pace and he remained in the hospital. In the meantime, Sunny and I had numerous conversations about whether Dad should return to work or retire. Ultimately, we agreed that only he should make that decision.

I was barely out of bed, dressed, and preparing for my first morning cup of coffee when River and Rascal set up a fuss with someone rapping on my door like a freakin' woodpecker rat-a-tatting against a tree.

Rat-a-tat, rat-a-tat. My grandmother yelled, "Tullah, unlock the door. It's Grandmother, and Charlie is with me." Tat, tat, tat. "We've brought breakfast." Tat, tat, tat.

I hollered, "Hold your horses."

After opening the door and inhaling the aroma wafting from the large tote bag in Uncle Charlie's hand, my mood lightened. We convened in the kitchen. While we enjoyed breakfast sandwiches and coffee, Uncle Charlie told us about his adventure in the woods.

He said, "When I was a boy, long before going into

145

foster care, I heard the old ones talk about a sweat lodge. As I have grown older, I have studied the ways of my father's Apache heritage, my mother's Inuit, and you and your family's Cherokee heritage."

He went on to explain that the holy men of the tribes believed sitting inside a sweat lodge helped them to connect with nature and to communicate with the spiritual realm, as well as providing moral and physical cleansing. "As a sacred ceremony, all that transpires in the lodge is left there and not shared elsewhere."

We sat in silence. Grandmother closed her eyes. She inhaled deeply, then spoke in a sing-song voice. "I am reminded of when I was a young girl and had chosen Samson as my husband. My mother and the elder women took me to the sweat lodge. A pit was filled with hot stones that were revered as ancient and spiritual in nature. Branches from cedar trees were burned, and sage tea was poured over the hot rocks. There was praying, singing, speaking from one's heart, and the door was closed and opened seven times before we could emerge from the lodge. We communed with the spiritual realm for moral and physical purification, the humbling of ourselves, and the healing of ourselves and others to achieve a specific need. In my case, to be worthy of Samson Six-Killer Goga. In the Cherokee language, *Goga* means Crow. I wanted to be a good wife to him and a good mother to our children."

When she had finished, she folded her hands around the coffee mug. Her eyes had taken on a faraway look as if she had lapsed into a different time and place. Uncle Charlie also seemed unaware that he was sitting in my kitchen.

The atmosphere was magical and reverent. I

hesitated, not wanting to disrupt this special moment. Keeping my voice low, and respectful, I said, "Two questions—are you suggesting I visit a sweat lodge, and where would I go to find one? I'm not opposed to the idea."

Uncle Charlie looked at me with thoughtful eyes. "That is why we have come at this early hour, Little Sister. I built a sweat lodge for myself and sought the Great Spirit Father. He spoke. I listened. The journey you will take is a dangerous one. This we know."

Grandmother interrupted. "You, Patty, and I must prepare ourselves for this journey. We must make ourselves physically, spiritually, and mentally strong."

The inclusion of herself and Patty concerned me. I shivered as if a cold wind had blown over me. "Uncle Charlie, are Grandmother and Patty in danger too?"

The wrinkles in his brow deepened. His ebony eyes seemed to grow darker, and there was a huskiness to his voice. "It never hurts to be prepared for the unknown."

What kind of answer was that? Goose prickles tracked up and down my spine. My instincts said I was about to do the limbo dance with death, and I told myself I had two other choices—one, allow my mother's murder to remain an unsolved mystery by sticking my head in the sand and calling off the entire trip; or two, branding myself a coward and living with guilt for the rest of my life.

Dad's words floated inside my mind—*Your mother would never expect you to avenge her death.* Realistically, I believed him. Spiritually, I knew mother had reached out to me, as had the other women's spirits.

Silence filled the kitchen. River and Rascal seemed to sense that now was not the time to whine or whinny for attention. Both animals lay quietly at my feet.

"Okay." I crossed my arms. "I'll do it. When?"

Grandmother reached to clasp my hand in hers. She gave it a squeeze. It was her unspoken gesture of approval. Uncle Charlie simply nodded. He said, "In two nights the moon will be full."

Grandmother nodded. "The hunter's moon. It is fitting."

Chapter Nineteen

A brief call to Ella gave me her reassurances that she could oversee the clinic, and that she didn't foresee a problem with Dr. Jesse Delight, our new intern. "Tullah, do what you need to do to find the fiends that killed your mother and those other women. If it were my mother, come hell or high water, you can bet your sweet patootie I'd be doing exactly what you're doing."

I wanted to reach through the phone and hug her. "You're the best, Ella. I'll never forget this."

The worry in her voice was obvious. "Tullah, don't talk like you're not coming back."

I explained about spending time at Uncle Charlie's sweat lodge. I also wanted to set her mind at ease. "Don't worry. I'll bring you a souvenir from New York."

We disconnected, and I rushed upstairs to pack a few essentials to take with me to Uncle Charlie's sweat lodge.

****

There's something uniquely serene about being somewhere that feels safe while the world beyond stands still amid its day-to-day hustle and bustle. That is not the way I felt as I followed behind Uncle Charlie when he turned off the main highway and traveled down a densely forested and rutted dirt road. Normally, he resided in an apartment over his establishment—the Whitehorse Saloon. With the schedule he had of supervising the kitchen, tending the bar, helping to serve customers, and basically being the chief cook and bottlewasher, he had no established work hours for himself.

Years ago, he'd purchased an abandoned lumber camp with the intention of renovating it into his permanent home once he retired. Part of the old building still remained. In fact, most of the wood had turned so dark with rot and age that the frame looked charred. He parked in front of a fairly new but rustic two-story cabin, and hustled around to the passenger side to assist Patty Sweet to the ground. A stiff wind greeted me as I departed my truck to help Grandmother.

The day had faded to dusk. Uncle Charlie hefted our meager pieces of luggage in his massive hands. Patty followed toting a large wicker basket. Layers of dried leaves crunched beneath our heavy shoes as we followed him through a weed-speckled trail.

The cabin overlooked a gurgling stream. We all stood in awed silence when a doe and her fawn eased from their hiding place and stepped to the water's edge for a quick drink before retreating into the woods.

Grandmother seemed to sniff the air. She whispered, "I believe I smell sage leaves."

Uncle Charlie cocked his gaze her way and merely smiled as he pointed a few feet away. Sheltered in a flat area amongst a stand of poplar trees stood what amounted to a large tarpaulin draped over poles to resemble a cave. "Ladies, your sweat lodge awaits. I'll take your bags inside the cabin."

"Charlie," Patty said, "That wicker basket is loaded with sandwiches and pastries. I'm sure we'll be starved by the time the sweating ceremony is over."

Uncle Charlie nodded. He added, "I've got a large

pot of chili in the back of my truck. I'll bring it up after you ladies get settled in the lodge."

I stood there, grave-silent, staring at the makeshift sweat lodge. With a deep sigh, I squared my shoulders and said, "We might as well get this over with."

Much to my surprise, Grandmother and Patty bent low and managed to enter the structure without assistance. For our convenience, Uncle Charlie had furnished us with bean bags covered with blankets rather than letting us sit on the cold ground as done in the olden days.

He said, "If you need me, I have pitched a tent nearby. I will take your luggage to the cabin. When you are ready to leave, call out and I will answer." And then he withdrew, leaving us alone.

He had built a small firepit in the center of the lodge. A bucket of water with a ladle sat next to the pit, and next to it was a ceramic bowl filled with sage leaves.

"Grandmother," I said, "Will you lead us in this ceremony?"

She nodded. Her voice flattened. "We shall disrobe to make ready for the cleansing of our bodies and our souls."

As previously planned, we had worn bathing suits underneath our regular clothes. Once settled, Grandmother leaned forward and gathered leaves from the bowl, then rubbed them on a cool stone in her hand, held over the already heated stones. She dipped the ladle into the bucket and slowly poured water over the herbs on the hot stones. Beads bubbled and hissed against the rocks and crushed sage. This created steam and humidity conducive to sweating.

"What do we do now?" Patty wanted to know.

Due to their ages, I was concerned for the health and wellbeing of my grandmother and her aged friend. The normal time to remain in a sweat lodge is typically five hours. I hoped neither of these dear women suffered from a heart attack or respiratory problems, but no amount of talking had deterred them from accompanying me in this ritual.

Grandmother relaxed in her seat. "Patty if you feel faint or ill in any way, do not put yourself at risk. We will call for Charlie to rescue you."

Patty reminded me of an outraged hen ruffling her feathers when she scoffed, "Not on your life, Tanti Crow. I'm in for the long haul."

I admired the spunk of these two octogenarians and was about to say so when Grandmother admonished us to silence. "We will not be like the jabbering bluejay. We must now begin our physical and spiritual purification."

She poured more crushed sage leaves and water over the stones. "The heat will detoxify our bodies. We will sweat out the impurities. This will rev up our blood flow."

Her eyes were dark and serious when she faced me. "This circulation of blood flow may trigger spiritual insight and visions. Do not allow fear to become your enemy."

Given my empathic abilities, I wasn't certain if I was ready to receive messages or see images pertaining to my trip to New York. A chill slithered over me, in spite of the heat inside our small domicile.

Grandmother shuttered her eyes and began to chant. Although I did not understand the words, I knew she was singing the language of the ancient Cherokee. Except for a few cousins, most of her family was gone. I wanted to ask if she missed living in North Carolina, but now was the time for silence and meditation, not questions.

Outside, Uncle Charlie beat a drum and shook a rattle, which added an eeriness to the ceremony. I closed my eyes and settled into the beanbag, allowing my mind to drift. Regardless of where my thoughts did or did not take me, I would always treasure this experience.

In spite of the brisk wind outside, perspiration trickled down my neck to seep between my breasts. Sweat beaded across my forehead. I wiped the moisture that threatened to sting my eyes. I breathed in the heady sage-filled air.

The muscles in my body relaxed. My mind drifted, and waves of memories swamped me. Flashes of events that had happened during my childhood darted through my mind, making me smile.

Not all memories were good, however. As much as I wanted to hang on to those happy thoughts, they sprouted wings and flew away. An ache formed in my heart, and tears choked my throat, and then anger welled inside of me as I stood at my fiancé's grave. I saw myself standing there a long time before saying, "Goodbye, Bryce."

And I thought, No matter what, I won't ever think of him again.

Like an old-timey movie, the scene flickered and rolled upward. A man stood in my kitchen, his back toward me. He was cooking and I was eating, which suited me just fine. I felt the shell around my heart softening. His inclusion in my life gave me a sense of balance.

"Who are you?" I asked.

A sudden gust of wind rattled the leaves. Sweat

drenched me from head to toe, yet I shivered. My gaze swept up his long legs. He was lean, his shoulders broad and muscular. There was the shadow of a beard suggesting that he hadn't shaved in a few days. His hair was obsidian black and hung past the nape of his neck. His face was tanned, his chin strong and stubborn. His features were finely chiseled, and he was handsomer than he had a right to be. I imaged he would be trouble for any woman who tried to tame him.

My heart slammed against my breast when he turned his deep blue gaze toward me. In that short moment I saw something else—pain flashed there momentarily; then it was gone. I wondered what his story was, and I wondered why I cared.

The feral virility in his eyes held me captive as he stepped toward me. Outside, a wolf howled. Words stuck in my throat when I tried to ask his name.

His hand feathered through my hair. A whisper of a smile reached his lips as they touched mine. I heard his name though he did not speak—Wolf. I blinked and he was gone. Outside, the wolf's bay sounded like *shunkaha.*

I heard the rattles of a snake, and the low throbbing of a beating heart.

Shadow Woman stood before me. She lifted one hand, palm outward, and made a motion that seemed to encompass the space around me. She said, "There is danger all around you. The grandmothers weep for the destruction of their granddaughters."

Hands grabbed me. Many hands. I was in a dark place, and watched in horror as sinister figures tormented me, whispered vulgarities at me. I saw myself hung upside down, my throat cut. I could hear the drip...drip...drip of my blood as it pinged inside a metal bowl.

I reached toward her. "Shadow Woman, don't leave me."

She looked at me with her all-seeing, all-knowing eyes as if assessing my features. Then she lifted the blood-filled metal bowl, dipped the fingers of her left hand in it, and drew three red marks across my cheek. She spoke three words, "The wolf comes."

The face of a fierce warrior began to shift and meld into the features of someone I had once known. I found it difficult to draw in a full breath. My body trembled with bone-chilling fear. I tasted death in my mouth like a bitter bile that threatened to choke me.

I tried to close my mind to these visions. I wanted...I *needed* to get away from this place.

A darkness blacker than any I had ever known surrounded me. The air was thick with my fear. A scream formed in my mind. I tried to call for help.

Chapter Twenty

Something solid trapped my arms in a vise grip. I tried to twist my body sideways, looking for a weapon. I couldn't find one. "Nooo! Get away!"

"Shh, it's all right. It is only me. You are safe, Tullah." Grandmother knelt beside me, gathering me close. "You are in no danger. It was only a hallucination."

I could barely speak above a whisper as I buried my face against her shoulder. I felt small and defenseless. "Are you sure?"

My eyes must have been wild with fright. Grandmother crooned and rocked me in her arms. "Very sure. Charlie and Patty are here, too."

Grandmother's grip tightened around me. My tremors melded with hers, and I was certain the ground beneath us was vibrating.

Charlie smoothed his hand over my head. "You are truly safe, Little Sister. Come inside the cabin. I imagine all of you are hungry."

Wrapped in blankets, we crawled on our hands and knees from the sweat lodge. I stared up at a star-speckled sky. The moon glowed full and bright. I heaved in a cleansing breath. The brisk air chilled me to the bone. I drew another breath and on bare feet hurried to the cabin.

The minute we entered the house, Grandmother drew me back into her embrace. "Granddaughter, oh my sweet child, I can't imagine what terrible things you saw."

I tried to hide my tears. I related about being at my fiancé's grave. As much as I didn't want to relive my own death, I managed to stammer, "I saw myself being murdered."

Grandmother and Patty's faces paled. Patty let out a tense breath. "Oh, my mercy, tell us everything that happened."

Grandmother grabbed my hand and held it tight against her breast. Fresh tears moistened my eyes. She admonished Patty. "That can wait, Patty. We must give Tullah time to collect herself." She continued, her voice, low and commanding, "Let us go upstairs and get into some warm clothing."

Uncle Charlie added, "I'll heat the chili, and make a pot of coffee."

Halfway up the stairs, I glanced over the railing. "Uncle Charlie, what time is it?"

I followed his eyes to a large Alpine clock hanging over the fireplace mantel. He said, "It is four o'clock in the morning."

We had arrived before noon, and now it was the wee hour of a new day. I had been locked in a terrifying hallucination for sixteen hours. With a deep sigh, I squared my shoulders and continued upstairs to dress.

Normally I can chow down two bowls of Uncle Charlie's chili without hesitation. Not tonight. Tonight, the kidney beans felt like rocks rolling down my throat, and the red color reminded me of my own blood. Without words, Uncle Charlie seemed to read my thoughts. He quietly removed the untouched bowl of food. Perhaps he thought one of Patty's lemon curd donuts would better suit me when he placed two on a plate and set it in front of me.

My stomach begged for nourishment; my tastebuds equated the sugar to gritty sand in both taste and texture. I wasn't trembling as much now. I managed to lift the cup of coffee and get it to my mouth without sloshing it down the front of my shirt. After several sips, the caffeine from the strong, dark liquid began to fortify me.

"Fear is the enemy, Little Sister. You must never let it win."

Uncle Charlie's calm voice and his words seemed to fortify me. I reached across the table to place my small hand into his giant paw. It wasn't the first time he'd spoken those same words to me. Funny how I had forgotten about that until now. I released my hand and pushed from the chair to walk to the kitchen window. I drew a deep breath and stared into the darkness, unaware of the passing of time. I forced open my mind, allowing happy memories to flood my thoughts.

Six waiting eyes, all filled with expectation, stared at me when I turned from the window. "Tomorrow, I will tell you what the spirits have shown me. Please excuse me. I am awfully tired."

Upstairs, I folded back the quilt and settled on the bed. It took a few minutes before I realized my grandmother was speaking to me from the doorway. "I'm sorry, Grandmother, I guess my mind was elsewhere."

She sat on the edge of the bed, tiredly brushing a strand of hair from her face. "I'm here if you need me."

I lifted the quilt. She wrapped me in her arms and held me as she had done so many times when life got in my way. Before sleep came, I saw my mother's face. She lowered her head as if it were too heavy to hold upright. Her silent words pierced my heart. "It's never a good day to die, my daughter."

I must have cried out because Grandmother said, "Shh, it's only a dream. Remember, the wolf comes."

With a deep sigh, I wondered how Grandmother knew about the wolf.

****

The morning was strangely peaceful after my horrifying experience in the sweat tipi. I was alone in the bed I had shared with Grandmother, and the twin bed where Patty had slept was empty. The aroma of bacon teased my nose, prompting me to quickly dress and hustle downstairs. Dread interrupted the peace I had felt earlier, knowing I was expected to share the visions that had visited me.

All eyes were on me when I entered the kitchen. Apparently, the forced happy face I wore failed. Uncle Charlie pointed to an empty chair, a cup of coffee in his hand. "Dark circles under your eyes speak loudly, Little Sister. We will save the talk until after we have fed our stomachs."

It took a plate of scrambled eggs, bacon, two donuts, and a large mug of coffee to help me feel up to the task of conversation. Fortified with another cup of coffee, I followed the others into the living room to relish the warmth of the fireplace.

I stared into the flickering fire. The dancing blue-and-orange flames evolved into images of women. I didn't recognize my own voice as I spoke of the attack in a dark alley… "And then a wolf came. A large black wolf with…blue eyes."

After the telling, I was so wired I was certain I would

explode. Although the fire warmed the room, it took all my efforts to keep my teeth from chattering.

Grandmother broke the silence. "I, too, had a vision. It was an old dream that had been rewritten." She grasped my hand and lifted the palm to her cheek. Tears and fear filled her eyes. I was afraid to speak. Grandmother isn't given to dreams or prophecies. Her hands were cold and she trembled. While I waited, I vowed to never participate in another sweat lodge ritual.

A little voice inside my head whispered, "You know not what you speak." And I silently screamed, *Shut up!*

Finally, Grandmother spoke. "In my vision, a bald man commanded a band of jagged lightning bolts. They obeyed his orders." She squeezed my hand until I thought my fingers might break. "Be careful, Tullah. A fire lives in this person's soul. I believe he will kill without conscience."

All of these warnings hung heavily over me. I dreaded the rising of the hunter's moon. At this point, what I wanted most was the security of my home with my animals.

Chapter Twenty-One

By the time we arrived at the hospital to check on my dad, I was more than ready to rid myself of the visions. In two days, Grandmother, Patty, and I would board a plane bound for New York.

While the waters were still muddied with questions about the mysterious bald man, the lightning bolts, and the blue-eyed wolf, we had linked some of the dots that hopefully would lead to my mother's killers.

The day was ending, and I had a nagging feeling that I was neglecting something important. Dad was still in isolation ICU. Although he sat in a chair, a blanket draped over his lap, he was unlike the vibrant man of a few days ago. Pale and frail, he fussed with the oxygen tube in his nose. The cleft in his chin looked deeper, and his eyes appeared sunken. I worried about leaving him. He mouthed *I love you.*

I put on my brightest smile and returned his love by shaping my hands to form a heart. I closed my eyes for a brief moment and when I opened them Sunny was helping him to bed. She motioned for me to wait.

We walked to cafeteria for coffee. "Be honest, Sunny. How is Dad?"

She seemed to concentrate on opening a packet of sugar. "He's tough."

"Yeah, and?"

"The damage to his heart from that old stab wound

and now with this…" Her voice drifted off.

"What are you not telling me, Sunny?"

"Henry is like most men—they think they're invincible. As much as I want him to retire, it's not my decision." She emptied a packet of sugar into her coffee and then reached for another packet. "He takes his duties very seriously. If he gets into a fight or has to do any strenuous running—oh, Tullah, I'm afraid he might not survive another issue with his heart."

I shared her fear. Where were the spirits when I needed them to show me how to protect my father? "Does he know I'm going to New York?"

Sunny grimaced at the taste of her sugary coffee and pushed it aside. "He doesn't know when, only that you are. He's worried about what might happen to you, and frankly, so am I."

There was no need to cause concern where it wasn't needed. "Grandmother and Patty are going with me. We'll attend the art show, perhaps take in a Broadway play, do some shopping, and…" I ran out of excuses and finished by saying, "Easy peasy. I'll bring you and Ella something special. What do you think she'd like, and what would you like?"

We chit-chatted a few more minutes about inconsequential souvenirs before hugging goodbye.

All the way home, I argued with myself. Part of my brain cautioned me to cancel the trip to New York. The other part insisted that the time was right to accomplish my mission. Once home, I checked on the post-surgery animals and fed the horses. In the quiet of the barn, I listened to the horses snuffling as they munched their grain. It was a satisfying sound. When they finished eating, I made certain their turnout blankets were snug.

The weather forecast predicted a cold night with the approaching hunter's moon.

I had been away a mere thirty-six hours, yet it seemed like a lifetime. I gave River and Rascal some much neglected attention. My dog and teacup donkey followed me upstairs. They watched every move I made as I packed my suitcase. "Hey, guys, I'll miss you. I really don't want to go, but it's something I have to do. If I don't find the creeps that killed my mother and those other women, well…well, I'm afraid their spirits will continue to haunt me."

A part of me hoped that once I solved this case this mysterious empathic gift would disappear—forever.

My pets cocked their ears back and forth as if hanging on to my every word. I laughed aloud and planted kisses on their foreheads. "As if either of you can understand what I'm saying."

River whined and wagged his tail; Rascal let out one of his silly snuffling brays. I snapped my fingers and pointed. "Okay, off the bed. You have your own," I commanded.

I was about to get ready for a shower and then to bed when I had an unexplainable urge to visit the front porch. River emitted a low throaty growl. The hackles on his neck rose. He scrambled from his bed with Rascal hot on his heels. I immediately followed. My animals are as in-tune with the unknown as I.

My heart thudded as I raced down the stairs and to the front door. River's wagging tail cued me that whatever presence was outside apparently meant me no harm. Yet I eased the safety bolt back, opened the door, and peered into the twilight.

Seeing nothing, I stepped outside, wishing I'd

thought to grab a jacket. The night was peaceful and serene. At the tree-lined drive, a breeze whispered through the bare limbs. It wasn't difficult to imagine someone or something hiding in the shadows. In fact, it wouldn't be the first time the spirits of warriors, and other ethereal specters had visited me on such a night. Seeing nothing, I had just decided to return to the warmth of my house when River growled and hugged against my leg. I grabbed his collar and held tight so he couldn't bound off the porch.

I squinted into the darkness. The crackle of leaves drew me to the steps. A massive shadow moved toward me. Breath hung in my throat as a ray of moonlight outlined a regal stag. His rack of antlers was expansive. This was no ordinary Kentucky deer.

Many animals have visited to warn me of an impending murder or death. Never a deer. Unafraid, but cautious, I held out my palm. The stag stepped forward and sniffed, then backed away. He pointed his neck skyward and bugled a long eerie sound. The moon's pale golden orb lit the sky.

Every fiber of my survival instinct warned me to run for safety. My voice held a slight tremor. I was frightened, and that annoyed me. "Why are you here?"

The stag was perfectly at ease, and the look in his eyes said he had no intention to harm me. I asked, "Are you real or a spirit? Are you here to warn me?"

This beautiful animal began to morph. The first to go were the antlers, and the rest followed until it had transitioned into the image of Shadow Woman.

"This is ridiculous." I didn't attempt to hide the annoyance from my voice. "Why didn't you simply appear and say what you have to say instead of playing these stupid charade games?"

"You would be wise to learn the history of your heritage, Tullah Crow."

"I'm not a mind reader. What are you here to teach me?"

When she spoke, she sounded a bit like my mother. "The Great Spirit Father knows what you are going through. Have faith."

"So the deer was a representation of the heavens— is that what you're trying to teach me?"

"It is your lesson to learn, Tullah Crow, and you are a wise woman."

"Yeah, well, I'm confused. Are you my mother or Shadow Woman?" Tears stung my eyes. I fiercely blinked them back. I would not insult her with my emotions when she was clearly in charge of her own.

The moon wasn't quite full, but it would be by the time we arrived in New York. "Does this mean I'm not in danger?"

Her image began to flicker. I knew it was time for her to go. "Wait," I cried out. "Don't leave. You haven't answered my question."

"Tullah Crow, do not kill the wolf spider."

And then she was gone.

My whole encounter with Shadow Woman had taken less time than a pot of coffee would take to brew. I returned to the house, taking my two animals with me. Once inside, I considered calling Grandmother but decided not to worry her. Instead, I dialed Uncle Charlie.

After six rings, I had almost hung up when he finally answered. I decided to forego the part about the stag morphing into Shadow Woman. Instead, I briefly explained about a spirit visiting me. "Uncle Charlie, in

Native American lore, what do spiders represent?"

"I am not much learned in all beliefs of the People, Little Sister. What exactly did this Shadow Woman say about spiders?"

"She warned not to kill a *wolf* spider."

"Aho, this spirit woman is wise. In another life she must have been a priestess." He went on to explain that wolf spiders were hunters and would go after their prey. "They don't mind showing their fangs. They rear up on their legs and attack, mostly at night."

We were silent for a few seconds. I tried to absorb what Uncle Charlie had said. "I'm not sure what this has to do with my trip to New York. I'm also not sure spiders live in the city, especially big hairy ones."

"Wolf spiders can live anywhere, Little Sister. I believe the spirit was trying to tell you that the wolf spider is a friend, a protector."

"Thank you, Uncle Charlie. I'll see you in the morning. Seven sharp."

I was glad he had offered to drive Grandmother, Patty, and me to the airport.

Chapter Twenty-Two

It was still dark when I arrived at Grandmother's apartment. I parked, unloaded my one suitcase, and locked my truck. Before I could ring the doorbell, Grandmother opened the door and beckoned me inside. Patty sat at the small dining table. Both women looked bright-eyed and ready for an adventure.

Grandmother's voice lilted. "Tullah, I have a gift for you. We have a few minutes before Charlie arrives."

"My birthday has come and gone, and Christmas is still several weeks away."

She handed me a small white box. I cast her a skeptical eye, and she gestured. "Go ahead; open it."

The box was too small to hold anything of consequence. I thought perhaps a piece of jewelry; though I couldn't imagine why she would give me such a gift. Earrings, perhaps. Boy, was I wrong. A beautifully beaded doeskin bag lay on a bed of cotton. Curiosity filled me as I lifted the bag from its nesting place. "Is it a medicine bag?"

"Yes. I made it especially for you, just as my grandmother did for me. Except I was entering my teen years when she made it. Open it."

I blinked several times to clear my vision, then opened the bag that was about the size of a plum. Grandmother pointed to a napkin and motioned for me to reveal the contents. She said, "You are more precious to me than life. I regret every day that Josie never had a medicine bag to protect her in her travels." She hesitated a moment as if steadying her emotions. "Each item holds a special meaning. Because you are a lover of animals and nature, I believe I have chosen wisely."

She pointed and explained that she had selected items from the plant kingdom, the animal kingdom, the mineral and human kingdoms.

The first item she pointed to was the dried body of a bee. Her lips quirked into a mischievous smile. "The queen bee is a messenger from Mother Earth. Not only is she a spreader of good omens, she brings love and joy, and…she is a symbol of fertility."

I rolled my eyes. Negative thoughts buzzed inside my head. Grandmother was still worried that my ovaries had shriveled up and I'd never have children. I decided to keep my thoughts to myself.

A bundle of sage leaves was tied together with a yellow ribbon. I waited for Grandmother to speak. "Sage represents immortality, virtue, health, and wisdom. I've secured the bundle with yellow because the color is sacred to our people and stands for willingness to fight to the death, intellect, and heroism. From the mineral kingdom, I have chosen a turquoise stone to protect you from negative energies. Also use it to call upon the spirits for guidance. And lastly, from the human kingdom, I have included this small black key with a purple ribbon."

When she stopped speaking, I glanced toward Patty. Her lips formed a smile that reminded me of a cat that had just eaten a canary and got caught with feathers in its mouth. Not wanting to interrupt this meaningful ceremony, I remained silent.

Finally, Grandmother leaned forward to barely

touch a fingernail to the key. "Your grandfather was the only love in my life. Since his death, I have never yearned for another man. I wish the same for you, granddaughter. The key will open your heart to a warrior who will be your soulmate. The purple ribbon means this lucky man will be intelligent, brave, protective of his family, and he will respect the ways of our ancestors."

I was certain that a man such as this existed only in fictional romance novels because he certainly didn't live in Enigma, Kentucky. Still, I remained silent. Grandmother seemed to be enjoying this little ceremony, and I didn't want to interrupt her joy.

Reverently, she placed each item inside the bag and drew the drawstrings to close it. Overwhelmed with emotions, I struggled to find my voice. I bowed slightly so she could place the thin leather thongs around my neck. Strangely, a warm power flowed through my body as the little doeskin medicine pouch nestled between my breasts.

And then I remembered Shadow Woman's words that I should learn the lessons of my people. I wrapped my arms around Grandmother. "I thank you, Grandmother, for these are treasures that will forever remind me of my birthright. I will revere them and allow them to be my guide in times of tranquility and trouble. And when I am a grandmother, I will honor my heritage by gifting such a treasure to my first-born granddaughter."

Patty left her place at the dining table. She wrapped her arms around Grandmother and me, and then whispered, "Beautiful."

A series of raps sounded against the front door, Uncle Charlie's signature knock. Our emotional session had ended, or so I thought.

I opened the door. "You're early, Uncle Charlie. We don't need to leave for another few minutes."

"Aho, I know." He motioned for us to follow him to the dining table where he set a green leather bag on the table. From the bag he withdrew three feathers. "Little Sister, this journey is more than a trip to honor the spirit and talents of your mother. It is also about discovery."

Uncle Charlie isn't a man given to jokes or frivolities. Perhaps it's his Apache-Inuit heritage that causes him to always wear a perpetual frown; or perhaps it was aftereffects of the war, or even sad memories from his childhood. Regardless of his facial expressions, next to my dad, Uncle Charlie is the most kind, brave, and honorable man I know. I waited for him to explain the meaning of the three feathers.

He aligned the feathers on the table, and lifted each one with its explanation. "The owl will let you see your way; from a hawk: he will protect you; and one from an eagle: Trust in the Great Spirit Father and wait with confident anticipation and hope. For if you do, He will give you such faith-filled confidence that you will soar with wings like an eagle to ride out any storm and reach the blue skies of victory."

He returned the feathers to their case and handed it to me.

I placed the leather bag inside my carry-on tote. "I am honored, Uncle Charlie." And then, I thanked him in the language of the Cherokee.

****

My mind was filled with questions, which made me glad that Uncle Charlie was driving us to the airport. We rode in silence. I tried to let go of the puzzles in my subconscious and allow my mind to digest the significance of Grandmother's and Uncle Charlie's gifts, as well as Shadow Woman's visit. But every time I tried to relax, I came back to the information in my mother's evidence file which created a strong sense of anger and anxiety. I was on high alert and there was little I could do to quit worrying.

I decided to focus on the passing vastness of the countryside. A dilapidated sign hanging askew from a rotting post captured my attention. The real estate sign was nowhere in sight. "Uncle Charlie, did someone buy the Second Chance Ranch? The sign is gone."

As the owner of a busy bar and restaurant, Uncle Charlie was always up on the latest town news. An idea cooked inside my brain to the point that I thought it would boil over from excitement.

Without taking his eyes off the road, he said, "Probably a bunch of hooligan kids stole it. As far as I know, the ranch is still for sale, and getting more rundown every day. It's too bad. Good pastureland, and from my understanding the bank has taken possession of the property."

"Do you think the bank would be willing to negotiate the price?"

"What's your sudden interest, Little Sister? You planning to build a new clinic and move the business away from your house?"

"Not on your life."

Grandmother had scooted forward in the back seat. "Yes, Granddaughter, I'm all ears. I've heard the house and barns are in bad shape. I guess the yuppie nephew didn't want to keep the payments up after his uncle willed it to him. Surely, you don't plan to renovate and then resell."

It took all my effort to keep from laughing out loud. The medicine pouch hidden beneath my shirt seemed to pulsate. In all my studies of Native American history and folklore, medicine bags were meant to protect, to heal, and to give wisdom to the wearer. Maybe it was working.

"Grandmother didn't you say that sage was for wisdom?"

She graced me with squint-eyed skepticism. "I did."

"Since you are the creator of the contents of the pouch, you are partly responsible for my idea." Before she could respond, I hastened on. "I think we are all in agreement that Dad should retire as sheriff. We also agree that he is a stubborn man and will resist all efforts if he thinks he's being forced to step down before the next election. So, here's my idea...

"Uncle Charlie, you and Dad have often mentioned that you'd like to start a rehabilitation facility for wounded veterans. Well, a few months ago, two women, retired military, approached me about buying horses for them. They planned to turn the old Second Chance ranch into a rehab for just that—wounded veterans. Once the women discovered how much they didn't know about horses, ranching, and all the things that go with running such a place, they changed their minds.

"Don't you see? It's perfect. Even the name— Second Chance Ranch—is perfect. You've talked about selling the saloon, that you're tired of all the odd hours, and the hassle. What about it, Uncle Charlie?"

"Little Sister, your friend Natalie Fletcher, who owns Happy Hooves Equestrian Center—didn't she open a rehab place for wounded vets? Enigma isn't big enough to support two such places."

I was quick with my response. You know, strike while the anvil is hot, so to speak. "While her heart was in the right place, it didn't pan out. Instead, she decided to expand her center to accommodate both disabled children and adults. Besides, I'm certain there are grants you could apply for to help with the funding. You and Dad were both wounded. Thankfully neither of you suffer from PTSD. The thing is, you know what it's like to not have the support that's needed for most of these guys, especially the ones with no family."

Uncle Charlie glanced at me. He wore an expression that told me he was giving serious thought to my idea. He wasn't a man to be pushed. He would need time to chew on the idea.

Grandmother said, "Granddaughter, I always knew you were a genius. The sage is truly boosting your wisdom."

Patty had remained quiet all this time. Finally, she said, "You know, I'm getting a little bored with traveling all the time, and I miss being in the kitchen. I'd happily volunteer to teach the Second Chance recruits how to make yummy good pastries."

"And, Ella and I would take care of all the veterinary needs. It would be our contribution to the cause."

I began to worry because Uncle Charlie was taking his sweet time mulling over the idea. I was almost afraid we'd arrive at the airport before he'd comment yea or nay.

"You know, Little Sister, it's a worthy idea. After I drop you ladies at the airport and return to Enigma, I think I'll pay Harmon Everett at the First National Bank a visit."

It's rare that Uncle Charlie smiles. This time a broad

grin graced his tanned face. He said, more to himself than to us, "Yep, it's a danged good idea."

And then he grinned at me. "I'm gonna pay Henry a visit and drop a bug in his ear. Knowing him, after he mulls it over a while, he won't think twice about hanging up his badge. Yep, it's surely a danged good idea."

A few minutes later, Uncle Charlie pulled in front of the airport's passenger drop-off entrance. He helped us with our luggage and promised to pick us up in a week.

Before he pulled away from the curb, he rolled down the window and yelled, "Second Chance Ranch. I like it!"

Part II: Clay Wolfchild Bannister: Memories

*"Some days the memories still
knock the wind out of me."*

~Anonymous

Chapter Twenty-Three

So many images floated around my head…broken, bloody dolls. Alive, happy, smiling—once. And yet, they remained like living memories.

The bailiff's voice interrupted my musings. He said, "All rise. The Honorable Judge Mercedes Raulo presiding."

Wise and merciful. Judge Mercedes Raulo was certainly wise. Merciful, not so much when it came to sentencing hardened criminals. Today was my lucky day.

As soon as we were seated, the court clerk called my name. I approached the witness stand. He held out the Bible.

I placed my left hand on the holy book. He said, "Do you swear to tell the truth, the whole truth, and nothing but the truth?"

"I do."

"For the court, please state your full name and occupation."

"Clay Wolfchild Bannister. Detective. Dallas

Sheriff's Department."

"You may be seated."

A sharp twinge stabbed me in the back when I stepped on the witness platform. I slowly released my breath as I eased into the chair. My eyes went directly to the piece of shit sitting next to an even shittier lawyer. Barton Siegle had a reputation for operating on the outer fringes of the law but not enough to get him disbarred. My Lakota Sioux blood screamed for revenge.

My knuckles ached. Siegle cocked an eyebrow at me. I gripped the sides of the chair to keep from leaping across the room to rip out the smirking bastard's throat.

District Attorney Elizabeth Cahill spoke my name, twice, before I actually heard her. "Detective Bannister?"

I cleared my throat. "Yes. My apologies, Ms. Cahill."

Well acquainted with the facts of the case, she offered a barely perceptible sympathetic smile. She said, "Detective Bannister, are you acquainted with the defendant?"

I cut my eyes toward Dwight Harvey. "Not personally."

DA Cahill's back was to Harvey. She didn't see him when he formed his right hand into the shape of a pistol and pointed it toward me.

The action however did not escape Judge Raulo. She slammed the gavel against the sound block so hard that it sounded like a gunshot.

She scolded Harvey's attorney. "Mr. Siegle, control your client. I will not tolerate such threatening intimidations in my courtroom. If you cannot control Mr. Harvey, I assure you that I will have him and you removed from my courtroom. Plus, I will add contempt of court to your client's already long list of infractions."

I wanted to shout, "Atta girl!" but remained silent, knowing I wouldn't earn any brownie points from the judge.

She said, "Is that understood, Mr. Siegle?"

Siegle adjusted the knot in his tie. "Yes, your Honor. I apologize for my client."

She merely nodded her head, then said, "You may continue, Ms. Cahill."

DA Cahill said, "Detective Bannister, do you recall your whereabouts on June twenty-first, two years ago?"

"Yes, inside the First Alamo Bank."

"Is that where you know Mr. Harvey?"

"As I've said, I am not personally acquainted with Mr. Harvey. You might say I'm one of his many victims."

Attorney Siegle, immediately stood and blustered. "Objection! Hostility toward my client."

I cocked an eyebrow toward the arrogant asshole. "I withdraw my last remark."

DA Cahill commanded the court reporter to strike my last sentence. She also cautioned me to contain my anger.

"Detective Bannister, without elaboration, please tell the court how you know the defendant."

Again, Siegle stood and said, "Objection."

Cahill stared at him. She addressed the judge. "Your Honor, my client hasn't answered the question. Just exactly what is Mr. Siegle's objection?"

Judge Raulo responded. "Overruled. Please answer the question, Detective Bannister."

Harvey leaned over and whispered in Siegler's ear.

I could only imagine what he was saying.

After adjusting my posture to relieve the pain in my back, and as instructed, I answered without elaboration. "On the day of June twenty-first, Mr. Harvey shot me."

There was an audible gasp from the audience. Judge Raulo reminded the spectators to remain silent and to keep their emotions contained.

Cahill said, "In your own words, Detective Bannister, please tell the court, in full detail, the events that led up to the shooting."

Siegler again called, "Objection, your Honor. Speculation."

Cahill turned to the judge, who said, "Overruled. I'll allow it."

Cahill nodded for me to continue with a reminder not to embellish the facts. I had relived that day a thousand times. As a lawman, I've seen death up close more than I care to remember. I knew this day was coming, knew I would need to testify. In my mind, I had rehearsed the facts over and over. Still, I was not prepared for the emotional impact that slammed against my heart, leaving me almost breathless. I blinked several times to banish the image of my bride lying like a broken doll in a pool of her own blood.

The pain in my back escalated. I wasn't sure if the bullet lodged in my spine was the cause or if it was psychosomatic. The first thing I noticed was the silence. I scanned the expectant faces of the jurors and the audience.

Drawing in a deep breath and letting it out slowly, I began. "On the aforementioned day, my wife and I—"

DA Cahill interrupted and said, "For the record, please state your wife's full name."

I began again. "On the aforementioned day, my wife, Bethanne Saunders Bannister, and I entered the First Alamo Bank. We had an appointment with a loan officer. It was my day off. My service revolver was locked inside the glove compartment of my truck. We had been inside the bank approximately five minutes when the defendant and three other men entered the bank. All were dressed in navy-blue business suits and wearing black ski masks—"

"Objection!" Siegler spouted. "If the men were wearing masks, Detective Bannister cannot possibly know which man, if any of them at all, was my client."

Cahill was clearly exasperated at the interruption. She huffed her statement. "Your Honor, if allowed to continue, Detective Bannister will answer Mr. Siegler's question regarding the defendant's identity."

Raulo nodded. "I'll allow it. You may continue, Detective."

Again, I adjusted my posture to relieve the pain shooting down my left leg. "All three men were armed with assault rifles. One man locked the bank's entry doors while the other three demanded the tellers fill each of their briefcases with paper money only.

"Unfortunately, the loan officer, Mr. Nicholas Jones, came out of his office and wanted to know what was going on. I can only surmise that one of the tellers had pressed a silent alarm, because two security guards entered the lobby. One of the armed men fired his weapon. Both guards were mortally wounded. This action appeared to create a frenzy of panic causing the other armed men to begin firing in spraying motions.

"My wife was hit multiple times. The coroner's report states she was dead before collapsing to the floor.

I lunged for a revolver that one of the downed guards had dropped, and managed to take out two of the perpetrators.

"My back was turned away from the guy guarding the door. He put four bullets in me—one of which is permanently lodged in my spine. He had fired multiple rounds, killing several innocent people; women, men, the loan officer, a child. When his rifle jammed, I lunged toward him and pulled off his mask. He slammed the rifle butt against my head. Before I passed out, I got a good look at his face. It's a face I will never forget."

"How so, Detective?" Cahill asked.

"The shooter had a large, red, strawberry-shaped birthmark on the left side of his face."

Cahill stood quietly facing the panel of jurors, and then she slowly pivoted to look at Dwight Harvey before turning toward me. I'd witnessed this specific tactic many times in other court trials. This type of momentous delay allows the jurors to absorb the witness's testimony. An effective move by this court-smart District Attorney.

All eyes turned toward the defendant.

She said, "Detective Bannister, is that man in this courtroom?"

"Yes!"

"Would you point to him?"

"Gladly."

"Let the court records show that Detective Clay Wolfchild Bannister has identified Dwight Harvey as the man who willfully shot and killed Bethanne Saunders Bannister, two bank security guards, a loan officer, three women, four men, and…a toddler."

Her hesitation when mentioning the child was another deliberate act to drive home the heinous act of

Dwight Harvey.

Judge Raulo banged her gavel several times to quiet the outrage from the audience. Finally, she asked Siegler if he had any questions, to which he declined. I was excused from the witness stand, and Harvey was shackled, handcuffed, and led from the courtroom.

****

One month later, I returned to the courtroom. Dwight Harvey stood, handcuffed and wearing leg bracelets. Judge Raulo passed the ultimate penalty. I should have been satisfied, but knowing how the system works, I also knew Harvey would sit on death row until he was allowed to use his one appeal. How many years that would take was up to the U.S. Appeals Court. I could only pray he'd meet his end in prison.

Chapter Twenty-Four

I awoke from a troubling dream. Only fragments remain—left over from the anesthesia, I supposed. The room was frigid. My mouth felt like a desert, my throat ached when I swallowed. I managed to rasp, "I'm cold."

"Ah, Detective Bannister, you're awake. I'll get you a blanket from the warmer."

Within minutes, a matronly nurse draped a toasty warm blanket over my shivering body. I thanked her and asked for a drink of water.

She smiled. "I'll bring you some ice chips. No water for a couple of hours."

I gladly accepted the icy crystals. I coughed to clear the rasp from my throat. "How did the surgery go?"

Again, she accommodated me with a robotic smile. "You're about ready to be transported to your room. The doctor will be in to see you shortly."

I said, "Is that a nice way of saying the surgery wasn't a success?"

"Oh, not at all." She adjusted the blanket. "I'm the recovery room nurse. I don't have the answers to your questions." She patted my shoulder.

The recovery room was a cacophony of sounds. A phone rang. A male nurse answered. He walked to stand next to my bed. "Your limo is arriving, Detective. Enjoy the ride."

I'm not sure how long I slept. I awoke to an

attendant setting a tray of gourmet hospital food in front of me. Gourmet—I say that with tongue in cheek, of course.

I was finishing the last of my red gelatin when the doctor strolled in. "Well, Detective Bannister, how're you feeling?"

Doctor Heather Griffin looked more like a fashion model than a neurosurgeon. We weren't exactly buddy-buddies, but this wasn't the first time she'd operated on me. I felt comfortable in saying, "I'd feel better if I had a steak, rare, instead of red jiggly water."

She brushed off my snide attempt to make a joke. "Maybe tomorrow." Then she commanded the nurse to help me turn onto my side.

After a series of painful grunts and worrying about the short nightgown exposing my butt crack, I said, "Okay, Doc, give it to me straight. What's the verdict?"

A few gentle pokes, prods, and questions about what sensations I felt along my spine, she finally said, "The verdict is that if you eat right, exercise, and stop getting shot, you might live to a ripe old age."

Thankful for the painkiller dripping into my vein, I eased back to lie flat. "Do I hear a *but* in there?"

When she didn't immediately answer, I said, "Good or bad, give it to me straight."

She crossed her arms over her white coat. I heard the sincerity in her voice. "Remember what we discussed pre-surgery?"

For a moment it seemed the world stopped as I recalled our conversation. All I could utter was, "Yeah." I was weary and didn't want to hear *I'm sorry*, again.

But she said it, "I'm sorry, Detective Bannister. No more running after bad guys, no more scuffles, leaping over cars, jumping out of second-story windows, or getting shot."

"Listen, Doc, I'm not ready to be a desk jockey. Chasing down bad guys is what I do."

The silence became awkward. Reality struck me—hard. The drug was kicking in, leaving my lips feeling fuzzy. I ran my tongue over them, and forced my brain to function. "You weren't able to remove the bullet."

It wasn't a question. It was a fact, a possibility, that I'd known before signing consent forms for surgery. The bullet was not in an accessible location. She had warned me that any meddling with it could cause permanent paralysis.

I looked at Dr. Griffin from aside and saw that in her mind she was revisiting and reaffirming her original diagnoses. I cleared my throat. "Yeah," I say feeling defeated.

The pain in my spine became a background noise. Everything in my life seemed out of balance. Her voice interrupted my thoughts. "We'll get you up tomorrow. You know the drill."

Sure, I knew the drill. Baby steps until working up to an hour of grueling physical therapy. Still, I wasn't ready to sit behind a desk and shuffle papers.

"How soon can I return to work?"

She cocked an eyebrow and shot me a scowl. I corrected myself. "If I promise to swap my revolver for a pen?"

"Four to six weeks; and be aware that your captain will be advised of my recommendations. Any line-of-duty assignments are strictly up to him." She turned to leave, then apparently changed her mind and with a slow exhale said, "You can either be smart or stupid. The choice is yours, Detective Bannister."

I refrained from asking if she was insulting my intelligence. I was certain I knew what she meant, except I needed to hear it. "Choice?" I ask.

"Yes. Wheelchair or walking."

And with that, Dr. Heather Griffin walked out the door, leaving me to wrestle with my thoughts as I drifted into a drug-induced neverland.

****

Later that evening the two women I loved most in life came to hospital. I wasn't in the mood for lectures and said so. Sure, my father had been a deputy. He was knifed to death while breaking up a barroom brawl. I understood my mother's and sister's concerns.

Mama lifted my hand into hers. "Fauni and I have talked to the doctor, Clay Wolfchild. You have enough time in to retire."

"Listen to Mama, Clay Wolfchild. Since Poppa's death she worries about you. I do too, and with Wes away, I double worry." Fauni's voice hardened. "Would you take such chances if Bethanne were still alive?"

The mention of my deceased wife struck a raw nerve. I wanted to rail at my sister to keep Bethy out of this conversation. Yet, with my brother-in-law as a Marine Raider, Fauni lived with the stress of never knowing what dangerous mission he was undertaking, or when he might have time to come home for a short visit. Part of me felt selfish, and the other part felt my mother and sister were equally as selfish for asking me to give up a job I enjoyed. Taking down bad guys gave me the same adrenalin rush that hanging on to a rank bull for eight seconds brought. I'd had to hang up my spurs and quit rodeoing after I'd been shot. Now, I was being told

185

to ride a desk...push a pen...pound the keys on a computer. The most danger I was in might be from a paper cut.

"Fauni, you and Mama stop worrying. I may be bullheaded, but I'm not stupid."

It was all a bunch of bullshit! Except, it wasn't.

Chapter Twenty-Five

Healing took a bit longer than I expected. Four weeks later, and after a day of physical therapy, I relaxed in a rocking chair. A western novel lay open in my lap. I could relate to the deputy marshal hell-bent on finding the men who had murdered his wife. In fact, when my cellphone rang, I almost didn't answer because I wanted to find out what happened next in the story.

I looked at the caller ID. "Afternoon, Cap'n."

"How you doing, Clay?"

"Bored. Ready to get back in the saddle."

"Yep. We'll talk about that later. Right now, I have some news that might perk you up."

We were quiet for a second or two. An uncomfortable quiet because I feared the worse—mandatory retirement. "All right. What you got?"

"Remember Dwight Harvey?"

I harrumphed. "The bullet in my spine is a constant reminder of that scumbag. What about him?"

"He's dead."

I searched through my mental calendar. His execution date was still a year away. "What happened?"

"One of the cons assigned to laundry duty found Harvey stuffed inside an industrial clothes dryer with ligature marks around his neck."

"Wish I could say I was sorry." And then I added, "At least whoever did Harvey in saved the State from having to pull the plug on him."

I had actually lived in fear that when the day of execution arrived Dwight Harvey might have found a loophole in his plea that would cause the governor to stay the execution. A sense of relief washed over me.

"Thanks for letting me know, Eric." Eric Bell was not only my captain, but a good friend. "Eric?"

"Don't ask, Clay."

"You have the final say."

"Whatever I decide, I hope you'll know it's because I have your best interest, and the department's, at heart. Clay, don't make this any tougher than it already is."

"Yeah, sure. See you in two weeks."

A dark cloud moved across the sun, dimming the light. The November air had grown cool. I stood. The forgotten western novel slid to the floor. It didn't take a genius to know that Captain Eric Bell had decided to assign me to desk duty—permanently.

It wasn't in my nature to be idle. The conversation with Eric left me feeling at loose ends. I meandered to the barn where my tobiano gelding stuck his broad head over the stall gate and whickered. I opened the grain barrel and filled Domino's feed bin with a large scoop of sweet oats.

As much as I desired to saddle the ol' boy, I remembered how much pain I'd experienced a couple of years ago while I was recuperating from when Dwight Harvey shot me. Thinking back to the rodeo in Kentucky and the day when a bull named Diablo had charged, knocking my horse out from under me; the day Diablo had killed his rider; and the same rodeo where I had saved the life of...my mind went blank. I remembered her eyes—blue—almost colorless.

I couldn't help the smile crinkling my cheeks as I recalled how she'd scolded me. I also remembered that rare moment when I'd somehow morphed into a wolf and saved her life from a rogue bull. I grabbed the curry comb and began brushing my black-and-white pinto.

"What was her name, Domino?"

The horse flicked his ears back and forth as if he was contemplating the answer to my question.

"You know, she did that chiropractic thing to your shoulder? Whatever she did, it sure helped didn't it, ol' son."

Why couldn't I remember her name? Maybe because, at the time, I was still grieving the recent loss of my wife. I thought about Bethanne and how much I now regretted allowing her to be buried in Kentucky. She was Cal and Annette Saunders' only child. The sunshine of her parents' lives. Naturally, they wanted her near them. Yeah, I regretted my decision; regretted not being able to visit her…talk to her…tell her how much I missed holding her in my arms and making love to her.

I held the brush midair. "Domino, she was a veterinarian. What the hell was her name?"

Domino looked over his shoulder at me. He answered with a soft nicker. I continued brushing and talking as if the horse understood every word I said. "That's right. Her father was a sheriff. He was named after a famous outlaw, and he had a tall Apache friend. Her name was—"

"Clay Wolfchild?"

My sister's voice interrupted my thoughts. I clamped down on my teeth, then forced an unruffled tone to my voice. "Down here, sis."

Fauni chided. "Who are you talking to?"

"The only person that'll listen without talking back." I placed a gentle slap on Domino's rump.

Her face was suddenly taut with anxiety. I said, "What's up, Fauni?"

She thrust an envelope forward. "It's from Wes. He won't be home for Thanksgiving."

"Another mission?"

She nodded. It hurt my heart to see her tear-filled eyes. I gathered her in my arms. Fauni is two years younger than me. Like our mother, she, too, is a teacher. Her husband is a Marine Raider, first lieutenant. He's a career Marine, loves his job. But his secret missions, and the rarity of his personal leave time is an emotional strain on my sister. As a ten-year Marine veteran, I understand his devotion and love of duty. Sometimes, I regret having left the Corps. As a civilian, I understand both sides of the situation. As a big brother, and the stress that Wes's job causes my sister, I sometimes want to punch my brother-in-law in the nose.

Fauni pulled away and huffed a sigh. "I'm thirty-three. My biological clock is ticking." She looked up at me. "I want children, Clay Wolfchild."

She shushed my comment with a simple glare. "I know it's selfish to want children. Because of his career, a son or daughter might never really get to know their father." Her voice hitched. "Or they might never know him if he gets…killed."

She grabbed my hand and clasped it so hard I nearly grunted. Her next words took me by surprise. "We've been married fifteen years, and in all that time, we've probably spent less than five years together. I've given it more thought than you can imagine. I'm not a wife, I'm not a widow, and I'm not single. I'm…nothing. Clay

Wolfchild, would it be terrible of me to divorce him?"

I drew my eyebrows together. This was awkward. "When was the last time you and Wes were together?"

"Two years ago. He was on R&R in Germany. We were supposed to have a month together. One night…one uneventful night," emotion laced her voice, "is all we had when he received a phone call, and then with barely an 'I'll be in touch,' a hug and a kiss, he was gone."

She had a death grip on the letter. I was afraid she might hyperventilate. When she finally drew a breath, she said, "In all this time, I've been faithful to Wes. I've deprived myself of sexual pleasures. I've kept myself busy with college, teaching, volunteering—crap! Clay Wolfchild, I live at home with our mother."

She plopped onto a bale of hay. "I feel like a total bitch." She wiped at the tears that slid down her cheeks. "I'm sorry. This is embarrassing; I didn't mean to rant and rave like a depraved hellion."

Waves of memories swamped me. I dragged my thoughts out of the past to concentrate on my sister's dilemma. In the ten years I'd deployed to various places around the world, I admit to dipping my stick in honeypots to satisfy my manly urges. And so did many of the guys in my unit. Most of them married. At least I was unattached. Regardless, that didn't solve my sister's problem. I hated watching her slowly withering away.

"Have you written Wes to let him know your feelings, and that you're considering divorce?"

She looked at me as if I'd grown three heads. "No! His job is dangerous enough. I'm afraid if I say anything it'll cause him unnecessary stress and put him off his game. If he were killed because of my letter, I don't think

I could live with myself because it would be my fault."

Her shoulders shook with silent sobs.

Propped against the stall gate, I kept my voice low and calm. "Fauni, whatever your decision, as your big brother, I'll back you a hundred percent. I also realize that because of Wes's job you're afraid of endangering his life. Over the holidays, fly home to Wyoming. Seek advice from the tribal shaman. Standing Bear is a wise man."

Fauni wrapped me in a hug. "And you, my brother, are also a wise man." She stood on tiptoes and kissed my cheek. "Mama is making chicken and dumplings for supper. She'll accuse us of lollygagging if we stay out here much longer."

Chapter Twenty-Six

The next two weeks dragged by at a snail's pace. Tired of reading western novels, I switched to romance, and boy, was that an eye opener. I never considered myself a woman's hero, but I sure did enjoy all the smokin' hot love scenes. In fact, some of those scenes made me hornier than hell. Since my wife's death, I have basically become a self-imposed celibate.

Reading seems to calm me. I marked the current novel's page and closed my eyes. The face drifting in my subconscious wasn't Bethy's. Instead, it was the face of a raven-haired beauty with eyes the color of clear blue water. Like a scene in the current romance novel, I was reaching for her…our lips were…and damned, the buzzing of my cellphone shattered that sensual moment.

I gruffed. "This better be good."

Captain Eric Bell's voice chided. "Well, aren't we in a cheery mood."

"Bite my ass, Eric. Especially if you're about to tell me I'm permanently relegated to riding a desk chair and staring at a computer all day."

"I'm glad we're pals, Clay, or I might take offense at your tone."

I decided to let a few seconds of silence elapse before I responded. "I'm a man of action, Eric. Sitting around all day doing nothing and waiting to hear if I've been cleared for active duty or not is beginning to wear on my everlasting nerve."

"Been there, done that. I empathize. It's the waiting that's the worst."

"Thanks for understanding, Eric. Still, that doesn't explain why you're calling a week before my official date with the department's medical review board."

"Yeah, about that. Does the name Diego Villatoro sound familiar?"

"Yup, super-bad dude. Too bad he beat the system on a damned technicality. What about him?"

"We picked him up ten days ago—extortion, assault and battery with a deadly weapon, and operating a drug pipeline from Laredo to Dallas. One of our snitches put us on to him."

"What does this have to do with me?"

"Hold your horses, good buddy. I'm gettin' to it." Eric cleared his throat and continued. "A Captain Leland Stein from New York Precinct contacted me. It seems our friend Villatoro is wanted for three counts of murder one, and the State of New York wants this slime ball in their custody."

"So…why doesn't Stein send one of his officers to Dallas to escort Villatoro back to New York?"

"Stein said they're holding a prisoner that appears to be of Hispanic origin. Apparently, the guy speaks no English. Either that or he's putting on a good act. Stein also said they've tried Spanish, Spanglish, and Spanish street slang, and the guy stares at them and simply shrugs."

"What about ID?"

"The only thing the forensics team found on him was a worn, dirty slip of paper with the word *tejas*. Mean anything?"

"Sure," I said. "Tejas is the old pronunciation of Texas."

"Uh-huh. That's what the translator in New York thought, but again, the guy simply shrugged his shoulders when asked if he was from Texas.

"This is where you come in, Clay. Not only are you fluent in several international languages, but you're also fluent in some of the South American countries' lingo. I know you're still officially on medical leave. However, I'd take it as a personal favor if you would deliver our friend Villatoro to New York and then assist in finding out all you can about Stein's nameless prisoner."

"Just what did this nameless prisoner do?"

"I'm glad you asked, Clay. According to Stein, a call came in from a woman that lives in one of the slum boroughs. She claimed she heard another woman screaming for help. When officers arrived on scene, the perp was standing over a slashed and bashed, bloodied body of a female of undetermined age. He was holding a blood-covered machete, and the perp was splattered from head to toe. Forensics determined the blood matched that of the victim.

"Because of that piece of paper with *tejas* written on it, Stein figured that my department might have someone who can communicate with this guy." Eric cleared his throat. "That, my friend, is where you come in."

I listened patiently until he finished. "Eric, surely a linguistic expert from one of New York's fancy colleges can speak to the guy."

I was certain I detected a bit of disgust in Eric's tone when he said, "I don't get you, Clay. You're the one always bitchin' about not wanting to sit behind a desk. I thought sure you'd jump at this opportunity. In fact, this might just be your last hurrah, Clay, and you *didn't* hear it from me."

Shit, I thought. Here it is. At last, out in the open. I wasn't sure if Eric had known all along the department medical review board's decision to retire me from active duty, and had accidently let it slip, or if his spilling the beans was deliberate.

Either way, it appeared he was trying his best to cover his ass by saying, "Free plane ride, round-trip, hotel, meals, and miscellaneous expenses. Think of it as an all-expense paid vacation."

A sick feeling formed in the pit of my stomach. I let out a tense breath.

Eric's next words were authoritative. "If it were me, Clay, I'd jump on it."

A litany of profanity curled around my tongue which I had to bite to keep those words from spewing out of my mouth. I also wanted to say, *But you're not me, asshole.* "Yeah, sure. When do I leave?"

Part III: To Catch a Killer

"There are people out there who act good
but deep down are pure evil."

~Anonymous

Chapter Twenty-Seven

The doors all along the hotel hallway to the elevators were shut. There was no sound except the tread of my shoes against the carpeting. The trip to the airport, the excitement of the flight to New York, and the nerve-wrecking cab ride to the hotel had exhausted Grandmother and Patty.

After getting settled in our suite, we ordered room service and enjoyed an afternoon tea lunch complete with assorted petit fours to satisfy our sweet tooths. Grandmother and Patty opted for a nap while I decided to pursue the real purpose behind my decision for visiting the Big Apple.

I stepped from the hotel lobby, zipped my jacket against the chill, and then consulted the map that the doorman had drawn to the police precinct. Instantly, I regretted refusing his offer to hail a cab. I'm not claustrophobic, but the crush of shoulder-to-shoulder people seemed to suck the air from my lungs, and served as a reminder that I was truly a country girl who loved fresh air and the wide-open spaces.

As I jostled along, my thoughts ran the gamut, including *This is what a herd of steers must experience when caught in a stampede.*

By the time I arrived at the police station, my ears hurt from all the honking horns and people screaming at each other. I was relieved when I entered the building, or so I thought. My nostrils were assailed by odious body scents. People of all ages, sizes, and bodily hygiene lined the benches. There was profanity, sobbing, moaning and groaning. Don't get me wrong, I'm not squeamish when it comes to rank odors. As a veterinarian, blood, guts, and manure are part of the job. Yet there's something nauseous about having to step over a pile of puke because the person didn't make it to the trashcan or the bathroom. I felt sorry for the poor cleaning woman who was diligently trying to mop up the area without spreading the contents of someone's stomach all over the tiled floor.

I stepped to the counter that separated potential offenders and complainers from the office area. "May I help you, ma'am?"

The name tag on his uniform identified him as Officer Brent Doyle. "Yes, Officer Doyle, I'm Dr. Tullah Holliday, and I'd like to speak with Captain Jerald Adams, please."

I speculated the young officer, with thick glasses that magnified his eyes, hadn't quite mustered up to more than a desk officer. He said, "Sorry, Dr. Holliday, but the captain retired two years ago. It was before my time, but I think he moved to Arizona for his arthritis."

Well, crap, I thought. "Who is the current captain?"

"That would be Captain Leland Stein."

"Okay," I said. "Then I'd like to speak to Captain

Leland Stein."

"Sorry, ma'am, he's not seeing anyone without an appointment." The young officer pulled a form from a drawer, and with a limp smile said, "If you like, I'll schedule an appointment for you, except he doesn't see anyone unless it's of utmost importance. I could refer you to Sargeant James Upchurch, except he's out on sick leave—got the flu."

"What about your chief—is he available?"

Officer Doyle's smile grew limper. "Ah, no, ma'am. He's in a meeting with the Mayor and the Police Commissioner. Besides, you'd have to go through channels to see him."

"Channels?"

"Yes, ma'am. You start with filling out this form, and—"

I was certain I was getting the royal run-around. To say I was feeling a bit peevish would be an understatement. I leaned forward, and to keep from grabbing Officer Doyle by the throat of his stiffly starched collar, I balled my hands into fists and jammed them inside my jacket pockets.

I inhaled and slowly exhaled before speaking. "Officer Doyle, fourteen years ago, my mother was brutally murdered in this city, in your precinct. Captain Jerald Adams was in charge. He did nothing, I repeat, *nothing,* but sit on his fat ass with his thumbs stuck up his nose, to find who eviscerated my mother and left her to die in a dark alley."

My temper was rising along with the tempo of my voice. At this point, I removed my hands from the jacket pockets and placed them on the counter. I leaned forward, almost nose to nose with Officer Doyle.

"Because of this department's negligence, her case has gone cold, and the hoodlums that killed her are more than likely walking around free and perhaps have viciously murdered more women."

I offered him my best squint. "If I have to leap over this counter and find Stein, I'll do it. Pick up the phone and buzz him—now!"

Doyle's eyes widened. He stepped back as if fearing I might actually live up to my threat. He glanced around. I thought he might be looking for another officer to come to his rescue. After a couple of attempts, he managed to clear the rasp from his throat. "Ah, miss, ah, Doctor...I'm sorry, what was your name again? I seem to have for...oh, yes, Dr. Holliday. Yes...yeah...sure...okay."

And he did. He picked up the phone and punched in a couple of numbers. He put his hand close to the receiver. I suspected he was trying to hide his words from me. He hung up. "Captain Stein can't see you today. The secretary said to make an appointment for next week."

I slammed my hand on the counter. A person sitting on a waiting room bench yelled, "Atta girl, lady."

I didn't want to leave Ella to run the clinic and mentor a student doctor, alone, for over a week before I could even see anyone in the police department. She would understand if I stayed as long as it took to either solve my mother's case or get some sort of satisfaction that my dad and I could live with. I was torn between loyalty to my mother and loyalty to my business partner, best friend, and stepsister.

My scalp itched. I wondered if the itching was from anger or if several ravenous lice had jumped ship and landed in my head while I was caught up in a stampede of people while hiking to the police station.

I virtually growled at the guy. "Make the appointment, and write it down on an official form. If I show up at the appointed day and time, and get the run-around again, tell your captain that he'll be hearing from my attorney, my congressman, and a newspaper reporter."

I turned to walk away, then decided to add one last word. "Tell him that's not a threat. It's a fact!"

Another person from the bench said, "You tell 'em, sista. I been sittin' here so long my ass done gone numb."

I would have laughed except anger overruled that part of my emotions.

Thankfully, the cleaning woman had managed to wipe up the messed floor and was wheeling her mop and bucket toward the door. I followed and was almost to the lobby when a masculine voice said, "Lost?"

The hairs on my arms prickled. The voice had a familiar ring. The word "lost" was a vague memory I couldn't quite remember—until I pivoted on the heel of my boot.

It was him. The warrior I had seen in the hospital's garden of peace on the morning I was waiting for my dad to recover consciousness. Except, it wasn't him. He wasn't riding a pinto horse, carrying a spear, or dressed in a breechcloth.

The dimple in his cheek deepened when he smiled. "Black-and-white tobiano gelding with a bad shoulder. You performed some kind of chiropractic miracle on him."

He was a tall man with broad shoulders. He had leaned up some since I'd seen him two years ago. There is always a vague tingle when a handsome man is staring at you. My visual memory did a rapid one-eighty of the wolf that had leapt on the back of a rampaging bull at the rodeo in Kentucky. The wolf had morphed into a man—this man.

Chapter Twenty-Eight

I returned his smile. "Of course. You are a long way from Texas."

It appeared that holding my gaze wasn't a problem for him. "I could say the same about you. What is a Kentucky girl doing at a New York City police station?"

At that moment, I wished I had refined the art of flirting. "I could ask you the same question."

"How about we enlighten each other over a cup of coffee?"

The police station had suddenly become a hive of activity. I glanced at the large wall clock, concerned about the growing lateness of the day. I didn't want to worry Grandmother and Patty. Meeting him like this was déjà vu. I reached to touch the medicine pouch beneath my sweater. I wasn't sure if it was the contents inside that was pulsating or if it was my heart. Whatever it was, he definitely had hold of my heart and my soul.

I took a deep breath. "As much as I'd love to swap tales with you, I left my grandmother and a family friend at the hotel. It's getting late and I don't want to cause them concern."

He reached to take my hand. His blue eyes appeared earnest. "I totally understand. If you don't mind my asking, where are you staying?"

My hand fit snug inside of his. I liked the feeling. I told him the name of our hotel.

His smile broadened and the crow's feet at the corners of his eyes deepened. "By coincidence, I'm there, too, and I happen to know their French blend is excellent."

I wasn't sure if he was joshing me about the hotel or not. Sometimes, my trust meter gets a little out of whack. A come-on or not, I said, "I'd love a cup of French blend."

He cupped my elbow and led me outside. The air had a bite to it. I said, "It'll be a chilly walk to the hotel."

About that same time, he let out a loud whistle and hailed a cab. "Why walk when you can ride."

I didn't object as he held the door for me to enter the back seat. Except for small talk about the weather, and a few snippets about the rodeo, we mostly rode in silence. You never know if the cab driver is an eavesdropper or not.

Whatever doubts I had about the detective staying at the hotel was diminished as soon as we exited the cab. The doorman hastened to open the door. I almost felt ashamed of myself when he smiled and said, "There's a message for you at the courtesy desk, Detective Bannister."

As we strolled to the desk, I chastised myself for not remembering his name. I think it started with a C— Conner, Calvin, Clu? Then the lightbulb flashed. Clay. Detective Clay Wolfchild Bannister. Whew! I thought as I touched my medicine pouch. There was no way I was letting him know I'd forgotten his name; especially when he'd remembered mine.

As if the message was of little concern, we made our way to the coffee shop, which looked more like an old-fashioned gentlemen's club room with its heavy leather chairs, dark cherrywood tables, and an electric fireplace with faux flames adding a warm and comfortable feature to the room. After we were seated and had placed our orders, I said, "Please excuse me while I send my grandmother a text letting her know I'm in the hotel."

He chuckled. "I was about to beg an excuse. I need to touch base with my boss." He removed his cellphone from an inside suitcoat pocket. "In fact, if you like, invite your grandmother and her friend to join us."

The tone of his voice indicated that his invitation was genuine. "Thank you," I said.

Grandmother's response to my text was a smiley emoji.

Bannister had walked a little distance away. He paced while he talked. I heard him say, "No, nothing yet. I'll keep you informed."

He returned and settled in a chair that faced me. "Sorry 'bout that."

"No worries." I added, "My grandmother is a bit feisty. In her younger years, she was a crime reporter. There isn't much she hasn't seen. In her retirement years, she got bored and ran for mayor of Enigma, our town. She has a natural curiosity and will probably plague you with questions."

In truth, once Grandmother met Bannister and his good looks, I was afraid she might bring up the topic of my dying ovaries. I uttered a silent prayer.

He interrupted my thoughts. "What about the friend you mentioned?"

"Oh, yes, Patty Sweet is as sweet as her name. She owned Sweets 'n' Eats Café and Pastry Shop, and was Grandmother's vice mayor. They're both eighty and still having the time of their life."

Our coffee arrived at the same time as Grandmother and Patty entered the room. Bannister stood and asked the waiter to remain, then asked Grandmother and Patty if they needed a menu to view the variety of coffees.

Grandmother offered a honeyed smile. She looked at the waiter. "I'll have a large hot chai tea latte, lots of whipped cream."

Patty mimicked Grandmother's order.

I made the introductions. "Clay Wolfchild Bannister, this is my grandmother, Tanti Waya Crow, and our friend, Patty Sweet. Patty is like the aunt I never had. And, Grandmother, Clay is a detective with the Dallas Sheriff's Department."

After shaking hands with both ladies, Clay settled in the chair. Grandmother said, "Don't let your coffee get cold."

We both lifted our cups for a sip. I have to admit I'm not a French roast kind of gal, but my tastebuds disagreed.

Grandmother said, "Tullah, isn't Wolfchild the detective Henry talked about helping solve the case involving your friend, Caleb Callaway?"

Clay didn't wait for me to answer. He said, "Yes, ma'am. I hope Tullah told you about the treatment she gave my horse, Domino. He had a sore shoulder, and she performed a little magic on him."

He was winning her over. Grandmother never graces any man she meets with *that* kind of smile. "Tell me, Wolfchild, who are your People?"

Here we go, I thought. The interrogation is about to begin. I hoped Clay understood that when she said *People* that she was referring to his Native American heritage.

Clay crossed one leg over the other. He drew a sip of coffee. He seemed completely at ease with her question. "My mother is Lakota, as were her mother and father. Her name is Lydia Elkhorn. She and my sister, Fauni Blue Butterfly, are teachers. My father was Clayton Bannister. He was a deputy sheriff."

When the waiter arrived with the chai tea lattes, Grandmother indicated that he should place them on the table between hers and Patty's chairs. Steam curled upward from the cup. "Was?" she asked.

"Yes ma'am. He was killed breaking up a barroom fight. That was some years ago."

"I'm so sorry." She lifted the cup and blew.

While we waited for her to enjoy a sip, Clay glanced at me and asked, "How is your father? Still sheriff?"

I explained that he'd come close to dying after a wacko had stabbed him in the heart. Then heaving a sigh, I said, "He's currently in the hospital recuperating from heart bypass surgery. There were complications due to the old knife wound. We're all hoping he'll retire."

He reached over and touched my hand. "It's tough losing a parent."

I was certain Grandmother hadn't missed the gesture, especially when she glanced at Patty and offered a quick wink.

Grandmother asked, "Are you married, Wolfchild Bannister?"

"My mother and sister call me Clay Wolfchild. Mama says it rolls off the tongue smoother than plain ol' Wolfchild. But, to answer your question—I'm a widower. My wife was killed during a bank hold-up."

Emotional pain registered all over his face.

Grandmother apologized, saying she didn't mean to

pry or to dredge up hurtful memories. She added, "Invisible tears are often the hardest to wipe away."

Sometimes silence is downright noisy. The crackling from the faux flames seemed to intensify. I searched for words to break the awkward hush. I finished the last of my coffee and settled the cup on the table. Finally, I said, "Would you excuse me, Clay? After walking up close and personal with a mob of people, some that stank like rotting fish, and looking as if their hair hadn't had an oil change in years, then the one guy in the police station that was constantly scratching under his arms, and through his hair, I feel the need for a shower."

He stood when I stood, and with a slight nod toward Grandmother and Patty, he situated the black Stetson on his head, and said, "Food seems to taste better when you're sharing it with lovely ladies. I'd take it as a favor if you would join me for dinner."

By the expression on Grandmother's face, I knew I was in for the third degree once we were alone in our room tonight. My first impulse was to refuse the offer. Grandmother beat me to the punch when she said, "We'd be delighted, Clay Wolfchild."

As we were walking away, Grandmother turned back and said, "Clay Wolfchild, in Cherokee, *Waya* means wolf, and wolves mate for life."

My cheeks burned with embarrassment. "Grandmother!" I chastised as I grabbed her by the elbow and guided her toward the elevators.

Patty almost choked on her laughter. I had to stop and pat her on the back. Between coughs and sputters she managed to say, "Tanti, you are shameless."

I punched the elevator button with force.

"Shameless isn't a strong enough word."

We stepped inside the elevator car. Grandmother wore a smug smile. "He's the one, Granddaughter. Let's pray your ovaries still have some life in them."

An hour later we met Clay in the lobby. As we walked toward him, Grandmother gave me a royal jab to the ribs. "If I were sixty years younger, I'd give you a run for your money, Granddaughter."

My first thought was that Clay Wolfchild had jumped out of the pages of a romance novel. As we walked toward him, I took full measure of his black jeans, impeccably pressed and creased. Under a black business style Western blazer, a silver arrowhead with turquoise inlay bolo tie adorned a crisp white shirt. The moment he spotted us, he removed the black Stetson from his sleek black hair and, with a slight bow, greeted us.

I wondered if I had conjured him up from the amorous pit of my subconscious. I arched my eyebrows. "Grandmother, behave yourself. If you embarrass me with your not-so-subtle innuendos about my ovaries and marriage, I promise I will sell my practice, house, and property, and move far away from Enigma, Kentucky. And if I ever marry and have children, you will never know."

She knows when I have *that* look on my face, and speak in *that* tone of voice, I mean what I say. I know how much Grandmother loves me. However, the implications that I'm thirty and getting past my prime had begun to wear thin. I muttered, "I'm not even close to being over the hill."

I felt a momentary pang of guilt when she looked at me—her brows were drawn together, meeting almost in a worried point.

Chapter Twenty-Nine

During dinner, we discussed our reasons for being in New York. Clay warned all of us, Grandmother and Patty particularly, that the city wasn't a safe place for unescorted ladies, especially after dark.

And then he looked at me. "Tell me more about your mother's art display."

"The Museum of Art is commemorating Indigenous Peoples art this month. Mother specialized in Native American paintings with an emphasis on animals and nature." I drew a breath to steady the emotional quiver in my voice. "She was gentle, giving, and kind, and so very talented. I can't imagine why anyone would harm her, much less do such horrible things to her body."

"I'm sorry, Tullah. I can see talking about her is painful for all of you. Let's change the subject, shall we?" He lifted his hand and signaled the waiter. "The dessert menu, please."

After indulging in surf and turf, we women decided to forego the classic dessert and ordered sophisticated and delicious chocolate martinis. Clay settled for a bourbon on the rocks.

I have to admit that as soon as the Irish cream and crème de cacao slid past my taste buds and hit my womanly nether regions, my ovaries awoke like a bear coming out of hibernation.

I fanned myself. "My goodness, someone needs to

turn up the air conditioning."

Grandmother and Patty finished their drinks and declared they wanted to explore the hotel's gift shop. Clay pushed back his chair and immediately assisted Grandmother and Patty. On a scale of one to ten, so far, he was batting a thousand.

Grandmother said, "Tullah, after the gift shop, Patty and I might head back to our room. Tomorrow is a big day. We've booked a trolley tour around the city, and then a little shopping. We'll meet you back here for dinner."

She touched Clay's arm. "My granddaughter can be a bit impetuous at times. Kind of like a wild mare that doesn't like being tamed." She then kissed me on the cheek, and whispered, "Remember what I said about him being a keeper."

"I admire Tanti's spirit." Before I could reply, he said, "The hotel has a solarium that overlooks the city. Will you join me there for a nightcap?"

Whether it was charm or calculation, I found myself smiling. Detective Clay Wolfchild Bannister, for all the fact that he was probably a one-night-stand kinda guy, was irresistible.

We rode the elevator to the top. When the doors opened, we stepped into an enchanted world of fairy lights, enhanced by a gurgling mini-waterfall complete with a koi pond and tropical plants. Clay ordered a carafe of coffee. Looking out the window panes at the city below was even more magical.

Clay slipped my hand into his. He said, "The stars remind me of a field of wildflowers that have been kissed by the dew."

Forget the wildflowers. I'd never wanted to be

kissed so badly in my entire life. It didn't happen. I wondered if he was talking to me or simply remarking to himself. It wasn't so much the words he said but rather the forlornness in his voice and the faraway expression in his eyes.

I didn't want to trivialize this magical moment with a sardonic remark. Grandmother's favorite saying is *Sometimes silence is your best friend.* I hope to be as wise as she, someday.

A waiter interrupted our interlude. "I've placed your coffee at table number seven. It's next to the koi pond and with a better view of the city."

I wanted to drown myself in Clay's subtle, sexy, manly cologne as he escorted me to the table. He lifted a carafe shaped like an oversized genie lamp and poured. "Tell me why you were so angry today at the station?"

I sipped my coffee, hoping to calm my twat twitches. Finally, I opened up and filled him in with explicit details about my mother's murder.

He seemed to think about all I was saying. "Personal question, Tullah?"

I nodded.

"While in Kentucky, your father told me about your special gift—is it still with you?"

I wondered why he wanted to know and was prepared to tell him that my gift wasn't for sale. I set my cup aside while mulling his question, and simply answered, "Yes.'

"The blue in your eyes has darken. Don't take offense, Tullah." He drew another sip from his cup. "I grew up on the rez and know the ways of the spirits, though neither I nor anyone in my family bear such gifts. What does it tell you about solving your mother's case?"

I filled him in about my mother visiting me in a dream, and about the spirits of the other women who visited me. "I find it reprehensible that hers and the other women's cases have never been solved, and personally, I believe it's because they were indigenous."

I further went on to say, "When phone calls to Captain Jerald Adams were either trivialized or never returned, my dad made several trips to visit Adams. Dad was never given the respect of his position as a sheriff or as a grieving husband." I huffed out a breath. "And that is why I was so angry. I felt like I was getting the royal run-around."

I lifted my cup to slake my thirst. Over the brim, I asked why a Texas detective was in a New York police precinct.

Clay had listened intently. When I'd finished, he answered my question with the explanation of his reason for being in New York. Then he said, "After I formally relinquished custody of my prisoner to the state of New York, Stein has a guy in a holding cell who speaks no English. I confess I've tried various Spanish dialects, and all he did was shrug, and then he lay down on the cot with his face toward the wall. Maybe as a woman—an indigenous woman—maybe you can communicate with him. Then afterward, I'll get you in to see Stein. And by the way, Tullah, I prefer Clay Wolfchild to plain ol' Clay. That is, if you don't mind."

Thrilled at Clay Wolfchild's solution to part of my problem, I didn't trust myself not to kiss him. Not even on the cheek. I shrugged at his suggestion. "Not sure how much help I'll be. I speak passable Cherokee, a little Apache, and very little Spanish."

I had a lightbulb moment and laughed. Clay

Wolfchild graced me with a bewildered look. I said, "I know one word in Welsh. '*Carrot.*' It means—'moron.' Perhaps I'll call Stein 'carrot.' "

Clay Wolfchild guffawed and slapped his knee. "From one wolf to another, you are my kinda gal, Tullah Holliday."

I was certain the medicine pouch beneath my blouse was pulsating. "It's late. Grandmother will worry. I should go."

Clay Wolfchild escorted me to the elevators. Against my protests, he insisted on seeing me to the door of my room. And then the unexpected happened. He leaned down, cupped my face with his hands, and kissed me full on the lips—a sensual kiss. My knees turned spongy and threatened to collapse.

When I walked into the room and locked the door, Grandmother, dressed for bed, sat in a chair, a mystery novel in her hands. "Granddaughter, you are smiling. I told you—he is the one."

Although I couldn't wipe the grin off my face, I repeated what I had said earlier. "Grandmother, you are shameless." But in my soul, I knew Clay Wolfchild was wiggling his way into my heart.

Chapter Thirty

Captain Leland Stein was shorter than Clay Wolfchild by at least three inches. Stein appeared to be a man in his early fifties, a slight pouch noticeable beneath his stiffly starched blue pinstriped shirt. A combover of his thin, graying hair failed to hide a balding scalp. It was his eyes that captured me—hazel, almost yellow—reminding me of a feral animal. Stein was definitely not a man I would trust.

"Captain Stein, I'd like you to meet Dr. Tullah Holliday. Since you were busy yesterday, and she couldn't get an appointment to see you, I thought I'd kill two birds with one stone."

"Two birds with one stone." Stein's smile was less than humorous. "And what was the second reason, Detective?"

Stein leaned forward slightly to sit in his large black leather office chair. When he did, I spotted a red tip peeking from beneath the collar of his shirt. A premonition touched me. It was different and had the feel of knowledge that the ancient grandmothers had brought me. Somehow, I knew the tattoo on his neck was a number seven.

Clay Wolfchild's posture reminded me of an animal on guard. His face remained stoic when he spoke. "Since neither I nor your linguist have had and luck communicating with the prisoner, I felt that Dr. Holliday might have some success. He might feel more at ease with a woman."

Stein's voice chilled me. It wasn't what he said as much as how he said it. "Yeah, an Indian one at that."

As much as I wanted to rail against his insult, a little voice cautioned me to swallow the argument rising in my throat. "Cherokee, to be specific, Captain." I met and matched his glare.

The look Clay Wolfchild sent to the captain could have melted steel. I wanted to laugh out loud. He came to my defense. "You are out of line with your insults. Either you want her help or not."

I think Stein was aware he'd met his match in men. "It's a joke. Where's your sense of humor?"

When neither Clay nor I responded, Stein must have realized that his attempt to apologize had failed. He said, "Yeah, sure, if she can get answers out of the weaselly bastard, then sure, okay."

He punched a couple of numbers on his phone, picked up the receiver, and said, "Doyle, escort Detective Bannister and the doctor to the holding cell where the idiot visitor resides."

Doyle's voice came through loud and clear. "Which idiot visitor would that be, sir?"

Stein cursed under his breath. "The one that doesn't understand English!"

Clay stood as soon as I rose. As we headed toward the door, Stein groused, "You said there was a reason why she was here. What is it?"

He addressed the question more to Clay than to me. I didn't miss the nearly invisible nod he directed toward me.

Clay answered, "Dr. Holliday's mother was

murdered in this city. The case has gone cold. After we finish meeting with the prisoner, I'd like to look at the case files for—" He stopped. He didn't know her name.

I spoke up, "Josie Crow Holliday. She was murdered fourteen years ago."

The captain merely nodded. When Officer Doyle arrived at the door, Stein commanded him to take us to the records room after we met with the prisoner.

We followed the young officer down a long hall, made a turn, and went down another hall. He pushed a button and a door opened. A uniformed officer looked up from a magazine that he immediately tried to stash in a drawer. Doyle introduced us, then said, "They're here to see the prisoner that doesn't talk."

The name plate on the desk identified the rather obese man as Sgt. W. Bedford. He opened a drawer and removed a ring of keys and commanded us to follow him. I asked, "Sergeant Bedford, do you have a notepad and a pen that I might use?"

He accommodated my request, then harrumphed. "Good luck. He uses the urinal, but he doesn't talk."

Clay asked if the prisoner was dangerous.

"Naw, he's more like a scared mouse."

The sergeant led us past a row of cells until we arrived at the last one on the block. He said, "Sing out if he gives you any trouble or when you're ready to leave."

I felt sorry for the man who immediately sat up from a cot and scooted against a corner of the cement wall. The cell was chilly. I noted one thin blanket on the bed. The man drew his knees upward and hugged them against his chest, and stared at us.

Even in a sitting position it appeared he was not a tall man. I estimated a little taller than five feet. His face was a river of reddish-brown wrinkles; eyes the color of onyx, and hair to match. In fact, it looked as if someone had turned a bowl upside down on his head to cut his hair. He was neither handsome nor ugly—just ordinary.

I immediately opened my phone, typed *Amazonian people,* then held the picture forward. He looked at the picture, and then at me. He shook his head—no.

I spoke to him in Cherokee. Again, his head moved—no. Apache and Spanish brought the same results. "I'm not giving up, Clay Wolfchild. It's obvious he's from a South American country. We just need to figure out which one."

"That was a smart idea about showing him the picture."

"Yes, but it didn't help much."

"Do you think he's faking it?"

I extended my hands, palms up to indicate that I didn't know the answer. And that's when the surprise happened. The little man extended his hands, palms up. He pointed to his chest, then pointed to me.

Excitement spiraled around me. I pointed to my ear, then to my mouth, back to my ear, then to him. I wanted to cry when relief shone on his face and he repeated my motions. I almost shouted, "Clay Wolfchild, he's deaf! Oh my god, why didn't someone figure out that the poor man can't hear?"

Clay lifted me off my feet in a bear hug. "Dr. Tullah Holliday, you are a genius. Now what?"

It was neither the time nor the place, but I felt his rock-hard chest muscles bunch as he pulled me against him. I wanted to wrap my arms around his neck and kiss him with all my years of pent-up passion. Instead, I smiled, patted him on the shoulder and cleared the rasp from my throat. "You can put me down now."

He set me on my feet. Above the thunderous thrumming of my heart, I think he murmured something about needing a stiff drink. And honestly, I wanted something stiff, too, but it wasn't a drink. I hoped Doyle and Bedford hadn't witnessed the split-second amorous pause.

Collecting my thoughts and redirecting my attention toward the man on the cot, I carefully printed on the notepad, *Do you understand sign language?*

He accepted the pad, then looked at me and shrugged. I remarked to Clay Wolfchild that our guy either didn't read at all, or didn't read English. He took the pad and printed in Spanish the same question.

Our guy smiled and used his hand to sign the word—little.

"What is your name?" Clay wrote in Spanish.

Tears welled in the little man's eyes. "Jose Luna."

He made cooing sounds as he reached for our hands and pumped them up and down.

Together, and as best we could, we managed to communicate with Jose that we would help him. It took almost an hour to connect with a linguist who could sign in Spanish. "Clay Wolfchild," I said, "I'd like to stay until the interpreter arrives. I don't trust Bedford or Doyle."

Clay pointed to his mouth, rubbed his stomach, then made a motion like he was feeding himself. Our little man immediately shook his head. He held up three fingers, pointed to his own mouth and rubbed his stomach.

Anger washed over me. "He hasn't eaten in three days? That's inhuman."

I yelled, "Sergeant Bedford!"

He waddled to the cell. "Ready to leave?"

"On the contrary. I'd like to order a pot of coffee, a bowl of soup, crackers and cheese, and an apple. Immediately!" I wasn't sure of Jose's origin or his dietary preferences.

"Prisoners don't get preferential treatment, lady. He'll wait just like the others and eat what is served; when it's served."

"I wouldn't argue with Dr. Holliday, Sergeant," Clay Wolfchild warned.

I did my best to hide my smile when he picked up the phone's receiver and shoved it toward the sergeant.

While we waited for the food and the linguist to arrive, we did our best to communicate with Jose. I showed him pictures of various South American peoples. His eyes lit when I scrolled to a series of Ecuadorian people. He pointed to a picture, then to himself, and nodded his head. We signed that we understood.

He also pointed to a woman and a group of children. "I believe he's saying he has a wife and children, or maybe a family."

Clay nodded his agreement. "It'll be interesting to find out how he got from there to New York, and if he really did kill that woman."

A half hour later, the food arrived. Jose practically swallowed the entire bowl of tomato soup in one gulp. He heaved a sigh. I poured a cup of coffee and handed it to him. While he waited for it to cool, he gobbled the crackers and cheese, then washed them down with coffee. He held out the cup for a refill.

When he'd finished his meager feast, he grabbed Clay's hand and pumped it up and down. Turning to me, he touched his forehead, then his heart, and then pointed at me. I was moved to tears.

"Tullah, I've seen a lot of murderers in my day. Jose doesn't fit the profile."

"I usually get special feelings about people. I did about Stein. I don't about Jose. Maybe because of his hearing impairment he's become a victim of circumstance."

"What do you mean about Stein?"

"I'll explain later."

The clack of footsteps on the tile floor warned us that someone was approaching. Officer Doyle said, "Sergeant, this is Dr. Elena Mendosa and her associate Dr. Luis Ortiz from the Lexington School for the Deaf."

In seconds, the two linguists joined us. I explained the situation with Jose, and why he was being held. Dr. Mendosa immediately signed and Ortiz translated, "She is asking him if he understands her."

I knew he did by the way his eyes lit with relief. His hands became a flurry of motion. Dr. Oritz suggested we transfer to a holding room where a table and chairs would accommodate all of us in a less hostile environment.

I was hesitant to leave Jose in the hands of the two interpreters for fear they might not protect him or his rights. I had my own agenda, and time was rapidly closing the gap between finding evidence that would lead me to my mother's killer and returning to Enigma. But my natural curiosity wanted to hear firsthand Jose's story.

Chapter Thirty-One

I sat quietly, fascinated by the movement of hands as Jose communicated with Dr. Mendosa. Dr. Ortiz translated into a tape recorder as a police officer videoed the session. Lieutenant Todd Amherst joined us in the session. Amherst stated that he was new to the department and learning the ropes.

We learned that, in spite of his wrinkled face, Jose was only thirty-five. We also learned that Inez Martinez, Jose's sister, was the murdered woman. In Ecuador, she was a teacher in the town of Quito, and he worked as a janitor at a local bank. He said it was his sister who had taught him to read. She had also purchased a sign-language book and together they had taught themselves how to sign.

Dr. Mendosa said, "Jose states that because he is deaf, he was quiet like a mouse, and no one took notice of him. He liked his job. One day, he saw the bank president take a sum of money from the vault and put it in his briefcase. Several weeks later he observed the same thing. When it continued to happen, Jose told his sister. She advised him to keep quiet.

"Jose says one night he was working late. The bank was closed. He decided to look inside the president's desk drawer. He found a ledger. He knew from all the figures that the president was stealing money, doing it bit by bit to keep from getting caught.

"Jose decided to report this to the captain of the Policía, but he happened to see a money exchange between *el presidente* and *el capitán*. Unfortunately, he was spotted and severely beaten, dismissed from his job, and his sister's life was threatened. A few days later a decapitated chicken was tied to the door of their house.

"Long story short, he and his sister had planned for years to come to the USA. They decided the time was right and paid a contractor to get them here and with a promise of a teaching position for Inez."

Lieutenant Amherst interrupted. "That's all well and good, but why did he kill his sister?"

His interruption annoyed me. Dr. Mendoza, however, arched an eyebrow and shot him a glaring look. "Guilty until proven guilty? Is that your philosophy, Lieutenant?"

I wanted to laugh out loud at his reddening cheeks. "Lieutenant," I said, "Jose Luna has been taken advantage of and mistreated due to his disability. I suggest you allow him to continue in his own words."

Then, as if purposely disregarding the lieutenant, Mendosa asked Jose if he had killed his sister. Dr. Ortiz continued translating. "Jose says he did not kill her. He said when they arrived in New York, they were dumped in that ratty, cockroach-infested room. Because they didn't speak English and he was deaf, neither of them could find work. His sister took a job as a cook in a local diner. But she was pretty, and young, and he thought she might be doing something unchristian."

"Like what?" I asked.

Mendosa heaved a sigh. "Prostitution. We see this more often than we'd like with immigrant women—legal or illegal—when the men can't find jobs due to language and education barriers."

There was a lengthy sign language exchange. Tears slid down Jose's cheeks. Mendosa handed him a tissue. The movements of his hands and fingers reminded me of a panicked bird flapping its wings. When the session was over, he had described the man he'd found leaning over his sister. When Jose entered the room, he said the man shoved the bloody machete into his hand and fled out the window and down the fire escape.

"Did the man speak or say anything to Jose?" I wanted to know.

Mendosa translated my question.

Jose's expression changed to anger. Ortiz said, "He says the man was angry but Jose couldn't understand the words he was shouting. The man slapped him, then poked the machete against his chest. Then when the woman from down the hall came, the man shoved the machete into Jose's hands and fled."

There was a brief pause before Jose's hands began moving again. Ortiz spoke, "He says the man had a pocked face and smelled of stale cigarettes. He wore a brown coat with a black fur collar that had a fox's head at the end and a funny-looking hat that was also brown, and he wore diamond studs in both ears, and had a gold tooth.

"When the woman saw him, he didn't know she would call the police. He was trying to tell her to get help for his sister, but she didn't understand. The police came and brought him here."

When he'd finished, Jose crossed his arms on the table and laid his head on them, then sobbed. No one in the room spoke. I seethed inside at the injustice done to another indigenous person. I asked myself what would happen to this poor man—would he remain in jail? If bailed out, where would he go? Frustration dug at me.

It was as if Dr. Mendosa was reading my mind. She said, "Lieutenant, in light of what we've just heard, I would like to post bail for Jose."

When Amherst's objection was obvious, she cut him off. "My family came here from Colombia. My father was a dentist, my mother a nurse. They didn't speak English. They were degraded to menial labor just to put food in our mouths and a roof over our heads, so I know how difficult it has been for Jose and his sister." She glanced toward Ortiz. "We see it every day with the children and adults whom we teach. I will take full responsibility for Jose."

I knew by the squint of her eyes and the set of her jaw that she meant business when she pierced Amherst with a glare that dared him to defy her. "I expect you to take charge of the investigation, find the man who killed Inez Martinez, and clear Jose of all charges. Will you do that, Lieutenant?"

"Well, Doctor, there's a process and paperwork. There's a hearing and a judge sets bail. I…"

Dr. Elena Mendosa cast a smile that reminded me of a cat about to pounce on a mouse. The tone of her voice was almost syrupy. "Lieutenant, I don't give a rat's ass about procedure. I have a connection with *The New York Times*. I'm sure he'd love to do a story about police brutality toward a deaf man."

Amherst shoved back his chair. He'd been cornered and we all knew it. "You've made your point, Doctor."

****

The morning had escaped us, and my meager breakfast had long since disappeared. Dr. Mendosa and

Ortiz left with Jose, with a promise to keep us informed. We stood on the sidewalk and watched them disappear inside a taxi. Clay offered to treat me to lunch. My hunger headache was growing. "As long as we don't linger. I really want to dig into the case files regarding my mother's investigation and also those of the other women."

He offered a smile. "Scout's promise. Tacos or Philly cheesesteak?"

"I don't care as long as we dine inside and out of the cold."

Before we could hail a cab, Lt. Amherst joined us at the bottom of the precinct steps. "I overheard you talking about lunch. I wasn't eavesdropping, mind you."

Clay shot him a *Yeah, right!* look, and Amherst hastened to say, "Hey, I don't blame you for thinking I'm an asshole." He glanced at me. "Sorry, Dr. Holliday."

I brushed it off. "Then why did you act like one?"

"Two blocks down, Tony Quang makes the best egg drop soup in the city, and his food is second to none. My treat."

"I'm not opposed to being treated to lunch, but why? I mean, why the sudden change of attitude toward us?"

"If you'll follow me, we'll talk on the way."

Heads down to keep the cold wind from biting our faces, we walked with a brisk pace that did not allow for conversation. We stopped in front of a restaurant with the sign "House of Quang." Amherst held the door for us to enter. A young man, definitely Amerasian, approached us. "Hey, Todd, my man, how goes it?"

Amherst introduced us. "Tony is my brother-in-law. We've also known each other since high school."

Tony Quang said any friend of Todd's was a friend

of his, too. Amherst asked to be seated in the back of the restaurant. Tony bowed and said, "Ah so, out of the range of listening ears." Then he smiled, patted Amherst on the back, and said, "You got it, bro." And he led the way to a table far from the others and facing the door.

"How's my sister?"

Tony smiled. "Why don't you ask about *me*? Cicely's craving pickles and chocolate-covered cherries, and I'm a nervous wreck. She's due any hour now."

"Don't worry. Call me. I'll be here with sirens blaring. We'll get her to the hospital in plenty of time."

The two men exchanged hugs and slaps on the back. Tony said, "I'll send Nancy Li to take your order." Tony Quang bade us good fortune and disappeared.

Chapter Thirty-Two

While we enjoyed our meal of seafood delight over fried rice, and copious cups of oolong tea, Amherst explained that when he'd made detective, he'd been transferred to Stein's precinct to fill an empty position. "I've been here six months. Long enough to feel there's something not quite kosher with the captain."

"In what way?" Clay Wolfchild asked.

A light-skinned man with a stylish Afro, Todd Amherst stood about an inch less than Clay's six-foot-three frame. And like Clay, he was well-built. "For one thing, he's definitely biased against people of color; especially women. I've also learned that he seems to enjoy using unnecessarily excessive force."

Uh-huh, I thought. He would be, with his Aryan looks. "Why doesn't someone on the force file a complaint against him?"

Amherst huffed. "I've been quietly asking those I think—I hope—I can trust, to find out what happens to anyone who even hints at filing a report against him or contacting the police commissioner."

"And?"

He gave me a look that spoke of doubt and the need to confess. Clay Wolfchild said, "You can trust us."

"I hope so. I don't relish getting my ass burned." Amherst drew his brows together.

The expression he wore caused me to think he was

trying to decide how far to go with his answer, or if he should sidestep the question and change the subject.

Finally, he spoke. "Apparently, two officers, both women of color, dared to stand up to him for harassment. Both were met in dark alleys and attacked. One didn't survive her injuries. From what I understand, after the other officer healed, she not only left the force, she fled the state."

While this information was feeding into my earlier premonition, I didn't trust the detective enough to reveal concerns about Stein. Instead, I explained about my mother's murder. "She was also killed in a dark alley. It's important that I see the investigative reports tied to her case."

Amherst said, "Dime to a donut that Stein will promise to make the files available."

I nodded. "Hopefully."

"Don't bet on it. When you return from lunch, to accommodate you, he'll pick up the phone and clear the way for you to visit the dead files morgue. He'll even write you a clearance slip to give to the duty officer. But...when you get down there, the officer will conveniently be gone, and the cage door will be locked. I've seen it happen multiple times since I've been here."

Clay Wolfchild let out an expletive. "So Tullah is about to get the royal shaft by a potentially crooked cop."

Amherst nodded as he opened his fortune cookie, read the fortune, and laid it aside. "I'm not saying he's crooked, just abusive. Also, he's a creature of habit. He goes off duty promptly at five. Give it fifteen minutes to make sure he's cleared the building." Amherst smiled and held up a key, then winked.

"What will happen to you if we get caught?" I

wanted to know.

"We won't cross that bridge until we come to it." Lt. Todd Amherst waved the waitress over and offered his credit card. He quirked a smile. "The two of you enjoy the rest of the day. I'll visit with Tony for a while before I leave. When you arrive, about five fifteen, ask the night desk officer to see me."

We stood to leave the table. Clay Wolfchild shook hands with the detective. I said, "Why are you really helping us? You don't know us from Adam's housecat."

Amherst seemed to ponder the question as if not sure of the answer. "Let's just say payback is hell, and leave it at that."

I had a feeling that it was more than he was willing to tell.

****

We arrived promptly at five fifteen. I asked the night desk officer to speak with Detective Amherst. A buzzer sounded. We spotted Amherst viewing a computer screen. Clay Wolfchild and I walked through the opened gate and proceeded to where he was seated.

Nonchalantly, he greeted us and said to follow him. We did, to an elevator ride down to the bowels of the building. Once we arrived at our destination, true to Amherst's prediction no one was on duty. Amherst unlocked the caged door and we entered. The basement room reminded me of a cave with its dark, stale, dank odor. The trashcan next to a desk was littered with empty coffee cups. A space heater warmed the area around the desk. For a moment we milled around accomplishing nothing.

I was amazed at the number of boxes that lined the metal shelves, and asked, "Are all of these cold cases?"

Amherst said, "'Fraid so. There's over thirteen hundred of them." He also added, "I hate to tell you there's no specific alphabetic arrangement. Let's split up and each take a different section. Sing out when you find the box."

"Detective Amherst, I'm also looking for files pertaining to two Hispanic women, one Asian woman, and two middle-eastern women."

He peered at me with arched eyebrows. "How would you know about them, and what are their names?"

Oops! How was I going to explain about my empathic abilities?

Before he could naysay, Clay Wolfchild spoke up. "Dr. Holliday has a special gift. Sometimes the dead reach out to her." His voice deepened a bit. "Don't give me that look, Amherst. She's the real deal."

"What does she have—laser vision or something?"

"Keep the sarcasm to yourself," Clay Wolfchild warned.

"Okay, yeah, sure. If you say so. But looking for those particular women will be like searching oysters for a pearl."

He was right, and we all knew it. Especially me. We split up. The thick dust in the aisle I chose made me want to sneeze. Still, I trudged forward. Because of my mother's name I selected aisles G, H, and I.

While surrounded by shelves of haphazardly stacked boxes, I cradled the medicine pouch beneath my sweater and sent up a silent prayer to the Great Spirit Father and the spirit grandmothers asking for their guidance in locating the boxes for the other women. *I don't know their names*, I beseeched.

Very slowly I proceeded down the aisle. "Detective,

do you know if the cases are catalogued by origin of nationality?"

He chuckled. "We could only wish. Honestly, I'm not sure anyone in the department really gives a rip. Besides, we're always understaffed and working on a slim budget. Cold cases get the least amount of attention."

"What about a database listing all the names with the victim's information?" I thought it was a logical question.

Amherst said, "Yeah, that's the sixty-four-dollar question, and the department's pat answer is always 'no funding available for nonessentials.' "

Like dead people aren't important. Keeping the thought to myself, I immediately searched for my mother's name. She was my first priority. While there were a couple of ladders leaning against a wall, I found the H's were all located on the middle shelf. Boxes were stacked three high. Amherst was correct when he said there was no true alphabetic system. It was as if the boxes had been randomly stacked. Thankfully they were in the correct alphabetic sections. I scanned each name carefully. My heart pitter-pattered when I was drawn to a cardboard container where several names had been X-ed through. One messily scrawled name in red drew me. I pulled the box forward. Although misspelled, the name was definitely Holliday. I toted the box to a table and opened the lid. Inside was a jumble of disheveled files. Although it was cold as a morgue in the room, no pun intended, sweat accumulated beneath my armpits; my hands trembled as I opened a manila envelope. My breath came in short gasps. I knew what was inside and I didn't want to see them.

"Clay Wolfchild, Detective Amherst?" I could barely speak their names.

Both men rushed to the table. Clay Wolfchild asked, "Your mother's?"

I nodded. I couldn't seem to get words past the large lump in my throat. Clay pulled out a chair and ordered me to sit. He took the envelope from my hand and removed several photos. "Damn," he said. Then, "Tullah, you don't need to see these."

He passed the envelope to Amherst, who made a gagging sound. "Sorry. I've never been to an autopsy, and I've only seen one dead body and it didn't look like these."

"How long have you been a cop?" Clay removed the photos from Amherst's hand and returned them to the envelope. He set it aside and lifted a stack of papers.

Although Amherst was a black man, his light skin had shifted to pasty white. He said, "I was a beat cop for five years. The most I ever did was write parking tickets, break up a few scuffles, and run down a shoplifting kid. I felt like I was in a rut. At my girlfriend's suggestion, I took classes, eventually got promoted to lieutenant, and last year made detective."

"You're a greenie, all right." Clay picked up a file folder marked Confidential. He flipped through the papers. I knew by the look he'd cast me that what he held was important.

"Amherst, is there any way we can take this with us? I want to carefully read every piece of paper to see what clues were ignored or missed."

"Sure, I can arrange that, as long as you include me. If I'm going to be an effective, crime-solving detective, I need to learn from someone experienced, like yourself,

Detective Bannister."

Closing the paper coffin that held my mother's remains, albeit not in a literal sense, we continued our search. It seemed hours passed. The dank room grew colder. I blew on my bare hands to warm them and sent up another prayer, this time thanking the Great Spirit Father for leading me to my mother. And then, asking the same for the five women.

I prayed silently, *Great Spirit Father and Shadow Woman, there is no way for my spirit animals to find me in this city of tall buildings or among these paper graves to lead me to the women whose souls cry out for justice. Send me a sign that will lead me to their information.*

"Meaning no disrespect, Dr. Holliday…are you like a witch or a fortune teller…or—" A loud crash interrupted the detective's question. He yelled, "Sonofabitch!" followed by a groan.

I stepped around the corner and over several boxes that cluttered the aisle to see what had happened. Amherst was sprawled on the floor. Scattered contents of an opened box lay on his chest and about his body. I squatted. "What happened? Are you hurt?"

He sat up. For a moment, his eyes looked crossed. He blinked several times as if trying to clear his vision, or maybe collect his senses. "There's no rhyme or reason why those boxes flew off the top shelf. If I didn't know better, I'd swear somebody deliberately pushed them on top of me." He touched the side of his head. "Hit me square on the noggin."

"Let me look." Inside, I was twittering and thanking the Great Spirit Father and Shadow Woman for answering my prayer. I asked him to follow my finger as I moved it back and forth in front of his eyes. "I don't think you have a concussion."

"There's no cut." I gently probed through his curly hair. "And I don't feel a lump. Does your head hurt?"

"Naw, I'm okay." He shifted to his knees. Clay Wolfchild stooped to help retrieve the strewn file folders.

I said, "Check the names. We're looking for two Hispanic, one Asian, and two Middle Eastern women."

Amherst shot me a skeptical look. "How do you know that, specifically?"

Clay Wolfchild answered for me. "It's part of her gift. Don't question it. Trust it."

To keep from experiencing an emotional spasm and hoping I didn't melt on the spot from the sincerity in Clay Wolfchild's eyes, I picked up several folders from the floor and arranged the tabs one behind the other, and was about to place them inside the carton when Amherst let out an expletive, then said, "I'm not believing this. Look…look!"

He said as he stared at the folder he held. "Lona Vargas. That's Hispanic, right?"

Clay Wolfchild waved another file and practically shouted, "Alita Vega."

I breathed a silent prayer of thanks. With Mother these two made three. Only three more names, I silently implored.

I followed the men to the table. Amherst spoke in jest. "My mammy was a Creole from New Orleans. I never much liked visiting her. She was into a lot of weird mumbo-jumbo and even kept a black cat she called Median. I hated that cat. Always hissed at me for no reason. Mammy'd box my ears if she ever heard me say I never put much stock in stuff I can't see or touch…you know, supernatural stuff."

Although I didn't bother to comment, I struggled to rise above his remark. "Let's keep looking. We don't know when the poor officer stuck in this dungeon will return."

Amherst agreed but added, "He's off for the rest of the night."

A noise somewhere in the darkness made us pause. I had the sensation of something watching us. Clay Wolfchild followed my gaze into the darkness. He whispered, "What is it, Tullah?"

I lifted a finger to my lips to caution him. Amherst looked unnerved. His hand rested on the hilt of his service revolver. He was probably thinking he shouldn't have jumped into the middle of this. Not good for a detective craving adventure. I had to admit that my own thoughts were a bit helter-skelter.

Clay Wolfchild motioned for me to go to the other end of the stacks. I listened carefully to whatever being was inside the room. All I could hear was my own heart pounding. In an unexpected moment, light flooded the dark cavernous room. We had not noticed Amherst edging his way toward the door, where he had just rotated the light's dimmer switch to full glow.

An unexpected flash of black sailed from the top of a shelf and landed smack dab on his chest. Between the yowling and the screaming, I wasn't sure who had attacked whom. Amherst was screaming, "Get it off! Holy shit…the devil has attacked me!"

Like a cartoon character, four legs splayed against the detective's chest, was a black ball of fur. Its tail furiously switched back and forth. Cooing softly to the cat, I gently wrapped my hands around its sleek body and in Cherokee bade it to release its claws from Amherst's shirt.

I cuddled the feline against my neck. The poor creature's heart thudded against my shoulder. I stroked the animal and murmured to it. And when I held it forward to look into its green eyes, I knew this was no ordinary mouser. Again in Cherokee, I spoke, "Lead me to the other women, Shadow Woman."

The black tabby leapt from my arms. I followed it to a stack of cardboard storage boxes stacked in a back corner of the room. The cat sat on top. It meowed several times. Had it not been for Shadow Woman disguised as a cat, we might have missed them so easily.

I gently lifted the cat from the top box, and in an instant it disappeared. There was a slight tremor to Amherst's voice when he asked, "The cat must be new. Maybe to catch mice." He rubbed his chest.

"Or," Clay Wolfchild smirked and continued, "maybe it was a spirit leading us to the other women."

Amherst cut his widened eyes toward me. "The only person I'm talking to about this is my mammy. Anybody else would suggest I see the department shrink."

I had opened the box and was fingering through files of deceased men's names until I reached the end. Nothing. If the women weren't here, why would Shadow Woman lead me to this particular crate?

I decided to straighten the files to keep them from falling against themselves, and that's when I spotted the folders that had slid flat and lay hidden beneath the other folders. I lifted them out. I almost shouted. "Look what I found!"

We counted. We had a total of five women and my mother's. Amherst said, "How do you know these are the ones you're looking for? I mean...there's over a thousand cold cases, and probably half of them are women."

I stared at him. "Read their names—one Japanese, two Hispanic, one Arab, and one Hindi, plus my mother. These are the women."

"Yeah, but *how* do you know, for sure?"

"Because they told me." I cast him a look that dared him to defy me.

Amherst merely shook his head. "I don't think anybody's gonna miss these. Let's take them with us, 'cause this place gives me the creeps."

Clay Wolfchild agreed that after the mystical way we'd located the files, he needed a stiff bourbon—maybe two.

Amherst said, "Let's go back to my brother-in-law's place. I'm officially off duty and could use a warm saki, and a bowl of soup. Tony'll see to it that we have plenty of privacy."

Chapter Thirty-Three

After we were seated, I sent my grandmother a text to let her know I was with Clay Wolfchild. I also let her know we'd located the folders and I had plenty to tell her.

Tanti: *Ask if you can make copies of the files. I don't trust that they might not disappear once they're out of your sight.*

Me, with a thumbs-up emoji: *Don't worry if I'm late. I'm in good hands.*

At Grandmother's suggestion, I asked if Amherst's brother-in-law had a copy machine. While we waited for our beverages, we viewed the information of our newly found evidence. Clay Wolfchild pointed to each place of death. "If this is too difficult for you, Tullah, we can copy the information and look at it another time."

Amherst savored his warmed saki. Clay Wolfchild and I settled for a carafe of coffee.

"Don't worry about me." In truth, I wasn't okay. It's not easy looking at once beautiful women whose faces had been mutilated and their bodies eviscerated.

As if choregraphed, together we leaned toward the handwritten police reports. Clay Wolfchild pointed to each page. "All of the women were attacked in an alley, at night."

Amherst said, "I don't think it's a coincidence that all the buildings where these alleys are located are in the

240

arts district and within walking distance of each other."

"Detective Amherst," I said, "is the arts district upscale, or is it rundown, an area that would invite this type of malicious attacks on women?"

"I hate to say it, Dr. Holliday, but all alleys, no matter what districts they're in, invite danger. The question is—why were these particular women in the alleys? Were they lured, did they go out for a smoke, or venture there by mistake?"

Clay Wolfchild suggested we look at their ages and occupations to see if we could find a correlation that would in some way link them together. "Good idea," I said.

I wrote as Clay Wolfchild read off the information. Lona Vargas was a doll maker from Oaxaca, Mexico. Like my mother, she was displaying her art, and like my mother was in her forties.

Alita Vega: age thirty-seven, Guadalajara, Mexico, attending a tourism convention.

Keyoko Hideki: age twenty, Japanese, candidate post masters/phD neuroscience at the university. Found in the same alley as my mother and Lona Vargas.

Melek Haddad: age forty-five, Arabic, medical doctor visiting her brother.

Rana Hari: age fifty-three, Hindi, tourist. Got separated from her tour group.

"Here's an interesting fact." Clay Wolfchild tapped his pen against each report.

When he didn't continue right away, I cast a look that expressed my impatience. He said, "They were all killed on a day that had a two or a seven in it, or in the seventh month, each exactly three years apart from the one previous and/or the one following."

It took a moment for the information to sink in. "My mother's death was November twenty-seventh." I researched calendars on my phone and opened several until I was satisfied, and held the phone to show the calendar. Keyoko Hideki died three years ago on the twelfth."

The edge in Clay Wolfchild's voice caused knots to form in my stomach. He continued, "All the buildings located or connected to the alleys have a seven in the address."

"Surely, that's no coincidence. It's an important clue—right?" *Think*, I chastised myself. *Think...think...think.* Important information lurked inside a dark place in my brain. I closed my eyes and tried to call it forward.

Clay Wolfchild wrapped his hand around mine. "Tullah?

Hastily, I gathered all the sheets of paper and shuffled them into a neat stack. "Detective Amherst, you said your brother-in-law has a copy machine. My brain hurts from all this information. It's late. My grandmother will be worried. Would you mind making copies of these? We'll wait here and finish the rest of our coffee."

I continued, "Besides, I'm sure you'll want to return the files before they're missed."

He accepted the papers. "That room is such a jumbled mess, I'm sure Arthur won't notice they're gone. Besides, I'm entitled to look at those files. But I do agree that it's late. The restaurant closes in about an hour."

He departed, assuring us he wouldn't be long.

"Tullah, your face is a mask of anxiety. Are the spirits talking to you?"

Clay Wolfchild's concern made me smile. I lowered my voice to a whisper. "I'm not sure how much I trust Detective Amherst."

"He's an okay guy. Green, but I don't feel he's untrustworthy."

"I don't mean like that. He's easily rattled, and I'm afraid under pressure he'll blab to Stein. It's Stein that concerns me."

"I'm not following you."

"It's the number seven." I went on to explain my grandmother's dream and the numbers two and seven, and how I'd researched the Aryan Brotherhood. "Seven is important to this particular gang. They're like neo-Nazis and hate almost everyone they consider different or not fitting *their* norm."

"Yeah. I'm more than familiar with them. We've tangled with 'em in Texas. Bad isn't strong enough to describe their members and their philosophies. How does this tie to Stein?"

I explained about seeing a red tip peeking above the edge of his shirt collar. "I'd bet my new saddle that tattoo is a seven." I grimaced when I swallowed the last of my cold coffee. "If push came to shove, I don't trust that Amherst has the guts to stand his ground against Stein."

Clay Wolfchild blew out a low whistle. "I'm not sure if you really want to open that can of worms, Tullah. Right or wrong, you're bound to get hurt…and maybe your grandmother, too."

"Cut the head off the snake, Clay Wolfchild." I didn't try to keep the sarcasm from my voice.

He countered, "Even the fangs of a dead rattler are filled with poison. This is bigger than you or me. The AB's have long arms and factions located in places you'd never suspect. Trying to prove Stein is a dirty cop is one thing, trying to prove he's tied to the Aryans spells—danger."

"You sound like my father."

"Then he's a wise man."

"I can't let this go, Clay Wolfchild. I promised to avenge my mother's death and the souls of the five women who sought me out. I promised!" A sob of frustration welled in my throat. Angry tears burned my eyes. I felt helpless.

Clay Wolfchild shoved back his chair. His knees buckled when he stood. His knuckles turned white as he gripped the table's edge to keep from falling. Pain flashed across his face. "Damn," He groaned as he struggled to remain upright.

"What is it? What happened?" I rounded the other side of the table to help him sit.

His words came out in small huffs. "I have a bullet lodged in my spine. I'll explain later."

"Do you have anything for pain?"

"At the hotel."

I was hovering over Clay Wolfchild when Amherst walked in. "What's going on? Did I miss something?"

"Clay Wolfchild has a bad back. He's been sitting too long and it's caused him a bit of pain." I pointed to the copies in his hand. "I think we should call it a night."

"Oh, sure thing." He held out the documents. I stuffed them inside my jacket pocket.

Clay Wolfchild's face was a study of pain. I slipped my arm around his waist, and commanded Amherst to go outside and hail a cab. Clay Wolfchild leaned heavily against me. Like linked puppets, we struggled toward the door. Except for a handful of stragglers, the restaurant was empty. No one seemed to notice, and if they did maybe they thought we'd had a little too much saki and were propping each other up.

Amherst held a cab door open. "Do you want to share the cab with us?" I asked.

"Nah." He patted the inside of his overcoat. "I've got paperwork to finish at the station. Plus, with only a skeleton night crew, it'll be safer and easier to return these right away." He winked and, before he slammed the door, said, "I'll be in touch."

I sent Grandmother a text explaining the situation and that I planned to stay with Clay Wolfchild until I was certain he didn't need to go to the emergency room.

We had only a short cab ride to the hotel, where the doorman rushed to open the door. I explained that Detective Wolfchild had hurt his back and was in a lot of pain. "Please help me get him to the elevator."

"Wait a second, Dr. Holliday." In a forceful voice he commanded the night desk clerk to bring a wheelchair. To me, he said, "We keep one for such emergencies."

The young clerk hustled forward with the chair, and the doorman asked, "Shall I escort Detective Wolfchild to his room, Doctor?"

I assured him his offer was appreciated, but I could manage. At the elevators, Clay Wolfchild lamented, "I don't like being helpless. Goes against my manhood."

The night clerk called after us, "Leave the chair outside the room door. One of the cleaning crew will return it in the morning."

I merely waved an acknowledgement and wheeled Clay Wolfchild inside the elevator and punched the button to his floor. After the short ride, and then once inside his room, he pointed to where he kept a vial of prescription pain meds. I returned with the bottle and a glass of water.

His hand trembled as he popped two pills into his mouth. "Let me help you to the bed. I'll remove your boots."

In spite of the pain I read in his eyes, he managed to quirk a mischievous smile. "I won't object if you'd like to undress me, too."

He reached for my hand and held it, palm open to the light. The scrutiny of his blue eyes made me uncomfortable. He drew a finger lightly from my wrist to the tips of my fingers. The power of his touch surprised me. He looked back into my eyes. "I haven't been with a woman since my wife died."

There was an element of sadness in his voice.

"Tell me about her." I hoped he couldn't feel my runaway pulse.

He gave me a lopsided grin that made him look much younger than his thirty-five years. "She was delicate, and beautiful, and afraid of everything."

Nothing like me, I thought. "You loved her very much." I loosened my hand from his and moved to the end of the bed where I lifted his foot and tugged until the boot slid free, and then I removed the other boot.

"Do you want children, Tullah?"

What an odd question. "Someday, if I ever find another man to love as much as I did Bryce."

He patted the side of the bed. I opted for the chair next to it. "Why did you ask me that question about children?"

The pain medicine was taking effect. I could tell by the way his body was releasing its tension. My frown must have tipped him off that his question had touched a raw nerve. "You're a bulldog, Tullah. I don't think anything scares you."

"I'm not sure if you're complimenting me or insulting me, Clay Wolfchild."

Outside the wind had kicked up. Puffs of snow splattered against the windows. I stood to leave. He grabbed my hand. "Stay…please. And, I apologize. I didn't mean for my question to come across as an insult."

I returned to the chair. He said, "Tell me about Bryce."

I countered with, "Tell me about the bullet in your back."

For the next few minutes, he relayed about the bank holdup, the shooting, his wife's death, his surgery, and the trial. He finished with, "This trip is my last hurrah, so to speak. When I return to Dallas, I'll either agree to become a desk jockey or take a forced medical retirement."

I liked the sound of his voice. It was deep and throaty. "Your turn. Who was Bryce?"

"He was a brilliant veterinarian. He died the day before our wedding. That was ten years ago. End of story."

Clay Wolfchild swung his legs over the side of the bed and stood. I didn't miss the grimace nor the set of his jaw when he lifted me from the chair. I was in his arms. I realized what a comfort it was to have his arms around me, how it felt to have his chest pressed against mine, and how much I craved the need to be desired.

The look in his eyes reminded me of smoldering blue embers. I was hot with anticipation. When his lips touched mine, I gave myself to the kiss. The heat that

247

followed was swift and demanding.

It was the chime on my telephone that kept us from burning past the point of no return. Clay Wolfchild had that effect on me. I gave a weak chuckle and broke away from him. "That's probably my grandmother checking on me."

He laced his fingertips through mine. "I keep thinking about what your grandmother said about wolves mating for life, Tullah."

"Don't go there," I cautioned. "We haven't known each other long enough for that kind of conversation."

He placed my hand against his heart. His tone was deep and feeling. "In my spirit, I feel like I've known you for a lifetime. I'm tempted to ask you to stay the night with me, but I'd never disrespect you in that way."

He followed me to the door. I really didn't want to leave him, and it scared me. Yes, I was afraid of my own feelings. I'd never felt this intimate with anyone—not even Bryce.

His dark eyes pierced mine for a moment. Before I walked down the long hall to the elevators, Clay Wolfchild said, "Don't go anywhere without me, Tullah, nor your grandmother or her friend. Meet me in the morning for breakfast and we'll finish reviewing the reports."

I'd forgotten about them. I removed the papers from my pocket and held them out. "I don't want Grandmother seeing these."

He wrapped his hands around the stack. "Tullah, I felt the medicine pouch. My cop instincts tell me you're in danger."

I tiptoed and lightly brushed his lips. The only danger I felt was from my own heart. "We'll see you at breakfast."

He was still standing at the door when I turned to look over my shoulder. I smiled as I walked backwards. "Four."

He frowned. "Four what?"

"Two boys—two girls."

He smiled back and winked. My heart flip-flopped at the warmth in his eyes.

I waved goodbye as I hustled toward the elevators. I touched the pouch beneath my sweater and smiled. My cellphone chimed. "I'm on my way, Grandmother." The scold in her voice was evident. "I'll explain when I get there. See you in a jiff."

Chapter Thirty-Four

Grandmother waited while I took a quick shower. I returned to the sitting room dressed in a long nightshirt, socks covering my cold feet. My sweet tooth craved something decadent, like raspberry-filled donuts. I settled for a cup of hot chocolate. Grandmother joined me.

"Patty is tuckered out from all the walking and shopping we did today. I'm ready to get home to the peace and quiet. Too many people, too much noise, and everyone is in a hurry to get nowhere fast." She sipped her cocoa. "Tell me about the files."

That was Grandmother—direct and to the point. Although I didn't want to talk about ugliness, I filled her in on how Shadow Woman had led me to the files. Grandmother chuckled at the part about the cat.

I blurted, "He kissed me."

Her eyebrows lifted in curiosity; she peered over her cup. "Who?"

"Don't pretend you don't know. Clay Wolfchild." I drained my cup and set it aside.

"Tullah, a long time ago, after Bryce died, I told you that someday a special someone would walk into your heart. Take off the blinders, Granddaughter, and open your heart. I'm not gifted the way you are, but I do know that you'll regret it for the rest of your life if you close the door on Clay Wolfchild. Men like him are rare gems."

I heaved a sigh. "Are you speaking from experience?"

She was pensive for a long while. I thought perhaps she might not answer me. She seemed far away when she spoke. "After your grandfather died, I buried myself in my work. I was following a story that led me to England. There I met and fell in love with a Brit. His name was Edward Faulkner. Clay Wolfchild reminds me of him— strong, virile, honest. He even followed me home. I was afraid, much like you, to open my heart again. Cousin Uma tried to tell me. I wouldn't listen and sent him packing."

Grandmother wrapped me in her arms. "Even when you are surrounded by people you love and who love you," she stood back and looked into my eyes, "loneliness is a terrible place to live, Tullah."

She released me and padded silently to the bedroom she shared with Patty Sweet. I climbed into my own bed and pulled the comforter to my chin. Sleep eluded me.

In a tiny corner of my heart, I wanted to be a victim of love, slain by the power of romance, and addicted to passion.

Everything Grandmother had said was true. Clay Wolfchild had walked into my heart. I think I knew it when we met two years ago at the rodeo, except I shoved it aside. I had returned to Enigma, buried myself in work and in using my unique ability to help Dad solve murders. And still mourning the death of his wife, Clay Wolfchild had returned to Texas.

I didn't want to cry. I hated crying. But tears slid down my cheeks.

Chapter Thirty-Five

Ready for the day, I stood at the window while waiting for Grandmother and Patty to finish dressing. The clouds over the city were slate gray. By the time we were ready to leave the room and join Clay Wolfchild in the dining room for breakfast, a light snow was falling.

Grandmother fastened the buttons on her jacket. She assisted Patty with an errant zipper while smiling at me in a mirror. Patty fretted, "I hope the weather clears before the gala at the museum tomorrow night."

"Not to worry, Patty." Grandmother assured her. "Our diligent doorman will have a cab waiting for us."

I looked down at Patty's blue-veined hands as she gathered mine. Her voice was filled with concern. "You have dark circles under your eyes, Tullah. All this cloak-and-dagger stuff is wearing on you. Tanti, we need to get our girl home." She shuddered. "That night at the sweat lodge haunts my dreams."

Haunts mine, too. I kept the thought to myself. A loud rap on the door startled us. "Who could that be?" Grandmother walked toward the door.

"Stop!" I didn't mean to shout. "Let me get it."

I wanted to laugh when Grandmother rummaged inside her handbag and withdrew a container of pepper spray. Her stance reminded me of a true warrior woman.

There was collective sigh of relief when I opened the door. Clay Wolfchild offered a dimpled smile. "Good morning, ladies. I thought we might all go down together. And by the way, Detective Amherst is joining us for breakfast."

Before I could protest that blood and gore didn't pair well with waffles and eggs, he said, "Amherst said he'd done a little covert snooping and thought we'd be interested in what he's found out about Stein."

By the time we rode the elevator to the dining room, Amherst was standing at the entry. "Oh, there you are. I was afraid I'd gotten the time wrong."

Clay Wolfchild made the introductions while we followed the hostess to our table. "Is everything all right, Detective? You seem a bit edgy." I noted the way he kept checking his phone.

"My sister is having labor pains. I'm expecting my brother-in-law to call telling me it's time."

I explained that Amherst's sister was pregnant with her first child. After the congratulations were over, and the waitress had arrived with coffee, we placed our breakfast orders. Amherst drew a notepad from his coat pocket.

Amherst said he was too nervous to eat. He added, "My apologies to you, ladies. I don't mean to discuss crime over breakfast. It's just that, well, I wanted to get this to you in person, and hopefully before I take off for the hospital."

"Let's have it," Clay Wolfchild said.

"I read all the files last night. It appears," he cast an apologetic look toward us, "from what I can glean, all of the women, including your mother, Dr. Holliday, were victims of a gang initiation."

I nearly missed my mouth, especially when he added, "Yeah, the Aryan Brotherhood required boys, anywhere from ages twelve to eighteen, to target a non-Caucasian woman, and…" There was a pink blush to Amherst's amber cheeks. He appeared uncomfortable, to the point that his pinstriped tie seemed to choke him.

The trooper she is, and maybe because of her past career as a crime reporter, Grandmother said, "Quit beating around the bush, Detective. We're all adults here. As a retired crime reporter, I've heard it all and seen even worse, and I've lived with my daughter's murder for all these years. Don't any of you think you're doing me a favor by shielding me from evidence, no matter how unpleasant."

She looked at Patty. "Patty, if you'd rather not, we'll understand."

"No siree-bob. Josie was like the daughter I never had. And I love Tullah as much as you do, Tanti Crow, so don't try to shoo me away." She ripped open two pink packets of sugar and dumped their contents into her coffee.

Amherst lifted his eyebrows as if surprised by the succinctness of these two elderly women. "Well, okay, then." He proceeded. "At present, Stein is forty-two years old. Dr. Holliday, that would have made him twenty-eight at the time of your mother's death. However, my source told me that Stein was a detective in Harlem and was reprimanded several times for using excessive force."

We all clammed up when the waitress arrived with our food. Waffles, eggs, and bacon for Grandmother, Patty, and me. Ham, home fries, and scrambled eggs for Clay Wolfchild. As soon as she was out of earshot, Amherst continued.

"How old was he when he joined the force?" I spoke

between chews.

Amherst flipped through his notebook. "Twenty-one. And before that…" His voice took on a conspiratorial tone. "His name was Leland Steinhaur. I checked the origin of 'Steinhaur.' It's German."

Before I could ask why the captain would change his name, Amherst's cellphone rang, or I should say it sounded like a siren. He answered, did an air fist bump, and said, "I'm on my way."

He shoved the notepad toward Clay Wolfchild. "I'm about to become an uncle. Maybe you can make sense of my scribbles. I'll be at the hospital if you need me."

He made a mad dash toward the door, then turned back. I shoved his overcoat forward. He offered a sheepish grin and weaved his way through the tables.

My first question was why would the captain change his name from Steinhaur to Stein? My other question was, "What is Amherst's motive—why is he suddenly interested in Stein's background?"

Clay Wolfchild related the incident about the two women officers. "It may be personal. I brought my laptop with me. After breakfast, I'll access the National Crime Information Centers database. It might reveal nefarious information about Stein, or he might be legit."

Due to the inclement weather, the dining room was becoming overly crowded. Clay Wolfchild suggested we adjourn to his room. I said, "Grandmother and Patty haven't experienced the solarium. We can stay as long as we like without being disturbed."

We agreed that if it, too, was crowded, then Clay Wolfchild's room was the alternate option. I sent up a silent prayer for the solarium. I didn't want to recall memories from last night's romantic encounter.

Before we left the dining room, I ordered a dozen assorted flavored donuts to be delivered to the solarium. "They won't be as good as yours, Patty, but my sweet tooth is craving donuts."

Clay Wolfchild agreed to meet us after he went to his room to grab his laptop. We parted at the elevators.

The solarium hostess greeted us. "Good morning, my name is Sarah. Do you have a special place you'd like to sit?"

A few people sat scattered throughout the large garden area. Most of them sat next to the viewing windows. I'd hoped for a window seat, but those available were too close together for a private conversation. "Detective Wolfchild will join us shortly, and we'd like a quiet corner."

We followed Sarah to an area that reminded me of a tropical jungle. She pointed and said, "If you'd like refreshments, the phone goes straight to my desk."

Sated from breakfast, we thanked her and waited for her departure. While Grandmother and Patty explored the various areas of the domed indoor gardens, I pondered possible reasons why Captain Stein would shorten his name. Anything to keep my mind from wandering back to last night. I glanced toward the door. My heart skipped a beat when Clay Wolfchild stepped out of the elevator. I watched him survey the room. When Grandmother and Patty spotted him, they pointed in my direction.

He strolled towards me with a mini-laptop in his hand. He greeted me with a genial smile. Not a smile that even hinted of last night's passionate kiss. My head itched with anger. Maybe I'd misread his honorable intentions. Maybe Grandmother was completely wrong about him. Either way, I was unreasonably angry at myself for being angry.

I was about to reach for the donut box when a wave of excitement filled the room. People were leaving their seats and rushing to the diamond-shaped glass windows. Grandmother stood, "What's all the commotion about?"

Patty fretted. "I hope it's not a fire. Maybe we should ask if there's a fire escape. I don't want to get stuck in an elevator."

Then a rush of voices yelled, "Crow…look at the crow."

Another person shouted, "I didn't know crows could fly this high."

Someone else exclaimed, "It must've got blown off course. In my entire life, I've never seen a crow in the city."

The medicine pouch beneath my shirt pulsated as I was drawn to the expanse of windows. Grandmother, Patty, and Clay Wolfchild trailed behind me. To my astonishment, a single black bird fluttered against a windowpane.

I rushed to the window and placed the palm of my hand against the glass. The black bird flew against the pane. This was no crow. It was a raven. My raven. Don't ask me how I knew. I just did.

The raven pecked against the window and furiously flapped its wings before dive bombing toward the ground. I turned to seek Sarah and bumped into her—literally. Once we had chuckled at ourselves, I pointed toward the street below. "Sarah, where does that street lead?"

My blood chilled when she said, "It leads to the Museum of Arts."

Loretta C. Rogers

I commanded Grandmother and Patty to stay in the solarium. Grandmother gripped my arm and whispered, "It's your raven, isn't it?"

She has learned too well about my spirit animals, and whispered again, "Do you think there's been a murder?"

"Possibly." I grabbed Clay Wolfchild's arm. He seemed to read the command in my eyes, and shoved the mini-laptop toward Grandmother. He also cautioned, "Tanti, whatever you and Miss Patty do, stay in the hotel."

The anxious look on my grandmother's face pierced my heart. I kissed her cheek. "Don't worry, Clay Wolfchild will look after me."

Grandmother reached out to grab Clay Wolfchild's sleeve. "The computer—is it password protected? Maybe I can do some research about you know who."

Clay Wolfchild grabbed a napkin, pulled a pen from his pocket, and jotted down a series of numbers and letters and shoved the napkin into Grandmother's outstretched hand.

Chapter Thirty-Six

The elevator ride to the lobby seemed to take forever. The moment the doors opened, Clay Wolfchild grabbed my hand and we sprinted toward the doorman. Clay asked, "What's the nearest way to the Museum of Art's alley?"

"Through the kitchen. It cuts off nearly a block. But…but…" The doorman's voice trailed after us.

We plowed through the kitchen toward the red exit sign. I was barely aware of the clanging pots and pans. Everyone appeared engrossed in their specific duties and paid us little attention. The air outside was colder than the night before. Although it was barely past noon, the sky was dark. The air felt heavy, but not pressing. My first reaction was the stench that rankled my nose as we stepped into an endless misery of brick walls and a narrow deteriorating road.

Clay Wolfchild still held my hand. For once in my life, I was thankful for my long legs. I matched him stride for stride as we raced through the trash-littered alley, feeling the hard broken asphalt beneath my heavy winter boots. Once we entered the street, we stopped to get our bearings.

He shot me a questioning glance. Lifting his black cowboy hat, he scratched through his thick black hair. "Tullah?"

"I don't know." I clutched my medicine pouch. I'm

not sure if I spoke the words aloud or if I beseeched her silently. "Shadow Woman, show us the way."

For a moment, I felt lost. Though I'm not easily startled, a gust of wind felt like a pair of rough hands against my back, shoving me forward. "This way." I hoped.

Two blocks later—no alley and no sign of the raven. Yet we were close. I could feel it in my bones.

Clay Wolfchild came to a screeching halt, still holding my hand, and the sudden stop whirled me around and slammed me against his chest. He cut a brief smile and said, "Did you hear that?"

"Hear what?"

Now wasn't the time to inhale his masculinity or snuggle against his chest. I turned from his arms and my eyes went straight to a store sign dangling lopsided from a rusted chain. "Look." I pointed. "Two Ravens Book Nook."

And then I *did* hear it. A light thumping coming from a narrow alley. The sound seemed to echo in my ears—a sound akin to the pulsating heart in Edgar Allen Poe's *A Tell-Tale Heart*. I tugged on Clay Wolfchild's hand. "This way."

He released my hand, unbuttoned his coat, and reached inside to remove a revolver from its holster. "Stay behind me, Tullah."

We entered a tight passageway. Backs against the wall, we inched our way into a chasm of semi-darkness. Holding the revolver in one hand, he signaled with the other to halt. We were looking at each other when the next series of thumps came again. This time followed by a low moan.

Clay Wolfchild pointed toward the sound and

motioned for me to follow. A dark figure lay face down. He held a can and was weakly beating it against the ground. Thankfully, the narrow slit opened to a wider space. Daylight from the other end was enough for us to spot the knife protruding from the victim's back. Clay Wolfchild and I knelt. He gently rolled the victim to his side.

"It's Detective Amherst," I cried out to Clay Wolfchild.

"Amherst…Todd…can you hear me? It's Clay Wolfchild."

Amherst didn't respond.

I felt his neck for a pulse. "It's weak. A least he's still alive. Judging from the amount of blood on his coat, I'm not sure for how long. How did he end up in an alley with a knife in his back? Why didn't he use his phone to call for help?" Questions with no answers flooded my mind.

"Where the hell are we? I didn't bother to notice the name of the street." Clay Wolfchild lamented as he whipped out his cellphone.

"Don't worry. Tell them the name of the bookstore. I'm sure the EMTs won't have trouble finding us."

Amherst had lapsed into unconsciousness and was shivering. Clay Wolfchild said, "Search for his phone and anything that looks like evidence while I call 9-1-1."

While listening to him talking to a dispatcher, I used the flashlight on my phone to search the area. A short distance from where he lay, I spotted what was left of his cellphone and the reason why he hadn't called for help. It looked as if it had been stomped on several times. I was reminded of Humpty Dumpty. All the pieces couldn't be put back together again.

"Whoever stabbed the detective didn't want him calling for help."

Clay Wolfchild cautioned, "Don't touch it. Maybe forensics can pull some prints off it."

"Detective Amherst…Todd?" I knelt and repeated. "Can you hear me?"

I looked up to see Clay Wolfchild returning to my side. "What's at the other end?" I asked.

He looked at me grimly. "The rear of the museum's building and another alley."

I'm not sure if it was the cold seeping through my jacket or if the chill invading my body was caused by a sudden anger sweeping through me. "He was supposed to be on the way to the hospital. Do you think we should contact his brother-in-law?"

Before he could answer, a deep masculine voice called, "Detective Bannister?"

"Yeah, back here. Hurry, he's in bad shape."

Following behind the medical team was Captain Stein, with two uniformed cops. "What the hell happened here?" gruffed Stein. "Is he alive? You didn't touch anything, did you? Can't have a bunch of out-of-towners contaminating the scene."

Stein's eyes bored into mine. I definitely disliked his insinuation. "Is it women you don't like, Captain Stein, or is it native women in particular that you disrespect?"

Stein narrowed his gaze on me. Clearly, he didn't appreciate my defiance toward him. He took a menacing step toward me.

"I wouldn't." The warning in Clay Wolfchild's voice was calm, firm, and carried the weight of an iron fist. The expression in his eyes reminded me of an alpha wolf protecting his mate.

I said no more because I didn't have to. I found myself amazed by Clay Wolfchild's composure even with the possibility that we were in the company of a murderer. Except for my dad, I've seldom known professional law enforcement types capable of maintaining such a calm and collective demeanor. I began to wonder whether his duties back in Texas extended into more than everyday detective work, and then I remembered he had once gone deep undercover, posing as a prisoner, to gather dirt on corrupt prison officials.

There was no smile on Clay Wolfchild's face. I'm certain only I read the humor in his dark blue eyes.

The lead EMT said, "We'll leave the knife in place, Captain Stein. Without knowing whether it's pierced his lung, or how close it is to his heart, I can't risk removing it."

"Aw right. Get him to the hospital. I'll check on his condition later."

I spoke up. "His sister is in labor. He was supposed to be on the way to the hospital to be with his brother-in-law. What hospital are you taking him to?"

"Sisters of Mercy on Fifty-Seventh, two blocks over."

I thanked the technician as he and his assistant hustled the stretcher down the alley to where the ambulance was parked. I heard him say to his assistant, "Let's hope nobody's stole the tires off the bus."

I detected a southern drawl from the assistant. "Yeah, or broken into the medical supplies. Man, soon as I get the chance, I'm moving back to Tennessee. Too much crime and noise here to suit me."

I distinctly heard Stein mutter under his breath, "Shit

ass." He looked up and shot Clay Wolfchild an uneasy smile, then said, "This is a crime scene, Detective Bannister, in which your presence is not needed."

Clay Wolfchild merely nodded as he cupped my elbow with his hand. "In Texas, it's customary for a witness to give a written accounting of the incident. However, since that's apparently not the case in your precinct, Dr. Holliday and I will be at the hospital checking on Detective Amherst, and then at our hotel, should you change your mind. And by the way, you'll find what's left of Amherst's cellphone about ten feet from where we found him."

With that, I allowed Clay Wolfchild to lead me toward where the ambulance had been parked. He said, "I'll hail a cab."

"No," I objected. "Two blocks isn't much of a walk. We'll take a cab back to the hotel once we check on Amherst."

By the time we entered the hospital's main lobby, I relished the warmth that greeted us. I was also ready for a cup of hot coffee. We approached the information desk. Clay Wolfchild said, "I'm Detective Clayton Bannister, here to check on the condition of Detective Todd Amherst, and could you also tell me if a Mrs. Tony Quang is a patient here. She would be in maternity."

The nurse receptionist typed in names. She looked up from the computer. "Do you have identification, Detective?"

Clay Wolfchild reached inside his coat and withdrew the case that held his badge and ID. She offered him a smile. "Precaution, you understand, Detective Bannister." Then she added, "Detective Amherst was taken to surgery upon arrival. Mrs. Quang is in the birthing room." She pointed and gave us directions to the waiting room for expectant fathers.

As I turned to leave, the receptionist called me back. "You have blood on your jacket. Do you need assistance?"

I briefly explained that I was a doctor, neglecting to say the veterinary type, and that the blood was from when I had examined Detective Amherst. She merely nodded her understanding.

On the way to the maternity wing, I spotted a sign that led to the cafeteria. Clay Wolfchild is an expert at reading minds, or maybe just mine. He suggested we detour for coffee.

"No, let's find Tony Quang first. He needs to know about his brother-in-law."

It took an elevator ride and a few turns down long halls before we stepped into the waiting room. I'm not sure how expectant fathers are supposed to look. "Haggard" is the word that came to mind. Tony recognized us the moment we entered the room.

He took in my appearance from dirty knees to blood on my jacket. Clay Wolfchild extended his hand. The two men shook hands. "Tony, how is your wife?"

"I just spoke to the doctor. There's a problem, so they're prepping her for a C-section. But why are you here? Where's Todd? I expected him an hour ago."

"You'd better sit down," Clay Wolfchild suggested.

Tony said, "There's coffee and cookies over there, Dr. Holliday. You look the way I feel."

My chuckle seemed to relieve some of Tony's tension. I asked if he wanted a cup. He declined, saying he'd already had enough to float a boat. Clay Wolfchild invited Tony to join him in a more private corner of the

Loretta C. Rogers

room. There was no need for others to hear the conversation.

I joined them and handed a steaming cup of coffee to Clay Wolfchild. He rolled the hot cup between his hands. I imagined they were as cold as my own. I sat in an empty chair next to Tony while Clay Wolfchild spoke in a hushed voice.

Tony listened intently. When Clay Wolfchild had finished speaking, Tony simply leaned forward, his face in his hands, and wept. We gave him time to collect his emotions. Finally, he said, "Except for me and my family, Todd is the only close family Cicely has. Oh, there's a few cousins that live somewhere…I don't know. She and Todd rarely speak about their family. It'll just kill her if he…you know—" He shook his head. "I can't say it, Detective. If I do, it might come true."

I wasn't quite sure how to console him. "Do you mind if we sit with you until you hear about your wife?"

I sensed the relief in him. "I would welcome it. My parents and one of my sisters are coming tomorrow. They will stay to help Cicely and the baby so Pop can help me run the restaurant."

I mentally scratched Todd Amherst off my suspect list. I felt a stab of disappointment coupled with relief.

Chapter Thirty-Seven

By the time we returned to the hotel, I felt like I'd had a date with a tough, sexy guy, but a date that had gone completely off the rails. I was hungry, filthy, and generally in a foul mood, and not necessarily in that order.

Clay Wolfchild's limp was noticeable as we walked down the hall. Nevertheless, he bestowed a brotherly kiss on my forehead and waited until I was safely inside the room I shared with Grandmother and Patty before he headed toward the elevators and his own accommodations. Because neither of us were in the mood for socializing, we agreed to skip lunch, and since it was snowing, we also agreed to meet in the dining room for dinner.

Grandmother gasped at the sight of blood on my jacket. "I'll tell you all about it, *after* I've had a shower, and Grandmother, I'm starved. Would you order room service? I don't care what you order as long as it includes French fries and dessert."

I spotted the laptop as I walked past the coffee table. The sight of it stopped me in my tracks. "Grandmother?"

Before she responded to my question, she spoke to room service. She winked at me and placed an order for a hamburger all the way with extra pickles, a double order of fries, a carafe of cola, and a carafe of hazelnut coffee. She added less enormous lunch orders for herself and Patty, then asked, "What's on your dessert list?"

She uh-huhed several times, then said, "Send three slices of pecan pie."

When she disconnected, she settled in a chair. "Food will arrive in about thirty minutes; enough time for you to shower and change. But, before you escape to the bathroom, tell me about the blood."

I gave her the shortened version of Detective Amherst's stabbing. "Give me ten minutes and I'll give you the all the details."

As I headed for the shower, I jokingly said, "Are all three pieces of pie for me?"

Patty, who had remained silent till then, spoke up. "You wish!"

By the time I returned, refreshed and ready to eat, the food service cart had arrived. Grandmother was setting out the meal. While we ate, I detailed the encounter with Captain Stein and moved on to less traumatic news. "Todd Amherst is critical but stable. We were able to speak with him for a few minutes before he succumbed to pain meds."

"What was he doing in an alley if he was on his way to the hospital?"

"He said he heard someone calling for help. It sounded like a woman in distress, and because it was in the alley nearest to the museum, and thinking about my mother and the other women, he went immediately to investigate."

I stopped to enjoy another bite of my hamburger and a swig of cola. "He remembered having his cell to call for help, but doesn't remember much after that. Whoever stabbed him attacked from behind. Before passing out, he remembered counting eight boots."

Patty said, "That means he was attacked by four ruffians. I hate to say this, but I'm ready to go home."

Grandmother chimed in. "It's a good thing the raven contacted you. Otherwise, the detective might have become another statistic. I'm glad he'll live to see another day. Now, what about his sister?"

"That's the best part of this story. Her name is Cicely. She and Tony, her husband, are the proud parents of a healthy baby boy. They named him Shen Li Anthony Todd; to honor both his Chinese and American heritage."

While Grandmother cleared the table, Patty set out the pie and coffee. I pointed toward the laptop. "Grandmother, were you able to research Captain Leland Stein?"

She shrugged. "Sorry, I couldn't get the password to work." After a brief pause, she said, "What about inviting Clay Wolfchild to dine in with us? The weather outside is terrible, and the two of you have had a harrowing experience."

I was about to buzz his room when a rat-a-tat-tat sounded at the door. "It's Clay Wolfchild." I tamped down the giddiness welling in the pit of my stomach. He stood, tall and handsome, and looking none the worse for our morning's events. He gave me a courteous peck on the cheek. I was disappointed, but what did I expect? A full-blown French kiss in front of my grandmother?

He accepted a cup of coffee. We made small chit-chat before settling down to business. He pulled out the notepad Amherst had thrust to him before rushing out of the hotel dining room. "His scribbles are a bit difficult to read. It appears Amherst has his own shorthand, or maybe he was afraid of getting caught and rushed to write this down. Either way…" Clay Wolfchild turned the small spiralbound notebook for me to see.

It looked more like hieroglyphics than handwriting. I read, "K. Steinhaur, IDJJ, IYC-Chicago."

I wrinkled my forehead into a frown. "What does all this mean?"

Clay Wolfchild was typing as I spoke. He looked over the top of the computer's screen. "This makes me think that our Captain Leland Stein was a bad boy in his younger days."

The screen opened to a national juvenile database. In the search engine, Clay Wolfchild typed "Leland Steinhaur." I'm not sure what I expected.

Clay Wolfchild read, "Karl L. Steinhaur, age sixteen. IDJJ, IYC, AC."

I said, "The name is different, and what do the initials mean?"

Clay Wolfchild typed again. "Illinois Department of Juvenile Justice, Illinois Youth Center, and…"

The frown on his face, and the fact that he'd stopped and looked at me caused me to ask, "Is it that bad…I mean like a sex offender or juvenile murderer?"

Clay Wolfchild heaved a disgusted sigh. "Neither. AC means Aryan Cell. We've dealt with them in Dallas. Bad doesn't even begin to describe them."

My words came out in a whooshed whisper. "My mother was murdered by Aryans."

Grandmother let out a little cry. "Is there a picture?"

It felt as if someone had dumped ice water over me. For a moment, I couldn't find my voice. My brain seemed to have become muddled. All I could think of was *why and how*? At that moment, I felt the need to punch someone in the face. This man, this bigoted idiot who might be connected to my mother's murder, was a gang-banger hiding behind a badge.

I finally managed to speak. "If he has a juvenile record that ties him to a dangerous gang, then how did he manage to become a policeman?"

"It depends on the extent of his record, what sorts of things he was arrested for, and it was a long time ago." He must have read the anger on my face. He hastened on. "I'm not defending Steinhaur. Besides, we're looking at a Karl L. Steinhaur."

"Steinhaur—Stein." I pfff'd. "He could have easily changed his name. I think that's what Amherst discovered. I also bet that somehow Stein found out and that Amherst's attack was deliberate." I pointed to the laptop. "Check the national crime database. Let's see what comes up for a Steinhaur and then for Leland Stein."

Clay Wolfchild's fingers flew across the keyboard. There was a brief silence as I watched him scroll from screen to screen, his face a study of concentration. He said, "I went back to the juvenile database and found this." He turned the laptop for all to see. Karl Steinhaur stood tall, overweight, a beige suit, a stiff collar, a beige tie, and without expression.

I pointed. "There's a date. Can you enlarge the photo so we can see it?"

Clay Wolfchild set the cursor and clicked until we could plainly see the date—nineteen ninety-four. "Holy crap! That's him. That's Stein. I don't care if he's listed as Karl Steinhaur. That's Leland Stein."

"Yep, and if I've got the math correct, he would have been about sixteen when this picture was taken, and wearing typical clothing supplied by the State."

I was more upset than I should have been. "I still

don't understand how he was accepted into law enforcement. The idea of that bigoted man who is supposed to uphold the law being responsible for my mother's death...and maybe *he's* the one who killed her..."

"Allegedly, Tullah. Don't go jumping the gun and making accusations you can't substantiate." Clay Wolfchild continued to scroll. "This may answer our questions."

He lifted his cup and emptied it before paraphrasing. "At the age of seventeen, Karl Leeyand Steinhaur requested his name be changed to Leland Stein. He asked the juvenile judge to grant him special dispensation to join the Marines. Stein's reasoning was to break away from a gang known as the skinheads. Stein expressed sincere regret for his involvement with the gang and said that his time at IYC had changed his life. The only way he knew to create a new life for himself was to get as far away from them as possible.

"Stein served eleven years as a military police officer. He also obtained a bachelor's degree in business administration. Upon leaving the Marines, he entered New Jersey's police academy. After graduation, Stein worked his way up through the ranks."

We watched Clay Wolfchild scroll down a couple more screens. His silence grated on my impatience. I was about to say so when he said, "Stein joined the NJPD. He was cited several times for excessive cruelty, especially toward people of color. After he received a suspension, he moved to New York where he started as a beat cop, then moved up the ranks. It appears that Stein has above average intelligence and scored well on all of his tests."

"How did he manage to become captain of a

precinct? Don't the people in charge thoroughly vet their applicants? I don't care how smart he is, he'd never pass muster with my dad."

The answer wasn't an easy one. I watched Clay Wolfchild weigh his words. "Sometimes the system doesn't seem fair—even to law enforcement officers, lawyers, and judges. I wish I had a better answer, Tullah."

Grandmother had listened quietly. When Clay Wolfchild finished speaking and silence permeated the room, her troubled eyes focused on me. "The only thing we've learned is why Stein changed his name, and that he doesn't seem to be a morally responsible cop. Other than that, there's no proof that he arranged for Detective Amherst's attack, and just because he had an early connection to the same bloodthirsty animals that killed my daughter, that doesn't mean Stein orchestrated it. Unless we have proof positive, all of this information means nothing."

Grandmother's reasoning was logical. At this point in time, logic wasn't in my wheelhouse as I commented, "Apparently, Stein thinks with his penis, and it's my guess there isn't a lot to work with."

"Tullah Josie Crow Holliday, the things that come out of your mouth!" Grandmother tried to sound serious in her scold. However, when Patty burst into laughter, Grandmother and Clay Wolfchild joined in. I hadn't meant for my insult of Stein's male anatomy to amuse anyone.

Clay Wolfchild stood. Between chuckles he said, "I hope you never get mad at me." He strolled to the door. "Unless you ladies wish to brave the snow to dine in a fancy upscale New York restaurant, I'd be honored if you'd join me in the hotel's dining room this evening."

That was fine with me. I wasn't in the mood for dressing up or fancy dining.

After he left, I was restless and wandered to the large glass window that overlooked the city. I missed my animals, especially River and Rascal. I missed going to work every day, and greeting friendly faces. Instead, my chest hurt with worry, and a gray fog seemed to settle over me. I watched a group of crows dart among the buildings like a dark cloud of evil. In the old folk tales, a group of crows were called a "murder" of crows. How appropriate, I thought. Only the dead enjoy the cold.

Grandmother walked over and put her arm around my waist, pulling me close. "What is it you see, Granddaughter?"

Her hands warmed my icy clutch. "Tomorrow night is the ceremony at the museum." I almost choked on my words, but they needed to be said. Grandmother always knew when I was holding back the truth. "The dark part of my brain tells me that if these killers' motive was the ritual of bleeding victims, they will want to kill in a place where they can play out their sicko ceremony."

Patty fussed about the room, placing dishes on the servicing tray. "Tanti…Tullah, it's not my place to stick my nose where it doesn't belong. It's just that, well…" She wrung her hands together.

Grandmother said, "Patty Sweet, we are closer than most sisters. Don't hold back. Say what's on your mind."

Patty motioned for all of us to sit. We found our places in the chairs we had claimed as our own the first day we'd arrived in the room. She cleared her throat, then met our gaze. "Tullah, God did not bless me with children. Instead, he brought you into my life. I love you as if you were my own. I mean no offense, and you can never speak to me again after this, and that's okay. I'll understand."

I had no idea where this was leading, and had to resist the temptation to ask her to fast forward and get to the point.

Patty's voice became crisp. "Those boys, the ones responsible for Josie and the other women's deaths, were in their teens. One as young as twelve." She shuddered. "I've lain awake these past few nights wondering if those boys' mothers had agonized over the evils done by their sons. It's been fourteen years and all of them are now in their late twenties or early thirties. Maybe they're all dead. Or maybe like Leland Stein they've left the gang and tried to clean up their lives."

Grandmother reached to squeeze Patty's hands. Tears were filling her eyes. Patty continued. "Tullah, you are thirty years old. Tanti is worried about your ovaries drying up and never blessing her with great-grands. I'm more concerned about how long are you going to keep living with the ghosts of the past?"

Chapter Thirty-Eight

The silence lingered on for a long time. Internally, I flinched at the pain in Patty's voice. The hard truth she had spoken was like a slap in the face—a wakeup call. The silence grew even heavier.

"This is a nightmare," I mumbled, more to myself than to Patty or Grandmother. "And it's getting worse every day. I keep hoping I'll wake up, that my life will return to normal…except I've almost forgotten what normal is, or how to get it back."

I jumped at the chiming of my cellphone and practically yelled, "Hello!"

"Tullah, it's Clay Wolfchild. What's wrong? You sound—panicked."

I sucked in a deep breath and forced myself to blow it out slowly. I didn't want to sound pathetic. "I'm fine. What's up?"

"Are you ready for this? I have a friend in Dallas, a real computer geek. He did some digging for me… Tullah, are you there?"

"Sure, what did your friend find out?"

"The names of the four boys arrested in your mother's attack."

This news perked me up. "Do you mind if I put the phone on speaker?"

"Better than that, I'm outside your door."

I practically jumped from my chair and rushed

forward. His signature rat-a-tat-tat sounded. I opened the door. Behind him a waiter stood with a service cart. Clay Wolfchild slipped a bill into the young man's hand. As I invited him in, a thick wave of fatigue washed over me and I was suddenly unsteady on my feet, almost woozy, much the way truck drivers describe their feelings of nearly dozing off behind the wheel.

Strong arms reached out to grab me when I wobbled. It was just past four in the afternoon, leaving several hours before time for dinner. Patty's words flashed through my mind as Clay Wolfchild led me to a chair. Grandmother followed with the service trolley.

She lifted the metal domed lid to expose a charcutier board filled with assorted cheeses, olives, meats, crackers, chocolate-covered nuts, and red grapes. "Clay Wolfchild, you are a keeper. What's in the carafe?"

He left me to help her. "Hot chocolate laced with Irish Cream."

Grandmother loaded a plate and handed it to me. She said, "You have the names of the boys?"

He nodded his answer to Grandmother, then handed me a cup of the aromatic hot chocolate. The caring sound in his voice felt like a warm caress. "Tell me why you're upset, Tullah."

I purposely loaded my mouth with food and took my time chewing. To relate Patty's statement about living with ghosts might come across as tattling. I knew she felt badly, and I didn't wish to make her feel worse. She beat me to the punch.

"I'm afraid it's my fault. I spoke out of turn by asking her how long she intended to keep living with ghosts of the past."

"It's a fair question," I managed to say. "The only

answer I have is that I don't purposely live with ghosts. I've never sought out the spirits that come to me. Whether they come in the form of animals or impressions, having them contact me is a heavy burden."

The alcohol-laced hot chocolate was soothing. If the liquid hadn't been scalding, I believe I would have drained the cup in one large gulp. "Let's change the subject. Tell us your news, Clay Wolfchild."

The information he relayed was almost prophesied by what Patty had said. He read from a small notebook. "The boys' names were Leroy Wick, Sheldon Campbell, and Eric Hampton. Wick and Campbell died in a gang war. Hampton was killed in a prison yard fight."

"The forensic files said there were four boys." In my spirit, I dreaded hearing the fourth name. "What was his name?"

When he didn't immediately answer, Grandmother said, "You've grown very quiet, Clay Wolfchild."

He cast a glance toward me. "Bernard Steinhaur, now age twenty-eight."

Hearing the name brought collective gasps. I managed to sputter, "Leland Stein's brother?"

"Yes."

"Is he still a member of the Aryans?"

Clay Wolfchild merely shrugged. "It appears he has dropped off the map. My friend checked under Stein and didn't find a match. He also checked birth certificates, driver's license, voting registrations, and tried to get a match from the nineteen ninety-four fingerprints for any that might be current. Nothing!

"At the age of fifteen, he was tried as an adult and sentenced to life at Rikers. Records indicate Steinhaur escaped five years ago. He was never caught. The theory is he may have drowned or been eaten by sharks, especially since great whites are known to frequent the waters around the prison."

Grandmother asked, "How long before a missing person can be legally declared dead?"

"Anticipating that question, I looked it up. In the State of New York, a person who is absent continuously for a period of three years, after a diligent search, and the fact that a person may have been subject to a specific peril, can be declared legally dead after the date their absence was determined."

"He's still alive, and I'm not going to argue the point. Trust me, Bernard Steinhaur, wherever he may be, is still among the living," I told everyone in the room.

Grandmother looked a little freaked. "Are you certain, Tullah?"

A darkness rippled over me. My voice sounded like I was speaking inside a tunnel. "Yes, he's a living, breathing ghost."

"What the hell is that supposed to mean?" I flinched at the bite in Clay Wolfchild's voice.

And I bit back. "It means he's among the living dead. If I had a crystal ball, maybe I could give you his description, too."

"Maybe like his brother he changed his name. A long time ago, I watched a movie where a guy got plastic surgery so no one would recognize him." Patty's expression suggested that after her last remark about my living with ghosts that she should keep quiet.

Although her remark had touched a sore spot, she did have a valid point. I set my cup aside and stood to give her a hug. "Patty, you are a genius."

I turned. "Clay Wolfchild…" My voice trailed off.

He said, "Way ahead of you, Tullah. I'll contact my friend and see if he can locate some old pictures of Bernard Steinhaur."

We discussed many possibilities surrounding the disappearance of Leland Stein's brother. All were plausible, but none answered the lingering question of why Shadow Woman, my mother, and the spirits had summoned me to New York, and especially on the anniversary eve of my mother's revival art showing.

Grandmother exhaled a deep breath. "Suppositions versus solutions. All of this has left me exhausted. I need a nap."

Patty agreed that she, too, was mentally exhausted. "I'll join you, Tanti."

After they had excused themselves and closed the bedroom door, Clay said, "You need a nap, too?"

"Actually, I'm wound tighter than a clock. If I were home, I'd saddle one of my horses and go for an all-out run across the swamp behind my house."

"Would you settle for an elevator ride to the solarium?" He glanced at his watch. "We have several hours before dinner."

"Give me a few minutes to refresh myself." I headed for the bathroom.

When I returned, the first thing I noticed was the way he rubbed his legs, and the grimace on his face when he stood. "When was the last time you took a pain med?"

"Last night."

My scold was harsher than I intended. "Stop trying to man-up, Clay Wolfchild. Getting relief from pain isn't a sign of weakness."

The agony behind his eyes was telling. "You sound like my mother."

"I'd love to meet her. I bet she's a smart woman."

Once we were in his room, I stood at the window while he refreshed himself and took his medication. Snow fell in inches to create small drifts around lamp posts. There was something placid and beautiful about falling snow to go with the sense of security I had knowing Clay Wolfchild was nearby. I clutched the medicine pouch beneath my sweater. *Why am I here, Shadow Woman? What danger am I in if all but one of mother's torturers are dead? Bernard Steinhaur doesn't know I exist.*

Clay Wolfchild's voice interrupted my musings. One look at his face and I pointed to the sofa and said, "We're staying here. Remove your boots while I get a couple of pillows to make you comfortable."

"No, I'm…"

He cracked a smile when I said, "Doctor's orders."

"Yeah, but you're a veterinarian."

"Shh, we'll let it be our little secret." I surprised myself. I was actually enjoying this thing called flirting. And then, as saturated as I was with cocoa and coffee, I asked if he needed anything.

He said, "Yes…you."

For safety from my own emotions, I scooted the chair next to the sofa out of touching distance, and remembering the last time I was in his room and the passionate kiss we'd shared, I felt awkward and shy. With his thick dark hair, dark lashes, a smile on his full lips, he was beautiful. Not a term I would generally use to describe a man, but in his case it was true. He was beautiful and masculine.

"A penny for your thoughts?"

How was I supposed to tell him I wanted to have sex

with him—mindless, passionate, very physical sex. *Wow*, where had that come from? I shoved that thought aside. "Oh, nothing important."

His comment took me by surprise when he blurted, "Tullah, I'm in love with you."

His simple declaration made me want to cry. But I wasn't relationship material. "That's not possible. We don't know each other. I mean, other than our brief encounter two years ago, and now working on a mystery case together, we're strangers."

"Oh hell, this isn't the way I had planned to court you."

"Stop. Stop it now! There is no courting, because there will never be an *us*."

Questions coupled with pain lined his face. "You feel exactly what I feel, Tullah. Don't deny it." His hand snaked out and grabbed my wrist. He pulled me on top of his supine body. I struggled to right myself and gain my composure.

Hot blood pounded through my veins as I stared into the passion in his blue eyes. I ached for him, yet I knew this was wrong. Wrong in every way.

"I can't, Clay Wolfchild. I refuse to love you or any man." I tried to loose my wrist from his iron grip. "Let me go!"

He held tight. "Why is loving each other wrong? Make me understand."

The rush of anger I felt was unreasonable. "It's not you, Clay Wolfchild. It's me—what I am. Patty was correct when she said that I live with ghosts. I never know when a spirit will contact me or what crime or death they will want me to solve. How long before you become disenchanted with me because the spirits will always come first? The spirits are demanding. They never leave me alone.

"And, as much as I want children, I will never bear a child for fear that I'll pass this curse on to them, and perhaps my grandchildren, too. I can see it written on your face. You're already denying that you'd never leave me, that wolves mate for life. Well, we're people. Not animals."

I forced myself to swallow the sobs that begged to be released, squared my shoulders, and heaved a long sigh. "Shadow Woman has warned that I am in danger. My mother's spirit and the spirits of Keyoko Hideki, Alita Vega, Melek Haddad, and Rana Hari have all cried out to me. All but one of their killers are dead, and I don't know why I'm here. Is it for me, or some other poor woman?"

The pitch of my voice had risen. "You have no idea what it's like to be me."

He released my wrist, and swung his legs over the sofa to sit up. His voice was calm. "Tullah, be quiet for a moment and listen to me."

Emotionally exhausted, I obeyed. My hands gripped the arms of the chair.

He apologized for upsetting me. "It's true, I don't know what it's like to live inside your skin. What I do know is that the love I feel for you is different, and deeper than what I had for my first wife. I'll ease off, Tullah, and after the art show tomorrow evening, I'll return to Texas."

He reached over, took my hand, and kissed the palm. This simple act of affection brought tears to my eyes. I didn't know what to think or say. For lack of anything better to offer, I said, "Don't retire, Clay Wolfchild. Stay with the department as a cold case investigator." I searched for something else to add. "In time, you'll forget about me. I'm certain there is a special someone out there waiting for you to find her."

With that, I walked to the door. I turned the knob, then turned back. "I'll tell Grandmother and Patty you decided to dine in your room—because of the pain in your back."

He merely nodded his agreement. Our gazes locked. The heartrending pain in his eyes threatened to choke me. I walked through the door, easing it shut, then leaning against it to regain my equilibrium.

My soul ached. I wasn't certain I would make it to the elevators before I collapsed into an emotional puddle right in the middle of the hallway.

Chapter Thirty-Nine

I wasn't in the mood for talking and was glad Grandmother and Patty were still sleeping when I returned to our room. I lifted the carafe of whiskey-laced chocolate and shook it. Although I wasn't hungry or thirsty, I needed a jolt of something to calm frayed nerves. Thankfully, there was enough for a full cup.

While I waited for the liqueur to work its magic, I decided to place a call to Tiny. He answered, "Good to hear from you, Tullah. How's New York?"

"Not my favorite place." I glossed over the small chit-chat and brought out the big guns. "Tiny, you're an expert at ferreting out information from the national crime database. Information that other people often don't know the right questions to ask. I need your expertise."

I brought him up-to-date on our latest findings about the four boys.

"Let me get this straight—three of those punks are dead, and this Bernard Steinhaur guy has seemingly gone deep incognito, and you need me to locate him—if he's truly still alive—correct?"

"Exactly, Tiny. If anyone can find the missing piece to this puzzle, you can."

"Thanks for the vote of confidence, Tullah. Rest assured I'll do my best." He chuckled. "I assume you need this yesterday?"

"And pictures, too, if available."

"Listen, before we disconnect, there's a surprise waiting for you when you, Tanti, and Patty get home."

"A surprise? What is it?"

Deputy Tiny Goodbody's chuckle is as big as his six-foot-seven stature. "My lips are sealed."

"Hey, no fair."

"The tease is on purpose. We're all hoping you haven't been bitten by the lure of the big city."

"Not on your life, Tiny. I'm ready for green grass, and the sound of something other than honking horns."

He guffawed. "I'll get back with you asap, Tullah."

I prayed asap meant before tomorrow evening's gala at the museum. I rinsed my cup and set it on the service cart, then pushed it outside the room for the cleaning staff. The bedroom door opened. Grandmother and Patty looked refreshed from their naps.

Grandmother's mouth twisted into a lopsided grin. "How was your visit to the solarium?"

I almost groaned. Clay Wolfchild was a topic I didn't wish to discuss. To sidestep her inquisitiveness, I said, "We didn't go. His back is acting up again. In fact, he's not joining us for dinner tonight. I'm tired, Grandmother. I don't feel like being around people or listening to a lot of loud voices. You and Patty go and enjoy the dining room. I'm just very tired."

"I know," she muttered. "I know."

My whole body seemed to droop as she repeated the words. She put her arms around my shoulders. "I don't know how you cope as well as you do—always burdened by dead people yammering after you. It's wonderful that Clay Wolfchild has come into your life." She pecked me on the cheek. "He's a good man, Granddaughter. I don't think it was happenstance that the two of you met again here in New York, of all places."

And then with a mischievous smile, she added, "The two of you will make beautiful children together."

That was my undoing. I twisted away from her embrace, and flung my hands forward, despairingly. "Stop! Just stop. There is no *two* of us, and there will never be any grandchildren. Not with Clay Wolfchild or any man. Don't you get it, Grandmother? Patty's right, I live with ghosts in the present and the past, and possibly into the future. It's my burden to bear—alone."

I collapsed on the sofa and cupped both hands around my face. My shoulders shook with pent-up sobs. "If I could rid myself of this curse, I would."

Patty gathered my hands as she sat beside me. Her voice was quiet. "Oh, Tullah, me and my big mouth. It's not a curse, a burden, yes, but not a curse. My dear, sweet girl, look at the good you've done, and the criminals you've helped capture." She burst into tears. "Forgive me, Tullah. One last thing, and I'll keep my peace. You are loved by so many people—Tanti, Henry, Charlie, Sunny, Ella, and me, to name a few. Take it from an old woman who let the love of a good man slip away— there's a huge difference between being loved by friends and family and being cherished by a life partner. You can surround yourself with spirits of the dead, friends, animals, family, and still be lonely, Tullah. Take it from me, the worst place in the world to live is—loneliness."

Once again she hugged me and whispered, "I'm so sorry."

Something in it made me shiver when Grandmother smiled a sober smile and said, "I agree with Patty. While we're spilling our hearts all over the floor, I might as well speak my piece, too."

Sometimes the way Grandmother gathers herself reminds me of a hen ruffling her feathers. I didn't know how much more of this soul browbeating I could withstand before I fled the room to seek solace elsewhere. I sat silent and listened.

She took a moment, as if gathering her thoughts. Though she spoke succinctly, there was compassion in her voice. "I believe the reason the spirits of the dead reach out to you is because you unwittingly opened that door. After Bryce's death, you shut yourself off from the world. You buried yourself in your studies, you became a brilliant forensics doctor, and not satisfied with that became a successful veterinarian and business woman.

"It was your loneliness that opened the door to the nether world. The dead spoke and you listened. Patty is correct when she speaks of the good you have done, but Tullah, oh my wonderful girl, there is more to life than communing with the dead and solving crimes."

I still had my mother's remaining killer to find, and what was I to do about the other women whose spirits asked for my help? My voice sounded hoarse and unlike myself. "Grandmother…Patty, how do I close that door?"

Grandmother said, "Clay Wolfchild Bannister loves you with every fiber of his being. It's written in his eyes, and the eyes are the windows to the soul. Open your heart and accept his love, Granddaughter."

"It's too late."

Grandmother and Patty exchanged questioning glances. Their words came out like an echo. "What do you mean?"

I didn't hold back any details when I related my earlier conversation with Clay Wolfchild. "His business is finished here. He only stayed to help me find more evidence about mother's murder. Tomorrow, he'll return to Texas because I've sent him away."

After I drew a breath, and collected my senses, I told them about the phone call I'd made to Tiny. And then I said, "I'm such a fool. I'm afraid I've erased all possibilities of a life with Clay Wolfchild."

Grandmother picked up my cellphone and handed it to me. "Call him. No, better yet, march yourself out the door and to his room. Once you're there…" She smiled, and I swear there was a twinkle in her eye when she said, "You are a woman. He is a man. Let nature do the rest. If you get my drift."

Oh, yes, I did get her drift. Loud and clear.

I sprinted out the door, down the hall, and to the elevators. My heart soared as the elevator rose to Clay Wolfchild's floor. I was out the door the second it opened wide enough for me to exit. In less than two minutes, I was knocking on his door. No answer. I called his name. Still no answer. I removed my phone from my pants pocket and was about to dial his number when the door opened and a maid stood in front of me.

"If you are looking for the gentleman who occupied this room, he checked out."

The exhilaration I'd felt disappeared. "How long ago?"

"I'm not sure. Maybe one hour."

While walking to the elevators, I chastised myself. All my stupid, self-righteous fault. Inside the elevator car, I opened my cellphone and speed dialed his number. The call went straight to voicemail. I didn't blame him for not answering. Not knowing what to say, I hung up. "Sorry," sounded trivial.

The doors opened and I punched the button for the lobby. I didn't feel up to facing Grandmother and Patty. I also hoped he might still be in the hotel—waiting for a cab. When I didn't see him, I approached the desk clerk.

"Excuse me, but how long ago did Detective Bannister check out?"

The clerk typed something into the computer, and confirmed what the maid had told me. Then he said, "You just missed him. He had to wait for a cab."

"Did he happen to say where he was going?"

"Ask the doorman. He might know."

I thanked him and walked to where the doorman stood. "Excuse me, did Detective Bannister happen to say where he was going when he left the hotel?"

"Yes, ma'am. To the airport."

My heart sank.

****

Grandmother and Patty offered to order room service. I needed some alone time and convinced them to enjoy their dinner without me. I showered, dressed in a pair of pajamas, and grabbed the mystery book I had purchased a few days ago. I'm not sure how long it was before I realized that I was still staring at the first page.

I was too upset to read. About the time I decided to dress and go for a walk, my cell pinged to indicate I had received a text. My heart did a slight flutter when I read the message from Tiny. He had notified me to check my email. I opened my laptop. The first thing I noticed was the attachment.

I was amazed that Tiny was able to locate information about Steinhaur in such a short time. I sent him a thumbs-up emoji, and a text message promising him a steak dinner when I arrived home. He responded with a smiley face.

After looking at the pictures and reading the patient intake report, my first thought was to call Clay Wolfchild, and then I remembered. He wasn't taking my calls. At least, I now knew why Bernard Steinhaur was among the living dead. He couldn't hurt me or anyone else.

That still left me with questions—why had Shadow Woman warned that I was in danger, and why did I see myself die when I was in the sweat lodge?

Chapter Forty

My spirits lifted enough that I phoned Grandmother and asked her to bring me something to eat. "Surprise me," I said.

She knows me too well. An hour later, she arrived with a to-go box filled with a container of tomato bisque, a double loaded grilled cheese sandwich, curly fries, and a slice of blueberry cheesecake.

Eager to share the information Tiny had located, I opened my laptop to the email and turned it toward Grandmother.

"I think you'll find this interesting." I made myself comfortable while she read aloud.

She looked from me to Patty, and said, "It's an intake patient report from Rose Mountain Healthcare and Rehabilitation Center, New Jersey."

I merely nodded while I enjoyed my late supper.

"It states that Bernard Edward Steinhaur, twenty-seven years of age, is a long-term care patient." I watched her scan the page. "Wow," she said.

"Don't keep me in suspense, Tanti Crow. What does it say?" Patty scolded.

"It says he was in a shootout, and to avoid being captured he decided to jump from the roof of a six-story building to an adjacent roof top and missed. He suffered a traumatic spinal cord injury which left him paralyzed from the neck down and cranial damage which left him in a coma. He's on a ventilator." She scoffed. "Some people never learn. He served ten years in prison, got out, rejoined his old gang, and look where he is now."

Grandmother closed the laptop. She sat quiet for a moment. "You were exactly right, Tullah when you said he was among the living dead."

"Odd that he's in New Jersey and not in a New York facility where Captain Stein could visit him or make sure he's getting good care," I said.

"You know the old saying, 'Out of sight—out of mind.' Maybe the captain doesn't want to be reminded that his own past is connected to his brother; I mean, being a cop and having a criminal brother isn't exactly good for the reputation."

"True. Not everyone is a good person." I gathered the empty containers and walked to the kitchenette to dispose of them.

Patty agreed with Grandmother's theory. Then she asked the same question I had been asking myself. "I don't understand. If all those little hellions are accounted for, then why is Tullah in danger, or even why are we here? Don't get me wrong, I'm looking forward to tomorrow's art gala. I'm just…confused about all this spirit and danger stuff."

"That makes two of us, Patty."

"Have you told Clay Wolfchild the news?" Grandmother wanted to know.

"Um, no. He checked out. The doorman said he caught a cab to the airport. I called Clay Wolfchild's number. He didn't answer." I let loose with a woe-is-me sigh. "I've made such a mess of things with him."

Grandmother opened her phone. She dialed. I cringed. "Please, don't, Grandmother. I don't need you to intercede for me."

She met my plea with a glare. There was a lilt to her voice. "Clay Wolfchild, this is Tanti Crow. We're looking forward to seeing you at the gala tomorrow night. Hope to hear from you, maybe at breakfast tomorrow."

Her voice came fast and aggravated. "It went straight to voice mail."

I swallowed the lump that had formed in my throat. "I suppose he's on his way back to Texas."

I'm not sure why I thought of my dad at this particular moment. Maybe because of my recent contact with Tiny. Both good lawmen, and both goodhearted men. When I was growing up, they and Uncle Charlie had shielded me from the worst of people as much as they could. A secret part of me was disappointed that Clay Wolfchild wasn't here to stand up for me, too.

In my heart, I knew it was my fault he was gone. I wanted him back. I wanted to leap into his arms and renew our passion. I wanted to tell him that I loved him, too. My phone rang and I was a little surprised to see the call was from Ella. I hoped nothing had gone wrong at the clinic or with the new resident intern. I answered and she got right to the point.

"Hi, Tullah, I know you'll be home day after tomorrow, but you're the first person I wanted to tell. No, wait, you're the third person. First was Andy, then my mother, and now you."

"Ella, what in the world are you babbling about?"

She shouted, "I'm preggers!"

"What...you're what?"

"Pregnant, as in having a baby."

"But how can that be?"

"Yeah, duh!" She giggled. "The usual way. You know...the birds and the bees and all that nonsense. Sex...Tullah! S-e-x."

If I was miserable before, I was now downright despondent. I didn't want to rain on my best friend's joyful news. After all, she isn't a mind reader and had no way of knowing I had virtually exiled myself to old maidhood by throwing away a good man—no, a great man.

I placed the phone on speaker and forced elation into my voice. "I'm so happy for you, Ella! Andy and your mom must be over the moon. How are you feeling? Morning sickness?"

We spent the next five minutes talking about baby names, whether or not she and Andy wanted to know if the baby was a boy or a girl, and then a brief update about Dr. Jesse Delight.

"If there's any way we can keep him, I think he'd be a great asset to the clinic, and now that I'm pregnant, I'll need time off with the baby." Ella hastened on. "Of course, that's months from now."

I handed the phone to Grandmother so she and Patty could offer their congratulations to Ella and Andy. Finally, Ella lamented, "You'll have to excuse me. I need to go pee, again."

We all snorted our laughter at the unexpected comment.

That night, I dreamed of tiny coffins filled with dead ovaries parading toward a barren garden.

Chapter Forty-One

I didn't sleep much that night. Grandmother and Patty were still in bed when I awoke. As usual, the morning newspaper had been pushed under the door. I placed a coffee pod in the coffeemaker, and while the aromatic liquid filled a mug, I collected the paper, then grabbed my coffee to settle at the window.

After yesterday's anxiety with Clay Wolfchild's departure, then the news of Ella's pregnancy, I was already expecting today to be even worse. With this expectation, I flipped to the horoscope page and skimmed down to Virgo.

Brace yourself for important information. It may be shocking, but you can handle it. All will soon be clear to you, if you are open-minded.

I read it again. Shocking news? Something I could handle? If this was about Ella, that was old news. It happened yesterday. Be open-minded? The jury was still out on that one.

I knew I shouldn't take my horoscope so literally, but still I had good reason to dread going to tonight's art show. I thought of a million excuses to keep from accompanying Grandmother and Patty to the museum. I told myself to buck up, and sat back to stare out the window, enjoy my coffee, and a few more minutes of quietude before Grandmother and Patty awoke and were ready to go down for breakfast.

It was refreshing to see the morning sun glistening off puddles of melting snow. It almost made me wish I'd brought a pair of running shoes. Maybe a nice long jog would clear my head. A second glance at the gathering hordes of people changed my mind. I wasn't naturally a people person, though I could handle it if I had to. I actually communed better with animals—and ghosts, apparently.

Grandmother interrupted my musings. "Good morning, Granddaughter. The sun is actually shining."

Patty wandered in. "I don't know about the two of you, but I'm feeling a little bit giddy this morning. Tonight is going to be spectacular. I can feel it in my bones."

"Let's go down for breakfast, and maybe a walk afterwards. I'm tired of being cooped up." Grandmother walked over and gave me a hug. She offered a smile. "Besides, our girl needs a little bit of cheering up. A walk will do all of us good."

We rode the elevator down to the dining room. We had become familiar with the hostess. She greeted us with a smile and showed us to our usual table. I found myself searching among the faces even though I knew Clay Wolfchild was miles away.

A hearty breakfast perked up my mood. We left the dining room, and greeted the doorman. He gave us a smile that was almost as sunny as the outdoors. I asked, "How far are we from Central Park?"

He grinned. "Two blocks. May I suggest that I contact one of the tour companies to give you a private tour. It will save you a lot of walking and you'll get to enjoy the full experience of the park."

We all agreed to his suggestion, and thanked him for

his consideration, although I was certain there was a little something in it for him. Nonetheless, I feared it wouldn't take long before Grandmother and Patty would exhaust their energy and be too tired to enjoy tonight's event.

In less than fifteen minutes, our horse and carriage arrived. Snug under lap blankets, we were off to enjoy crisp fall air and the city's winter wonders. We were awed at the sight of the Belvedere Castle, the iconic Bow Bridge, and we stopped at the world-famous Central Park Zoo where we went from tigers to polar bears, to goats and llamas, and I yearned to see my own animals, especially River and Rascal.

After a three-hour tour, sated with hot chocolate and then lunch at another famous restaurant, by the time we arrived back at the hotel, my mood had lightened, and I had almost forgotten about the possibility of facing a dangerous evening. That is, until I was departing the carriage and happened to look across the street.

He stared at me. At least, I was certain he was staring at me, even though I couldn't be sure because he wore dark sunglasses. A black sweater cap covered his hair, and his hands were inside the black trench coat's pockets.

There was something about him that seemed familiar. Grandmother sounded concerned. "Tullah, do you know that man?"

"No, ma'am." I willed the door to the dark side of my brain to remain closed.

"He's had several opportunities to cross the street. Maybe he's blind and needs help."

She started forward, and I grabbed her arm. I looked at my sweet grandmother. She didn't have a mean bone in her body. Before retiring as Enigma's mayor and after a career as an award-winning crime reporter, she had stopped watching cop shows, saying they were too phony. She enjoyed shows where judges picked people who competed in singing contests, where stars danced, and where people rehabbed old houses—like Uncle Charlie. And if Patty was addicted to anything, it was cooking shows.

I was about to cross the street to ask the guy why he was watching us when another man approached. The two conversed. I was too far away to hear. When the second man lifted his head, even under his black fedora, I recognized the grossly unpleasant police captain.

"That's Captain Leland Stein, Grandmother. Maybe the man he's talking to is an undercover detective or maybe a friend."

We hustled inside the hotel's lobby. Grandmother said, "I could use a nap before dressing for tonight." We all agreed that our chilly but exhilarating day in Central Park had left us refreshed and pleasantly tired.

Except for me. I couldn't shake the bad feeling I'd had all day. We were taking our time walking down the hall toward the elevators when a voice called out, "Dr. Holliday?"

Puzzled, I turned. Captain Stein approached. A scowl deeply imprinted the crevices on his face. He certainly couldn't be upset with me. My contact with him had been limited to less than thirty minutes, four days ago.

I introduced him to my grandmother and Patty. My negative attitude toward him hadn't changed. "What can I do for you, Captain?"

He removed his hat and coat. Stein was a man of medium height, with light hair fringed around his bald head. Even though he wore a suit coat, he was built like a tree trunk with heavy arms. His dark eyes narrowed. "Is there a place where we can talk privately?"

"Whatever you have to say can be said in front of my grandmother and friend."

"It's regarding your..." Lowering his voice, he hesitated.

"If it's about my mother, I've learned all I need to know. All of the boys involved were members of the Aryans, and they are all dead except for Bernard Steinhaur—your brother."

Stein didn't flinch when I met his stare. Someone should have told him I was a champion when it came to staring people down. He flinched and dropped his gaze. Chalk one up for me.

His demeanor softened slightly. Grandmother said she and Patty needed to rest before getting dressed for the evening and excused themselves. I followed Stein to the dining room for a cup of coffee.

His eyes became hard, and his mouth tightened. "I'll be the first to admit that it would be merciful if Bernie were to die. I've even thought about pulling the plug on him, except for our mother. She lives in Jersey, and prays for him every day. There's nine years' difference in our ages. He and I were the bane of her existence. I managed to get my life in order. Bernie is another story. I think he was born with the devil in him. Even as a toddler he was often out of control, and grew worse as he aged.

"I tried to talk him out of joining the Aryans; even took him to juvie hoping to do the 'scared straight,' thing with him. He thought it was cool."

Stein pointed to his starched collar. "I've tried to have the tattoo removed. What I have left is a scar in the shape of a seven as a permanent reminder of days I hate remembering."

He drained his cup and motioned for a waiter for a refill. "What about you, Dr. Holliday?"

I never turn down coffee. I also felt the need to say something poignant about his confession. Unfortunately, words failed me. I wanted to ask what all of this had to do with my mother. He continued speaking before I had a chance.

He gave me a black look. "Bloodletting was like a super high for Bernie. It's a terrible thing to say about one's brother, but I hated him, and have zero feelings toward him now. He was so violent that his first night in prison was spent in solitary confinement. And that was at age fifteen."

Silence passed as I searched for proper words. "I don't mean to be insensitive, Captain Stein, but what does this have to do with me?"

He fell silent, staring down at his cup. His face flushed from pale to deep purple. He cleared his throat. "Apologies don't come easy for a man like me. I've been remiss in my attitude toward you."

He stood. "I'm not making excuses, just take it for what it is. I'm deeply sorry about your mother, especially since my brother was involved. And the only excuse I have for the abundant cold cases is budgetary reasons and lack of manpower. We've tried to enlist the aid of retired cops. Those guys apparently have no desire to spend their free time in dank, dark dungeons, working on cases no one seems to care about."

I wanted to admonish him for his treatment of bicultural women. Instead, I held my peace.

He collected the check. I immediately said, "If you

have time, do you mind if I share what I've learned?"

His eyebrows lifted as if skeptical but interested. He sat down.

"We've learned that the killers always choose indigenous women. And the murders happen three years apart. I get the extreme bias toward these particular women. What I don't understand is the significance of the number three."

He considered my question. "In the AB, three means the courage to take on new challenges and push them to the limit. For the inductees, often teen hoodlums eager to prove their worthiness, the challenge is to blood-let, and it must be a woman who is non-white. It doesn't matter if she is young, old, disabled, pretty, or ugly, as long as she meets the skinhead standards. And the more violent their cruelty, the more the kids are able to prove their worth, get fully accepted into the brotherhood, and move up the ranks."

I felt the muscle under my eye twitch. "It's been three years, Captain Stein. I hope the ABs don't target my grandmother and me. We're leaving in the morning, and frankly, I can't wait to bid farewell to this city."

"I understand, Dr. Holliday, and that's why I'm assigning Officer Doyle to shadow you."

"Doyle? You mean the guy with the coke-bottle glasses?"

"Yeah, he's been itching to get in the field. In spite of his vision, he's smart, and qualified on paper to become a detective. This is his test run."

"That was Doyle you were talking to, earlier? The guy in the trench coat and dark glasses."

Again, Stein's face flushed. "'Fraid so."

I wanted to laugh as I thought about the old

television crime comedy where the main character was a bumbling secret agent. And if this was all Stein had to offer, I feared we were in serious trouble.

Chapter Forty-Two

It was a dazzling November evening. I was awestruck at the sight of the museum. I followed Grandmother and Patty in through the immaculate white-tiled entrance. The first painting that caught my attention was that of women toiling in cotton fields, their clothes soaked with sweat and their hair wrapped in colorful kerchiefs and yet they exuded femininity.

Although I had resisted much of Grandmother's attempts to teach me the art of feminine wiles, I did learn one important thing—a woman's aura of desirability is created first in her mind. Obviously, it was a lesson I had not cultivated.

Grandmother gripped my arm. She leaned close and whispered, "Remember, there is an art to entering a room at an important soiree. It is timing, attitude, and dress. We are among the elite. We will hold our heads high and meet every eye because we are Cherokee."

Grandmother was regal in her black ankle-length velveteen gown with its long sleeves and intricate gold-and-burnt-umber floral design. Her salt-and-pepper hair, braided and coiled, sat on her head like a tiara, and simple gold studs decorated her ears.

To honor our heritage, Patty wore a rust-colored suede dress decorated with a southwestern design around the neck and down the long sleeves.

I, on the other hand, had opted for a simple black,

western-cut pantsuit. On the lapel, I wore a heart-shaped sterling silver pendant of a mare and her foal, inlaid with turquoise, which had been designed by my mother. I wore my hair in a French braid.

We presented our invitations to a tuxedoed host. He viewed our cards and smiled. "Welcome." He motioned for a young attendant, and said, "Please escort Madames Crow and Sweet and Dr. Holliday to Monsieur Toussaint, *tout suite.*"

Coming in from the cold, the warmth of the party hit me like a fist. A server approached with a tray of champagne. We helped ourselves. Almost immediately Monsieur Armand Toussaint greeted us. I had pictured a tall, thin man with a thick head of dark hair. I had totally missed the mark. He was short and stocky and wore a petite handlebar moustache. In fact, he reminded me of Hercule Poirot, Agatha Christie's famous detective.

We followed Toussaint into a larger gallery. I was surprised at the number of people, all dressed in finery. Servers with trays of hors d'oeuvres floated in and among the group. Monsieur Toussaint approached the front of the gallery and tapped on his crystal goblet to gain everyone's attention. Voices ebbed as he motioned us to the front, along with other notables, to join him.

After a short speech recognizing my mother and other indigenous female artists far and wide—from the United States, Canada, Australia, and Japan—for their invaluable contributions to the world of art, he invited us to enjoy each showroom dedicated to that particular artist.

The moment we entered the gallery titled "Josie Crow Holliday" Grandmother gripped my hand and let out a small gasp. In front of us was a self-portrait of my mother so lifelike it felt as if she could step off the canvas. She stood in a field of wildflowers. Her hand was lifted toward the sky, and perched on her finger was a cardinal hen.

My heart clutched as I recalled the day at the hospital garden and the little burnished-red cardinal hen that had lit nearby as I thought of my mother. Filled with emotion, I squeezed Grandmother's hand. She said, "It's a sign, Tullah. My Josie is with us wherever we go."

As we meandered to each painting and stood absorbing the beauty and the depth of my mother's talent, I had that sensation one gets when it feels as if someone has walked across your grave. I turned and caught a flash of black overcoat. Officer Doyle, I thought. Yet I was caught off guard when a dark cloud of evil came over me. Not wanting to spoil the elation of being in my mother's presence, albeit through her artwork, I shrugged it off. I should have paid attention instead.

Emotion filled Patty's voice. "I had no idea Josie was so prolific." She placed fisted hands against her breasts. "Her work is so real I feel as if I'm part of every scene she has created."

We ended the first section of our tour, and when we walked to the opposite side of the moveable wall, my breath hung in my throat. "It's him!" I managed to say.

"Who do you mean, Granddaughter?"

I pointed at the life-size painting. "The warrior. The one who appeared on the rearing pinto horse the morning I was waiting in the hospital's garden to hear Dad would pull through after surgery. It's him. And he and his horse have all the same markings and colors."

I could almost hear the cadence of Uncle Charlie's

baritone voice the morning he had explained the significance of the warrior's symbols. I remembered his words as clear as day. "In the ways of the warrior people, the handprint on the horse's shoulder represents an oath of vengeance. I believe the water marks are hail. These marks symbolize a prayer for the horse and rider to fall upon the enemy like shards of ice. The snake symbol represents stealth when approaching the enemy, and the straight arrow signifies victory."

"Oh, my lord, Tullah!" Patty stood close to the painting. "It's…it's…no, it can't be."

Grandmother groused. "For heaven's sake, Patty Sweet. What are you babbling about?"

Grandmother and I waited for Patty's answer. She pointed. "I know it's just a painting, and there's no way on earth Josie could have known him. I mean he would have been a little boy when she painted this, and he's a man about thirty-five-ish."

"Patty?" I was beginning to think her mind had wandered off into neverland.

She persisted. "Look closely, Tullah. If I can see it, surely you can, too. Except for all the feathers, and warpaint, and being half-naked, it's the spittin' image of…" She hesitated. "Clay Wolfchild."

Patty's revelation was startling. To steady myself, I took a sip of champagne. The alcohol caught in my throat and I thought I was going to choke. My nose burned, and my eyes watered. He was a dark force, and no matter how much I tried to deny it, he affected me. I managed to gasp, "He has blue eyes, just like Clay Wolfchild." There was one exception, in the background, mother had painted the image of a howling wolf. I had to concede that the warrior in the painting looked exactly like the man I loved, and had sent away.

"Why now?" I asked self-pityingly.

Grandmother spoke with a hushed reverence. "It's like Josie knew the future and she painted him so you would know that he's the one. Except for her untimely death, you might have met him sooner."

Patty added, "Josie apparently had a secret sense that none of us knew about."

A creepiness drifted over me. Goose bumps rose on my arms and the hair prickled at the nape of my neck. "Grandmother, excuse me. I need to find the ladies' room."

She caressed my face like she always does when she knows I'm stressed. "Shall I go with you?"

I read the concern in her eyes. "We should return to the hotel. As soon as I return."

"Are we in danger?"

"I hope not."

At the end of the moveable partition, I turned to look at Grandmother and Patty. Over the past fourteen years I've become better at listening to my secret sense. At least I hope I have. And it was telling me we were in danger. Not just me, but Grandmother, too.

I approached one of the servers and asked for directions to the bathroom. She pointed toward a long hall. I detected a sound behind me. Maybe it was Grandmother or Patty. Maybe one of them had followed me. Despite the dreadful pounding in my heart, I said a few earnest prayers. I stopped and strained as hard as I could. Whoever was following me was not a skilled tracker.

Relief washed over me when I pushed open the bathroom door, then sequestered myself in an empty stall. I relieved myself and stepped toward the sink to wash my hands. I looked at myself in the mirror—minus the thick glasses, Brent Doyle's face was rising above mine in the reflection. He reached a gloved hand into his coat pocket.

Suddenly I realized I should be absolutely terrified. Before I could react, he'd placed his hands over my head and covered my face with a white handkerchief. In one breath, I felt as if I were falling off the edge of a precipice.

He whispered, "That's right, bitch. Inhale, but not too much. I need it to look as if you are my date."

"What did you give me?" My words were slurred.

"A hint of an opioid. Not enough to incapacitate you. I want you to see and feel what we're doing to you."

We're. I was coherent enough to realize he meant more than one was involved, and they were going to torture me like they had my mother. I retched.

"No puking allowed. Got it?" Doyle commanded.

"Why are you doing this?"

He laughed. "Because of what you are—a shit-eating bitch. A maggot. People like you are the ruination of our great country."

He led me to the exit door. The cold air revived me enough that I spun around, but before I could smash my fist in his face, he shoved me through the opening. I landed hard on the ground. Hands grabbed me and dragged me to a sitting position against a brick wall. I blinked several times to clear my vision. I surmised from the stench of litter and defecation that we were in an alley.

I struggled against the hands that gripped my arms. Whimpers and sobs drew my attention. Slumped against

309

an overflowing dumpster were three women, their hands tied, mouths gagged. I blinked again to clear my vision and was certain I recognized the artist from Torres Strait, Australia, her face adorned with the traditional Dot painting.

Doyle's voice was hard and mean. "If the good doctor tries to escape, hurt her. Not much. I want the old broad to watch what's gonna happen to her when we finish with her bitch granddaughter."

Fear hung in my throat when he pricked the underside of my chin with the tip of a knife. I winced against the pain. It was almost as if I could taste death in my mouth—like bitter bile that threatened to choke me. When I finally found my voice, I said, "How did you manage to become a cop?"

Doyle laughed. He removed the thick-lensed glasses and stuffed them in a pocket. "Ain't no effing pig, cunt." He continued laughing as if he'd pulled a funny joke on someone. "My name ain't Officer Brent Doyle. Nope, he's sleepin' with the fishes."

"I don't understand."

"'Course, you don't, stupid shit. I look enough like Doyle to pass for his twin. He arrested me once. It was like looking at myself in a mirror. Yeah, it was. That's when I got the idea to impersonate a cop, 'cause it makes me smarter than that dumbass Stein, and it gets me the inside dope on boogers like you."

One of the gang members hissed, "We don't like rats and roaches. We gets rid of 'em." To make his point, he smashed a can with the heel of his brogan.

I clutched the medicine pouch hidden beneath my camisole and silently called out to the Great Spirit Father and Shadow Woman. I couldn't bear the thought of these animals torturing my grandmother.

Doyle ordered, "Watch her. She's wily, and she's mine. Got it?"

I forced myself to remain calm. *Think, Tullah, think,* I admonished. My mind drifted to the words of my former psych professor. *A killer believes he is in charge, that he is smarter than the law. Break him down by talking how inferior he is, that he is a bully, that he's powerless over you. The more you can get under his skin, the greater the chance he'll slip up.*

Yeah, that's all well and good, Professor Van Aken. How do I apply this principle to six amoral punks?

I focused on the youngest boy. "Hey, you, what's your name?"

He smirked. "Jack Brown. Ask me again and I'll knock you down."

Smart ass. "Cute. How old are you—eleven?"

"Thirteen, bitch."

"You're not even old enough to grow peach fuzz, let alone shave. Why, you're barely out of diapers."

The other boys guffawed.

Even in the alley's dim light, I could tell I'd struck a nerve with my insult. He grabbed his crotch. "Suck my—"

Whatever he was about to say died when Doyle opened the door and shoved my grandmother to the ground. Rage and adrenalin fueled me. I rose to my feet and lunged at Doyle. My fingernails found their mark and raked bloody crevices down his cheeks.

Blood filled my mouth when he backhanded me. My face stung with pain. I stumbled backward, then stooped to place protective arms around my grandmother. "What's happening, Tullah? Are these the same animals that murdered my Josie?"

Doyle or whatever his name was, said, "Nah, old woman. We're the new-agers. They're all dead. Just like you're gonna be."

I managed to keep my voice calm. "You and these guttersnipes are the ones who will die."

I looked at the young ruffians dressed in combat boots and wearing trench coats too large for their immature bodies. Their heads were shaven clean. There was enough light for me to see the lightning bolts tattooed on their bald heads.

Grandmother managed to stand. She sidled against me. Like a woman warrior, she faced the enemy. "I pray for your souls because hell is a terrible place to live."

Doyle commanded, "Moody, grab the old bag's arms. Hold her while Carney drugs her. Beanie, you're the strongest and oldest. Help me with that one." Doyle pointed toward me. His eyes narrowed. "The rest of you newbies watch and learn. This is your initiation test."

Doyle pointed a long-bladed knife toward the young teens. "You don't want to know what's gonna happen if you fail to measure up."

Grandmother fought to keep the one called Moody from placing the opioid saturated cloth over her face. I struggled against Beanie's restraints. I wasn't about to go down without a fight. The remaining gang of neophytes circled around me, chanting—*die, die, die.* Doyle played a bowie-type knife from hand to hand. He grinned at me and I felt as if I were looking at the devil himself.

In desperation, I lashed out with my foot. The silver tip of my boot caught him between the legs. He lost his grip on the knife, grabbed his crotch, and sank to his knees.

Grandmother's laughter seemed to bounce off the brick walls. "Serve you right, little puppy. You're all bark and no bite."

A sudden gust of wind rushed through the dark alley, and then the whispers started. It sounded more like human voices than the wind. It was like that part of the city block had a secret story to tell.

We had been days without a moon, but now it was rising to cast shadows against the brick walls. The aboriginal woman cried out, "The bones of our ancestors will protect us."

In a heavily accented voice, another woman practically shouted, "Somebody, please tell me what's going on."

A tremor ran through my body like a fish coming back to life after it's been tossed back into the water. My teeth chattered. The wind's force increased and its temperature dropped to freezing. I shivered as though shaking with a fever. At the same time, shrieks and shrill cackles reverberated off the walls, and like wisps of smoke, spirits of the dead rose from the earth.

Primal fear blocked the scream in my throat.

Waves of panic rose and fell on the young gangsters' faces as they muttered in fear and exclaimed, "What the...?" and "Go away, Go away!"

"What's happening?" one of them cried, cowering to his knees and placing his hands over his head.

In the throes of terror, the young wannabe gangsters collided with each other as they scrambled to avoid assault by the icy fingers of the dead. A ghoul grabbed Beanie and swirled him around and around. Dropping him to the ground, she hovered over him, pursed her lips, and blew. Her breath came out like a cloud of ice. Covered in frost, Beanie stammered in a high-pitched voice, "D-D-Doyle…what the hell's going on?"

Seemingly in my imagination, I saw the shadow of a large wolf. Its growl echoed in my ears as it lunged toward Doyle. The attack was swift, leaving Doyle clutching his throat and sinking to his knees. A pool of blood collected around his body.

A crescendo of shots rang out. The moon darkened. I covered Grandmother with my body, and she moaned softly. In the darkness it was impossible to see if she or anyone else had been wounded.

Captain Stein's voice rang out. "Detective Bannister, have you been injured?"

The moon slipped free of the clouds and dimly lit the alley. I gasped when I spotted Clay Wolfchild sitting against the wall near me, and like some kind of supersonic spider I scuttled toward him.

When I touched his chest, my hand came back wet and sticky. "How bad is it?" I asked.

"Shoulder. Knife wound." And then he asked, "You and your grandmother?"

Even injured, he was more concerned about others than himself. Stein knelt beside us. "One of my officers called it in. Ambulances are on the way."

"The other women?" I asked.

"Other than scared out of their wits, they're unharmed."

"How did you know to come here?

"Detective Amherst. I went to visit him. It's a long story."

I looked around at the scattered bodies. Doyle lay on his back, his face a picture of fright, his eyes wide and void of life. He was a sad imitation of what he was. "The boys?"

We were all quiet for a long moment. Stein wasn't quick to speak. He said, "I don't know what the hell happened here. These kids look like they've been scared to death. I'm not sure I believe in zombies, and if anyone asks me what killed them...oh, hell, I'll leave it up to the coroner to figure it out."

Grandmother beseeched me. "Tullah?"

"I don't have any answers, Grandmother, except we saw what we saw and, by the laws of science and by all that is holy, I believe the Great Spirit Father and Shadow Woman heard our prayers."

Chapter Forty-Four

Clay Wolfchild lay propped in the hospital bed, the sun coming in through the windows. He'd been here two days. His shoulder was healing at an amazing rate. The old bullet fragment lodged in his spine may have saved his life. Apparently, the exertion of running to save me caused his legs to collapse, thus causing the knife to miss his heart.

Grandmother and Patty entered. "How are you feeling, Clay Wolfchild?" Grandmother asked.

"Good. Actually, great. The doctor says I'm healing faster than most people." He reached for my hand and held it firmly. "I was already inside the museum when Patty spotted me. She was frantic, saying the two of you had disappeared. I immediately contacted Captain Stein."

He pressed the palm of my hand to his lips. "All the way to the airport, I could only think of one thing—that I wanted you in my life, and I came back for you."

I didn't want to cry. I hated crying, especially in front of people. "I'm so glad you did."

He looked at me with cool eyes and a slight quirk to his lip. "Tullah Josie Crow Holliday, it's impossible for me to get down on bended knee, and this isn't the way I had planned to ask you to marry me, but—"

I forced a teasing note into my voice to hide the fact that my heart was pounding painfully in my chest. "Yes,

I'll marry you on one condition."

I could almost feel Grandmother's hackles go up.

Skepticism filled his blue eyes. I leaned down and kissed him. Really kissed him, all too aware of how close I'd come to losing him.

"And?"

"That we don't have a big fancy wedding, and that we spend our honeymoon in a cabin by a gurgling stream, no people, only you, me, and nature."

The dimples in his cheeks deepened. "How long does this honeymoon have to last?"

Emotions threatened to choke me. "For the rest of our lives,"

He looked at Grandmother and winked. Desire filled his eyes when he pulled me against his chest and touched his lips to mine.

Grandmother whooped. "Wolves mate forever."

Part IV: The Final Chapter

*"When you finish a book and realize you live
in a real world and not the book's world!"*
                                    ~*John Sinopoli*

Epilogue

Tomorrow's Thanksgiving turkey is prepped and ready to place in the oven. The children and Clay Wolfchild are upstairs asleep. I've decided to take advantage of the quiet time to put the finishing touches on my autobiography. While I stare at the computer's blank screen, my thoughts are like scattered leaves that refuse to be gathered and contained.

If you recall, earlier in the story, Tiny said he had a surprise for me when I returned home from New York. It was a wonderful surprise. He and my dad were retiring their badges, and Uncle Charlie had an opportunity to sell the Whitehorse Saloon for a substantial sum.

The best part of the surprise was that Dad had purchased the Second Chance Ranch. He, Tiny, and Uncle Charlie formed a partnership to turn the five hundred acres of dilapidation into a working rehabilitation ranch for wayward teens who are getting into trouble with the law because they have no one in their lives to offer them love, respect, and stability.

Six years ago, after the incident in the alley, and on

Thanksgiving Day, we saw no need to wait. Clay Wolfchild was well enough, and we held our small wedding ceremony at the cemetery. Yes, I know, weird. But due to her untimely death, my mother had missed out on numerous important events in my life. It was my way of having her celebrate this special occasion with me, and also my way of letting go.

We knew she was there to celebrate with us because the little tufted cardinal hen lit on mother's gravestone. She sat quietly until after the ceremony, and then, with a ruffle of her feathers, she chirped her song, which sounded like "Cheer, cheer, cheer," and flew away. I believe it was Mother's way of saying goodbye.

After our wedding, Clay Wolfchild's mother and sister moved to Enigma to be closer to us. Lydia Elkhorn and Fauni Blue Butterfly are teachers, which works out well because classes at the ranch thus can be held on site and under strict supervision. Our former office assistant, Jeff Dempsy, graduated with his degree, and completes the circle of teachers. Patty volunteers twice a week to teach culinary skills.

Odd things have happened. Uncle Charlie fell in love. I believe it was love at first sight for him and Lydia Elkhorn Bannister. Needless to say, he is no longer a confirmed bachelor but a happily married man at the ripe age of sixty-two. My hope is that one day Tiny will meet the love of his life.

I'm getting a little ahead of myself. You may be wondering about the true identity of Brent Doyle, and what happened to Captain Leland Stein. Doyle was identified as Rocky Groggans. I'm reminded of Madam Zahrani's warning about salt and sugar looking the same. He was able to pull off his ruse due to the unexpected retirement of Captain Jerald Adams and because Adams's immediate replacement, Captain Stein, had a less than stellar reputation. And Groggans did indeed resemble the late Doyle, whose body was never located. Groggans had not only stolen Doyle's identification, but the keys to his apartment and his personal vehicle, and his password notebook, all of which gave him access to Doyle's life.

Detective Todd Amherst wrote us that Stein had exercised his authority as guardian to have his brother taken off life support. It was his understanding that Stein's mother passed away two days later. As for Stein, he seems to have dropped off the face of the earth.

The New York coroner's report stated that the deaths of all the young hoodlums on that fateful night in the alley was from traumatic heart failure, possibly caused by excessive inhalation and/or exposure to fentanyl.

Even as I write this, I know the truth. It wasn't a dangerous narcotic that killed those boys. The question is not what I believe, though, but what you the reader believe about vengeful ghosts. I bet you're wondering if the spirits still seek me out.

The answer is—not at all. I no longer see warrior spirits rising from the earth in my front pasture. There are no mystic visits from the owl and raven. I believe Grandmother was correct in her theory that with the tragic deaths of my mother and my fiancé I had willingly opened the door to the realm of the dead. It was easier for me to live in a world of loneliness because I felt guilty to be alive and successful. Happiness was a place I felt I didn't deserve. That part of my life is behind me.

When my dad retired, Andy became his temporary

replacement. It's been seven years and Andy is still sheriff. He's as admired and respected as my dad. He and Ella are the proud parents of three little boys, all with red hair and freckles. Ella is a few weeks away from delivering their fourth child—a little girl.

After their traumatic experience in New York, Grandmother and Patty became fearful of being alone at night. And while they are still full of piss and vinegar, there wasn't much resistance when I insisted they sell their apartments and move closer to me.

When Clay Wolfchild and I were on our honeymoon, lightning struck my house. All that remained were ashes. I believe the Great Spirit Father and Shadow Woman ordained the burning of my house. The fire was a sort of cleansing…an ordination that my mother was finally at peace and this was her final farewell.

In an unexpected gesture of generosity, Monsieur Toussaint gave me the painting of my mother with the little cardinal hen perched on her finger.

In retrospect, we had outgrown the house, and the stairs were difficult for Clay Wolfchild to manage. While rebuilding, we built a two-bedroom granny cottage behind our house. It's wonderful having Grandmother and Patty within spitting distance.

On a side note, Uncle Charlie, Clay Wolfchild, and Lydia Elkhorn officiated the Native American blood oath ceremony officially making my grandmother and Patty blood sisters. And while Ella and I are stepsisters, we, too, participated in the ceremony to bind our blood together as true sisters.

Stretching the kinks out of my body, I stop to refresh my coffee. River and Rascal follow me to the kitchen, where I reward them with a treat. Then, seated back at the computer, I think about my new life and smile as I recall my thirtieth birthday party where Grandmother declared she was worried about my ovaries drying up and dying. She needn't have worried. John Clayton, better known as JC, is five. His brother Justin is three, Josie and her twin sister, Jurnee, are nine months. I've decided it's time to retire my ovaries.

The clinic has grown. Ella and I hired Dr. Jesse Delight. He lives up to his name and is a tremendous asset to our practice. Clay Wolfchild decided to put his law degree to work and is now known as Judge Bannister. He presides over juvenile court and is instrumental in selecting candidates needing a second chance to reside at the Second Chance Ranch.

Because my mother's murder was never properly investigated, and upon experiencing firsthand how many cases go cold due to either lack of interest or lack of manpower, I founded HB (Holliday Bannister) Cold Case, Inc. Retired Sheriff Malachi Dotson, from Dixie County and a close friend, heads the unit. He has recruited other retired law officers who prefer staying active to playing golf or sitting at the local bar rehashing the good old days. We are determined that no dead soul is forgotten. I can't begin to tell you how many letters we have received from families expressing their gratitude for our solving what often seemed an unsolvable case.

My fingers hover over the keyboard. It's taken six books to tell my story, and I'm excited to write "The End!" to my autobiography.

Tomorrow is a special day. Not only is it Thanksgiving, but also Clay Wolfchild and I will celebrate our seventh wedding anniversary. I'm thankful my children will never know the loneliness I felt as a child. They have their cousins, aunts, uncles, and several sets of grandparents, and more animals than we can count.

It's past midnight and officially Thanksgiving morning. I'm ending the day by quietly checking on my sleeping children, then easing into bed. Clay Wolfchild is awake. He folds me into his arms, and whispers for me to remove my oversized sleep shirt. "You're as beautiful as you were on our honeymoon night."

Except for threads of silver in his black mane, he is still a handsome warrior, virile, and, like his name—protective.

His lips touch mine lightly. His arms tighten around me. It seems my whole life has been leading up to this moment. I wish I could express my true feelings for him. I feel so much that words fail me. "I do love you, Clay Wolfchild."

He props on his elbow. Flames of desire still flicker in his blue eyes. "Loving you has brought peace to my soul."

I fall asleep with my head resting on his shoulder. My last thought is: *Wolves mate for life.*

A word about the author...

Loretta C. Rogers is a fourth-generation Floridian. When not writing, she enjoys genealogy, reading, crossword puzzles, and traveling.

Thank you for purchasing
this publication of The Wild Rose Press, Inc.

For questions or more information
contact us at
info@thewildrosepress.com.

The Wild Rose Press, Inc.